WINTER'S CRIMES 11

WINTER'S CRIMES II

Edited by George Hardinge

ST. MARTIN'S
NEW YORK

Library of Congress Catalog Card Number : 79-623696

First published in Great Britain in 1979

First published in the United States of America in 1980

Printed in Great Britain

ISBN : 0-312-88238-6

Contents

EDITOR'S NOTE

The policy of *Winter's Crimes* anthologies is to publish new short stories: stories – written specially for the series – that will never before have seen the light of day except possibly in America.

As *Winter's Crimes* reaches the age of eleven its companion volume, *Winter's Tales*, appears for the twenty-fifth time, edited by Caroline Hobhouse. There will also be a special jubilee edition of *Winter's Tales*, chosen from the earlier volumes: published under the title *Best for Winter*, this will be edited by A. D. Maclean.

Winter's Crimes has been lucky all the way with its contributors, and the luck holds. I am very grateful to the authors who contributed to this volume, and I do not need to speak for them, since their names are well-known.

George Hardinge

Simon Brett

DOUBLE GLAZING

The fireplace was rather splendid, a carved marble arch housing a black metal grate. The curves of the marble supports echoed the elaborate sweep of the coving and the outward spread of petals from the central ceiling rose. The white emulsion enthusiastically splashed over the room by the Housing Trust volunteers could not disguise its fine Victorian proportions. The old flooring had been replaced by concrete when the damp course was put in and the whole area was now snugly carpeted. This was one of the better conversions, making a compact residence for a single occupant, Jean Collinson thought as she sat before the empty grate opposite Mr Morton. A door led off the living room to the tiny kitchen and bathroom. Quite sufficient for a retired working man.

She commented on the fireplace.

'Oh yes, it's very attractive,' Harry Morton agreed. His voice still bore traces of his Northern upbringing. 'Nice workmanship in those days. Draughty, mind, if you don't have it lit.'

'Yes, but there's no reason why you shouldn't use it in the winter. When they did the conversion, the builders checked that the chimney wasn't blocked. Even had it swept, I think.'

'Oh yes. Well, I'll have to see about that when the winter comes. See how far the old pension stretches.'

'Of course. Do you find it hard to make ends meet?'

'Oh no. I'm not given to extravagance. I have no vices, so far as I know.' The old man chuckled. He was an amiable soul; Jean found him quite restful after most of the others. Mrs Walker with her constant moans about how her daughter and grandchildren never came to visit, Mr Kitson with his incontinence and unwillingness to do anything about it. Mrs Grüber with her conviction that Jean was part of an international conspiracy of social workers devoted to the cause of separating her from a revoltingly smelly little Yorkshire terrier called Nimrod. It was a relief to meet an old person who seemed to be coping.

Mr Morton had already made his mark on the flat although he had only moved in the week before. It was all very clean and tidy, no dust on any of the surfaces. (He had refused the Trust's offer of help with the cleaning, so he must have done it himself.) His few possessions were laid out neatly, the rack of pipes spotless on the mantelpiece, the pile of Do-It-Yourself magazines aligned on the coffee table, the bed squared off with hospital corners.

Mr Morton had taken the same care with his own appearance. His chin was shaved smooth, without the cuts and random tufts of white hair which Jean saw on so many of the old men she dealt with. His shirt was clean, tie tight in a little knot, jacket brushed, trousers creased properly and brown shoes buffed to a fine shine. And there didn't linger about him the sour smell which she now almost took for granted would emanate from all old people. If there was any smell in the room, it was an antiseptic hint of carbolic soap. Thank God, Jean thought, her new charge wasn't going to add too much to her already excessive workload. Just the occasional visit to check he was all right, but, even from this first meeting, she knew he would be. Harry Morton could obviously manage. He'd lived alone all his life and had the neatness of an organised bachelor. But without that obsessive independence which so many of them developed. He didn't seem to resent her visit, nor to have complicated feelings of pride about accepting the Housing Trust's charity. He was just a working man who had done his bit for society and was now ready to accept society's thanks in the reduced circumstances of retirement. Jean was already convinced that the complaints which had led to his departure from his previous flat were just the ramblings of a paranoid neighbour.

She stifled a yawn. It was not that she was bored by Harry Morton's plans for little improvements to the flat. She had learned as a social worker to appear interested in much duller and less coherent narratives. But it was stuffy. Like a lot of old people, Harry Morton seemed unwilling to open the windows. Still, it was his flat and his right to have as much or as little ventilation as he wanted.

Anyway, Jean knew that the lack of air was not the real reason for her doziness. Guiltily, she allowed herself to think for a moment about the night before. She felt a little glow of fragile pleasure and knew she mustn't think about it too much, mustn't threaten it by inflating it in her mind beyond its proper proportions.

But, without inflation, it was still the best thing that had happened to her for some years, and something that she had thought, at thirty-two, might well never happen again. It had all been so straightforward, making nonsense of the agonising and worry about being an emotional cripple which had seemed an inescapable part of her life ever since she'd broken up with Roger five years earlier.

It had not been a promising party. Given by a schoolfriend who had become a teacher, married a teacher and developed a lot of friends who were also teachers. Jean had anticipated an evening of cheap Spanish plonk, sharp French bread and predictable cheese, with conversation about how little teachers were paid, how much more everyone's contemporaries were earning, how teaching wasn't really what any of them had wanted to do anyway, all spiced with staff-room gossip about personalities she didn't know, wasn't likely to meet and, after half an hour of listening, didn't want to meet.

And that's how it had been, until she had met Mick. From that point on, the evening had just made sense. Talking to him, dancing with him (for some reason, though they were all well into their thirties, the party was still conducted on the lines of a college hop), then effortlessly leaving with him and going back to his flat.

And there it had made sense too. All the inhibitions she had carried with her so long, the knowledge that her face was strong rather than beautiful, that her hips were too broad and her breasts too small, had not seemed important. It had all been so different from the one-sided fumblings, the humourless groping and silent embarrassments which had seemed for some years all that sex had to offer. It had worked.

And Mick was coming straight round to her place after school. She was going to cook him a meal. He had to go to some Debating Society meeting and would be round about seven. Some days she couldn't guarantee to be back by then, the demands of her charges were unpredictable, but this time even that would be all right. Harry Morton was the last on her round and he clearly wasn't going to be any trouble. Covertly, with the skill born of long practice, she looked at her watch. A quarter to five. Good, start to leave in about five minutes, catch the shops on the way home, buy something special, maybe a bottle of wine. Cook a good dinner and then . . .

She felt herself blushing and guiltily pulled her mind back to listen to what Harry Morton was saying. Fantasising never helped, she knew, it only distanced reality. Anyway, she had a job to do.

'I've got a bit of money saved,' Harry was saying, 'some I put aside in the Post Office book while I was still working and I've even managed to save a bit on the pension, and I reckon I'm going to buy some really good tools. I want to get a ratchet screwdriver. They're very good, save a lot of effort. Just the job for putting up shelves, that sort of thing. I thought I'd put a couple of shelves up over there, you know, for magazines and that.'

'Yes, that's a very good idea.' Jean compensated for her lapse into reverie by being bright and helpful. 'Of course, if you need a hand with any of the heavy stuff, the Trust's got a lot of volunteers who'd be only too glad to – '

'Oh no, no, thank you. I won't need help. I'm pretty good with my hands. And, you know, if you've worked with your hands all your life, you stay pretty strong. Don't worry, I'll be up to building a few shelves. And any other little jobs around the flat.'

'What did you do before you retired, Mr Morton?'

'Now please call me Harry. I was a warehouse porter.'

'Oh.'

'Working up at Granger's, don't know if you know them?'

'Up on the main road?'

12

'Yes. We loaded the lorries. Had trolleys, you know. Had to go along the racks getting the lines to put in the lorries. Yes, I did that for nearly twenty years. They wanted me to be a checker, you know, checking off on the invoices as the goods were loaded on to the lorries, but I didn't fancy the responsibility. I was happy with my trolley.'

Suddenly Jean smiled at the old man, not her professional smile of concern, but a huge, genuine smile of pleasure that broke the sternness of her face into a rare beauty. Somehow she respected his simplicity, his content. It seemed to fit that the day after she met Mick, she should also meet this happy old man. She rose from her chair. 'Well, if you're sure there's nothing I can do for you . . .'

'No, I'll be fine, thank you, love.'

'I'll drop round again in a week or two to see how you're getting on.'

'Oh, that'll be very nice. I'll be fine, though. Don't you worry about me.'

'Good.' Jean lingered for a moment. She felt something missing, there was something else she had meant to mention, now what on earth was it?

Oh yes. His sister. She had meant to talk to him about his sister, sympathise about her death the previous year. Jean had had the information from a social worker in Bradford where the sister had lived. They tried to liaise between different areas as much as possible. The sister had been found dead in her flat. She had died of hypothermia, but her body had not been discovered for eleven days, because of the Christmas break.

Jean thought she should mention it. There was always the danger of being thought to intrude on his privacy, but Harry Morton seemed a sensible enough old bloke, who would recognise her sympathy for what it was. And, in a strange way, Jean felt she ought to raise the matter as a penance for letting her mind wander while Harry had been talking.

'Incidentally, I heard about your sister's death. I'm very sorry.'

'Oh, thank you.' Harry Morton didn't seem unduly perturbed by the reference. 'I didn't see a lot of her these last few years.'

'But it must have been a shock.'

'A bit, maybe. Typical, though. She always was daft, never took care of herself. Died of the cold, she did. Hyper . . . hyper-something they called it.'

'Hypothermia.'

'That's it. Silly fool. I didn't see her when I went up for the funeral. Just saw the coffin. Closed coffin. Could have been anyone. Didn't feel nothing, really.'

'Anyway, as I say, I'm sorry.'

'Oh, don't think about it. I don't. And don't you worry about me going the same way. For one thing, I always had twice as much sense as she did – from a child on. And then I can look after myself.'

Jean Collinson left, feeling glad she had mentioned the sister. Now there was nothing nagging at her mind, nothing she felt she should be doing. Except looking forward to the evening. She wondered what she should cook for Mick.

Harry Morton closed the door after her. It was summer, but the corridor outside felt chilly. He shivered slightly, then went to his notebook and started to make a list.

He had always made lists. At the warehouse he had soon realised that he couldn't remember all the lines the checker gave him unless he wrote them down. The younger porters could remember up to twenty different items for their loads, but Harry recognised his limitations and always wrote everything down. It made him a little slower than the others, but at least he never got anything wrong. And the Head Checker had said, when you took off the time the others wasted taking back lines they had got wrong, Harry was quite as fast as any of them.

He headed the list 'Things to do'. First he wrote 'Ratchet screwdriver'. Then he wrote 'Library'.

Harry knew his own pace and he never tried to go any faster. When he was younger he had occasionally tried to push himself along a bit, but that had only resulted in mistakes. Now he did everything steadily, methodically. And now there was no one to push him. The only really miserable time of his life had been when a new checker had been appointed who had tried to increase Harry's work-rate. The old man still woke up sometimes in the night in the sweat of panic and confusion that the pressure had put on him. Unwillingly he'd remember the afternoon when he'd thrown a catering-size tin of diced carrots at his tormentor's head. But then he'd calm down, get up and make himself a cup of tea. That was all over. It hadn't lasted very long. The checker had been ambitious and soon moved on to an office job.

And now he wasn't at work, Harry had all the time in the world anyway. Time to do a good job. The only pressure on him was to get it done before the winter set in. And the winter was a long way off.

He read through all the Do-It-Yourself books he had got from the library, slowly, not skipping a word. After each one he would make a list, a little digest of the pros and cons of the methods discussed. Then he sent off for brochures from all the companies that advertised in his Do-It-Yourself magazines and subjected them to the same punctilious scrutiny. Finally, he made a tour of the local home-care shops, looked at samples and discussed the various systems with the proprietors. After six weeks he reckoned he knew everything there was to know about double glazing.

And by then he had ruled out quite a few of the systems on the market. The best method he realised was to replace the existing windows with new factory-sealed units, but, even if the Housing Trust would allow him to do this, it would be far too expensive and also too big a job for him to do on his own.

The next possible solution was the addition of secondary sashes, fixing a new pane over the existing window, leaving the original glass undisturbed. There were a good many propriet-ary sub-frame systems on the market, but again these would be far too expensive for his modest savings. He did some sums in his notebook, working out how long it would take him to afford secondary sashes by saving on his pension, but he wouldn't have enough till the spring. And he had to get the double glazing installed before the winter set in. He began to regret the generous proportions on which the Victorians had designed their windows.

He didn't worry about it, though. It was still only September. There was going to be a way that he could afford and that he could do on his own. That social worker was always full of offers of help from her network of volunteers, but he wasn't reduced to that yet.

Then he had the idea of going through the back numbers of his Do-It-Yourself magazines. He knew it was a good idea as soon as he thought about it. He sat in his armchair in front of the fireplace, which was now hidden by a low screen, and, with notebook and pencil by his side, started to thumb through the magazines. He did them in strict chronological order, just as he kept them stacked on their new shelf. He had a full set for seven and a half years, an unbroken sequence from the first time he had become interested in Do-It-Yourself. That had been while he was being harassed by the new checker. He chuckled to remember that he'd bought the first magazine because it had an article in it about changing locks and he'd wanted to keep the checker out of his flat. Of course, the checker had never come to his flat.

He started on the first magazine and worked through, reading everything, articles and advertisements, in case he should miss what he was looking for. Occasionally he made a note in his notebook.

It was on the afternoon of the third day that he found it. The article was headed, 'Cut the Costs of Double Glazing'. His heart quickened with excitement, but he still read through the text at his regular, unvarying pace. Then he read it a second time, even more slowly, making copious notes.

The system described was a simple one, which involved sticking transparent film on the inside of the windows and thus creating the required insulation gap between the panes and the film. There were, the writer observed slyly, kits for this system available on the market, but the shrewd Do-It-Yourself practitioner would simply go to his local supermarket and buy the requisite number of rolls of kitchen cling-film and then go to his hardware store to buy a roll of double-sided Sellotape for fixing the film, and thus save himself a lot of money. Harry Morton chuckled out loud, as this cunning plot was confided to him. Then he wrote on his list 'Kitchen Clingfilm' and 'Double-sided Sellotape'.

As always, in everything he did, he followed the instructions to the letter. At first, it was more difficult than it sounded. The kitchen film tended to shrivel up on itself and stretch out of true when he tried to extend it over the window frames. And it caught on the stickiness of the Sellotape before it was properly aligned. He had to sacrifice nearly a whole roll of clingfilm before he got the method right. But he pressed on, working with steady care, perched on the folding ladder he had bought specially for the purpose, and soon was rewarded by the sight of two strips stretched parallel and taut over the window frame.

He was lining up the third when the doorbell rang. He was annoyed by the interruption to his schedule and opened the door grudgingly to admit Jean Collinson. Then he almost turned his back on her while he got on with the tricky task of winding the prepared film back on to its cardboard roll. He would have to start lining the next piece up again after she had gone.

Still, he did his best to be pleasant and offered the social worker a cup of tea. It seemed to take a very long time for the kettle to boil and the girl seemed to take a very long time to drink her tea. He kept looking over her shoulder to the window, estimating how many more strips it would take and whether he'd have to go back to the supermarket for another roll to make up for the one he'd ruined.

Had he taken any notice of Jean, he would have seen that she looked tired, fatigue stretching the skin of her face to show her features at their sharpest and sternest. Work was getting busy. She had ahead of her a difficult interview with Mrs Grüber, whose Yorkshire terrier Nimrod had developed a growth between his back legs. It hung there, obscene and shiny, dangling from the silky fur. The animal needed to go to the vet, but Mrs Grüber refused to allow this, convinced that it would have to be put down. Jean feared this suspicion was correct, but knew that the animal had to make the trip to find out one way or the other. It was obviously in pain and kept up a thin keening whine all the time while Mrs Grüber hugged it piteously to her cardigan. And Jean knew that she was going to have to be the one who got the animal to the vet.

Which meant she'd be late again. Which would mean another scene with Mick. He'd become so childish recently, so demanding, jealous of the time she spent with her old people. He had become moody and hopeless. Instead of the support in her life which he had been at first, he was now almost another case on her books. She had discovered how much he feared his job, how he couldn't keep order in class, and, though she gave him all the sympathy she could, it never seemed to be enough.

And then there were the logistics of living in two separate establishments an awkward bus-ride apart. Life seemed to have degenerated into a sequence of late-night and early-morning rushes from one flat to the other because one of them had left something vital in the wrong place. Jean had once suggested that they should move in together, but Mick's violent reaction of fear against such a commitment had kept her from raising the matter again. So their relationship had become a pattern of rows and making up, abject self-recrimination from Mick, complaints that she didn't really care about him and late-night reconciliations of desperate, clinging sex. Always too late. She had forgotten what a good night's sleep was by the time one end had been curtailed by arguments and coupling and the other by leaving at half past six to get back to her place to pick up some case-notes. Everything seemed threatened.

But it was restful in Harry's flat. He seemed to have his life organised. She found it an oasis of calm, of passionless simplicity, where she could recharge her batteries before going back to the difficulties of the rest of her life.

She was unaware of how he was itching for her to go. She saw the evidence of the double glazing and asked him about it, but he was reticent. He didn't want to discuss it until it was finished. Anyway, it wasn't for other people's benefit. It was for him.

Eventually Jean felt sufficiently steeled for her encounter with Mrs Grüber and brought their desultory conversation to an end. She did not notice the alacrity with which Harry Morton rose to show her out, nor the speed with which he closed the door after her.

Again he felt the chill of the corridor when the door was open. And even after it was closed there seemed to be a current of air from somewhere. He went across to his notebook and wrote down 'Draught Excluder'.

It was late October when she next went round to see the old man. She was surprised that he didn't immediately open the door after she'd rung the bell. Instead she heard his voice hiss out, 'Who is it?'

She was used to this sort of reception from some of her old ladies, who lived in the conviction that every caller was a rapist at the very least, but she hadn't expected it from such a sensible old boy as Harry Morton.

She identified herself and, after a certain amount of persuasion, he let her in. He held the door open as little as possible and closed it almost before she was inside. 'What do you want?' he asked aggressively.

'I just called to see how you are.'

'Well, I'm fine.' He spoke as if that ended the conversation and edged back towards the door.

'Are you sure? You look a bit pale.'

He did look pale. His skin had taken on a greyish colour.

'You look as if you haven't been out much recently. Have you been ill? If you're unwell, all you have to do is – '

'I haven't been ill. I go out, do my shopping, get the things I need.' He couldn't keep a note of mystery out of the last three words.

She noticed he was thinner too. His appearance hadn't suffered; he still dressed with almost obsessive neatness; but he had definitely lost weight. She wasn't to know that he was cutting down on food so that his pension would buy the 'things he needed'.

The room looked different too. She only took it in once she was inside. There was evidence of recent carpentry. No mess – all the sawdust was neatly contained on newspaper and offcuts of wood were leant against the kitchen table which Harry had

19

used as a sawing bench – but he had obviously been busy. The ratchet screwdriver was prominent on the table top. The artifact which all this effort had produced was plain to see. The fine marble fireplace had been neatly boxed in. It had been a careful job. Pencil marks on the wood showed the accuracy of measurement and all of the screws were tidily countersunk into their regularly spaced holes.

Jean commented on the workmanship.

'When I do a job, I like to do it properly,' Harry Morton said defensively.

'Of course. Didn't you . . . like the fireplace?'

'Nothing wrong with it. But it was very draughty.'

'Yes.' She wondered for a moment if Harry Morton were about to change from being one of her easy charges to one of her problems. He was her last call that day and she'd reckoned on just a quick visit. She'd recently made various promises to Mick about spending less time with her work. He'd suddenly got very aggressively male, demanding that she should have a meal ready for him when he got home. He also kept calling her 'woman', as if he were some character out of the blues songs he was always listening to. He didn't manage this new male chauvinism with complete conviction; it seemed only to accentuate his basic insecurity; but Jean was prepared to play along with it for a bit. She felt there was something in the relationship worth salvaging. Maybe when he relaxed a bit, things would be better. If only they could spend a little time on their own, just the two of them, away from outside pressures . . .

She stole a look at her watch. She could spend half an hour with Harry and still be back at what Mick would regard as a respectable hour. Anyway, there wasn't anything really wrong with the old boy. Just needed a bit of love, a feeling that someone cared. That's what most of them needed when it came down to it.

'Harry, it looks to me like you may have been overdoing it with all this heavy carpentry. You must remember, you're not as young as you were and you do have to take things a bit slower.'

'I take things at the right pace,' he insisted stubbornly. 'There's nothing wrong with me.'

But Jean wasn't going to have her solicitude swept aside so easily. 'No, of course there isn't. But look, I'd like you just to sit down for a moment in front of the . . . by the fireplace, and I'll make you a cup of tea.'

Grumbling, he sat down.

'And why don't you put the television on? I'm sure there's some nice relaxing programme for you to see.'

'There's not much I enjoy on the television.'

'Nonsense, I'm sure there are lots of things to interest you.' Having started in this bulldozing vein, Jean was going to continue. She switched on the television and went into the kitchen.

It was some children's quiz show, which Harry would have switched off under normal circumstances. But he didn't want to make the girl suspicious. If he just did as she said, she would go quicker. So he sat and watched without reaction.

It was only when the commercials came that he took notice. There was a commercial for double glazing. A jovial man was demonstrating the efficacy of one particular system. A wind machine was set in motion the other side of an open window. Then the double-glazed window was closed and, to show how airtight the seal was, the man dropped a feather by the joint in the panes. It fluttered straight downwards, its course unaffected by any draughts.

From that moment Harry Morton was desperate for Jean to leave. He had seen the perfect way of testing his workmanship. She offered to stay and watch the programme with him, she asked lots of irrelevant questions about whether he needed anything or whether there was anything her blessed volunteers could do, but eventually she was persuaded to go. In fact she was relieved to be away. Harry had seemed a lot perkier than when she had arrived and now she would be back in time to conform to Mick's desired image of her.

Harry almost slammed the door. As he turned, he felt a shiver of cold down his back. Right, feathers, feathers. It only took a moment to work out where to get them from.

He picked up his ratchet screwdriver and went over to the

bed. He drew back the candlewick and stabbed the screw-driver deeply into his pillow. And again, twisting and tearing at the fabric. From the rents he made a little storm of feathers flurried.

It was cold as she walked along towards Harry's flat and the air stung the rawness of her black eye. But Jean felt good. At least they'd got something sorted out. After the terrible fight of the night before, in the sobbing reconciliation, after Mick had apologised for hitting her, he had suggested that they go away together for Christmas. He hated all the fuss that surrounded the festival and always went off to stay in a cottage in Wales, alone, until it all died down. And he had said, in his un-gracious way, 'You can come with me, woman.'

She knew it was a risk. The relationship might not stand the proximity. She was even slightly afraid of being alone with Mick for so long, now that his behaviour towards her had taken such a violent turn. But at bottom she thought it would work. Anyway, she had to try. They had to try. Ten days alone together would sort out the relationship one way or the other. And Christmas was only three weeks off.

As so often happened, her new mood of confidence was re-flected in her work. She had just been to see Mrs Grüber. Nimrod had made a complete recovery after the removal of his growth and the old lady had actually thanked Jean for insisting on the visit to the vet. That meant Mrs Grüber could be left over the Christmas break without anxiety. And most of the others could manage. As Mick so often said, thinking you're indispensable is one of the first signs of madness. Of course they'd be all right if she went away. And, as Mick also said, then you'll be able to concentrate on me for a change, woman. Yes, it was going to work.

Again her ring at the doorbell was met by a whispered 'Who is it?' from Harry Morton. It was Jean – could she come in? 'No,' he said.

'Why not, Harry? Remember, I do have a duplicate key. The Housing Trust insists that I have that, so that I can let myself in if – '

'No, it's not that, Jean love,' his old Northern voice wheedled.

'It's just that I've got a really streaming cold. I don't want to breathe germs all over you.'

'Oh, don't worry about that.'

'No, no, really. I'm in bed. I'm just going to sleep it off.'

Jean wavered. Now she came to think of it, she didn't fancy breathing in germs in Harry's stuffy little flat. 'Have you seen the doctor?'

'No, I tell you it's just a cold. Be gone in a day or two, if I just stay in bed. No need to worry the doctor.'

The more she thought about it, the less she wanted to develop a cold just before she and Mick went away together. But it was her job to help. 'Are you sure there isn't anything I can do for you? Shopping or anything?'

'Oh. Well . . .' Harry paused. 'Yes, I would be grateful, actually, if you wouldn't mind getting me a few things.'

'Of course.'

'If you just wait a moment, I'll write out a list.'

Jean waited. After a couple of minutes a page from his notebook was pushed under the door. Its passage was impeded by the draught-excluding strip on the inside, but it got through.

Jean looked at the list. 'Bottle of milk. Small tin of baked beans. Six packets of Polyfilla.'

'Is that Polyfilla?' she asked, bewildered.

'Yes. It's a sort of powder you mix with water to fill in cracks and that.'

'I know what it is. You just seem to want rather a lot of it.'

'Yes, I do. Just for a little job needs doing.'

'And you're quite sure you don't need any more food?'

'Sure. I've got plenty,' Harry Morton lied.

'Well, I'll probably be back in about twenty minutes.'

'Thank you very much. Here's the money.' A few crumpled notes forced their way under the door. 'If there's no reply when you get back, I'll be asleep. Just leave the stuff outside. It'll be safe.'

'O.K. If you're sure there's nothing else I can do.'

'No, really. Thanks very much.'

Harry Morton heard her footsteps recede down the passage

23

and chuckled aloud with delight at his own cunning. Yes, she could help him. First useful thing she'd ever done for him.

And she hadn't noticed the windows from the outside. Just thought the curtains were drawn. Yes, it had been a good idea to board them up over the curtains. He looked with satisfaction at the wooden covers, with their rows of screws, each one driven securely home with his ratchet screwdriver. Then he looked at the pile of new wood leaning against the door. Yes, with proper padding that would be all right. Mentally he earmarked his bedspread for the padding and made a note of the idea on the 'Jobs to Do' list in his notebook.

Suddenly he felt the chill of a draught on his neck. He leapt up to find its source. He had long given up using the feather method. Apart from anything else, he had used his pillows as insulation in the fireplace. Now he used a lighted candle. Holding it firmly in front of him, he began to make a slow, methodical circuit of the room.

It was two days before Christmas, two o'clock in the afternoon. Jean and Mick were leaving at five. 'Five sharp, woman,' he had said. 'If you ain't here then, woman, I'll know you don't give a damn about me. You'd rather spend your life with incontinent old men.' Jean had smiled when he said it. Oh yes, she'd be there. Given all that time together, she knew they could work something out.

And, when it came to it, it was all going to be remarkably easy. All of her charges seemed to be sorted out over the holiday. Now Nimrod was all right, Mrs Grüber was in a state of ecstasy, full of plans for the huge Christmas dinner she was going to cook for herself and the dog. Mrs Walker was going to stay with her daughter, which meant that she would see the grandchildren, so she couldn't complain for once. Even smelly old Mr Kitson had been driven off to spend the holiday with his married sister. Rather appropriately, in Bath. The rest of her cases had sorted themselves out one way or the other. And, after all, she was only going to be away for ten days. She felt she needed the break. Her Senior Social Worker had wished her luck and told her to have a good rest, and this made Jean realise how long it was since she had been away from work for any length of time.

She just had to check that Mr Morton was all right, and then she was free.

Harry was steeping his trousers in mixed-up Polyfilla when he heard the doorbell. It was difficult, what he was doing. Really, the mixture should have been runnier, but he had not got out enough water before he boarded up the door to the kitchen and bathroom. Never mind, though, the stuff would still work and soon he'd be able to produce more urine to mix it with. He was going to use the Polyfilla-covered trousers to block the crevice along the bottom of the front door. His pyjamas and pullover were already caulking the cracks on the other one.

He congratulated himself on judging the amount of Polyfilla right. He was nearly at the end of the last packet. By the time he'd blocked in the plug sockets and the ventilation grille he'd found hidden behind the television, it would all be used up. Just the right amount.

He froze when he heard the doorbell. Lie doggo. Pretend there's no one there. They'll go away.

The bell rang again. Still he didn't move. There was a long pause, so long he thought the challenge had gone. But then he heard an ominous sound, which at once identified his caller and also raised a new threat.

It was the sound of a key in his lock. That bloody busybody of a social worker had come round to see him.

There was nothing for it. He would have to let her in. 'Just a minute. Coming,' he called.

'Hurry up,' the girl's voice said. She had told him to hurry up. Like the new checker, she had told him to hurry up.

He picked up his ratchet screwdriver and started to withdraw the first of the screws that held the large sheet of chipboard and its padding of bedclothes against the front door. At least, he thought, thank God I hadn't put the sealing strips along there.

Jean's voice sounded quite agitated by the time he removed the last screw. 'What's going on? Can't you hurry up?'

She had said it again. He opened the door narrowly and she

pushed in, shouting, 'Now what the hell do you think you're – '

Whether she stopped speaking because she was taken aback by the sight of the room and her half-naked host, or because the ratchet screwdriver driven into her back near the spine had punctured her heart, it is difficult to assess. Certainly it is true that the first blow killed her; the subsequent eleven were unnecessary insurance.

Harry Morton left the body on the floor and continued methodically with his tasks. He replaced the chipboard and padding over the door and sealed round it with his trousers, sports jacket, shirt and socks, all soaked in Polyfilla. Then he blocked up the plugs and ventilator grille.

He looked round with satisfaction. Now that was real insulation. No one could die of cold in a place like that. Always had been daft, his sister. But he didn't relax. One more final check-round with the candle, then he could put his feet up.

He went slowly round the room, very slowly so that the candle wouldn't flicker from his movement, only from genuine draughts.

Damn. It had moved. He retraced a couple of steps. Yes, it fluttered again. There was a draught.

By the fireplace. That fireplace had always been more trouble than it was worth.

It needed more insulating padding. And more Polyfilla to seal it.

But he'd used everything in the room and there was no water left to mix the Polyfilla with. He felt too dehydrated to urinate. Never mind, there was a solution to everything. He sat down with his notebook and pencil to work it out.

Well, there was his underwear, for a start. That was more insulation. He took it off.

Then he looked down at Jean Collinson's body and saw the solution. To both his problems. Her body could be crammed into the chimney to block out the draughts and her blood (of which there was quite a lot) could mix with the Polyfilla.

He worked at his own pace, unscrewing the boxwork he had put around the marble fireplace with his ratchet screwdriver. Then he pulled out the inadequate insulation of pillows and

Do-It-Yourself magazines and started to stuff the body up the chimney.

It was hard work. He pushed the corpse up head first and the broad hips stuck well in the flue, forming a good seal. But he had to break the legs to fit them behind his boxwork when he replaced it. He crammed the crevices with the pillows and magazines and sealed round the edges with brownish Polyfilla.

Only then did he feel that he could sit back with the satisfaction of a job well done.

They found his naked body when they broke into the flat after the Christmas break.

He would have died from starvation in time, but in fact, so good was his insulation, he was asphyxiated first.

Gwendoline Butler

NORTH WIND

As soon as I saw Harry Trask I guessed what he must be. He was one in the line of descent, an inheritor, a successor.

C.I.A., I thought : *he's* the man sent here to replace Jim Olsen. (Jim had been a friend of mine. Or, anyway, we'd seen a lot of each other.) Then I thought : if he is the man sent to succeed Jim, he's come here to watch someone. So the thing to do is to observe whom he cultivates, whom he sees most of.

It took me some time to realise that person was me.

A bubble of speculation, floating airily above me, had suddenly turned hard and white and hit me, like a golf ball driven in from outer space during some celestial competition.

In fact there was a golf ball at my feet where I walked by the sea. I picked it up and threw it back towards the green. The dog followed it.

When you live a great deal alone by yourself in an isolated but intellectual community games get invented. I belong to such a group, living amidst schools, university and golf courses, and facing the bleak North Sea. The German Ocean, the Kaiser's Ocean, our grandfathers called it. We were far away from almost everywhere. The winds that lashed us came straight from the Urals.

The best game was about people, and I was the inventor. 'Bubbles' we called it. Half secret, half public was 'Bubbles'. We played it at drinks parties, on long quiet walks, in bed. You could play it together or alone. 'Bubbles' had no beginning and no end. So innocent, so inventive, so easy, a challenge to the imagination we thought it. In the time since, at moments when I have been alone, I have given much thought to the essential nature of the game we played and I would now call it destructive.

'A dangerous game it turned out to be,' I said aloud, stirring my coffee. The waiter, who did not understand very well, and small wonder, since I was but learning his tongue, thought I asked for sugar and brought me a bowl.

This particular 'Bubble' began at a party. A cold summer evening in a garden overlooking the sea, not a time to have drinks out of doors, but Clara and Jock ignored the thermometer's temperature when their roses were out.

Roses do bloom beautifully by the sea, but sometimes the salt spray burns and scorches them. This had happened now to Clara and Jock Oban-Smith's roses, so that the petals were brown and sere.

All the same, I picked one and sniffed. The sea air diminishes scents as well, but in this case the roses had triumphed. 'Lovely,' I said to Jock. 'Delicious. Better than ever. A good year.'

He was pleased; he knew it was a lie, roses, after all, aren't like vines and don't have a vintage, but he could accept a compliment to his own good husbandry. He and I were particularly good exponents of 'the game'.

There were about thirty people crowded into the small garden and I knew every one of them. There were no more variations to be played in our small circle, we had done them all. I suppose it was what made our game so essential.

One notable omission among the guests that evening, I observed.

'Who's not here?' I said, testing.

'Jim Olsen, of course.'

Jim Olsen was a fat young American who had come to teach geography at the local boys' prep school. He was always beautifully dressed in grey, with a good deal of white about him. He seemed too rich and sophisticated (and also just slightly too seedy, there was a hint of secrets about him) to be teaching in a boys' school. We could never quite understand his presence, so he was a natural for our game.

'Why of course?'

'He has to obey his masters. He's been called back home.'

'Ah,' I nodded sagely. 'What a good notion.'

In this bubble of our imagining, Jim Olsen swam round and round like a goldfish in a bowl with Jock Oban-Smith after

29

him. It was Jock's bubble really. I had just joined in, but I was taking it over. In it Jim Olsen was not really a school teacher but a representative of the C.I.A.

'Of course, if Jim *is* really C.I.A.,' I had said originally when we were just starting this bubble, Jock and I, 'then he has to be here doing something.'

'Oh, that's simple,' said Jock Oban-Smith easily. 'There's a Russian spy at the airfield. Or a security leak of some sort. The Americans are alarmed, you know they use the airfield, although we aren't supposed to admit it. They've sent old Jim over to watch a suspect.'

'Yes, I accept that,' I nodded judiciously. 'We all know that more things than they ever admit to fly in the skies over that field. I am sure there are spies. And so counter-spies. Yes, I like that, Jock.'

Although we never talked much about the airfield I, for one, never forgot its presence. My husband had been a flyer there. Had been or was : of which tense I was never sure – was it what he did or what he aspired to? To me, he seemed to have so many ambitions.

Now Jock Oban-Smith said : 'Look, Elizabeth, I know how dreary it's been for you since your man went away. Rotten for you. Let me know if I can help.'

'Oh, Jock, it's not so bad,' I protested. 'He's not dead or divorced. He's coming back.' (I wasn't totally convinced of this, but never mind.) 'It's only a polar expedition.'

'But twelve months !' He looked at me with sympathy. 'Tough.'

Jock had never been six months away from his wife, and probably never would be, but Clara had confided in me that she wished for silence and a period of quiet and would have been grateful if the North Pole had called Jock.

'Oh, I *know*,' went on Jock, looking at me with sympathy. 'I've seen you taking your long walks across the sands, head down, pushing against the wind.'

To divert him I said, 'We never worked out who Jim was watching, did we? He hardly seemed to know anyone but us.'

'Oh, not so. He had a tremendous circle : all the boys at the school, all the staff. Oh yes, he had his circle. They'll miss him.'

'And he's really gone?'

'On Wednesday. Flew out. Naturally he'd keep it quiet. Be discreet. The school was told his mother had died. But that's a cover story. Anyway, he's gone. With hardly a word.'

As I took my customary long walk across the dunes that ran towards the airfield, I thought : if Jim Olsen was truly C.I.A. and has now been withdrawn, then someone else will surely take his place, because the job is not done. I have only to watch and wait to identify his successor.

It was such an extension of our bubble that at first I decided to keep it to myself. The town seemed full of ghosts as I turned and walked towards it, leaving the sand dunes and the wild sea behind me. Some of them walked out of history, like Mary Stuart and John Knox, but others were my own private and personal hauntings. I think Jim Olsen had his own walk there.

By October a young American had arrived. He had short-cropped hair and an air of great neatness. He said he had been an army officer stationed in Athens, had become interested in antiquity and had come here to study the ancient Greeks. A likely story.

All right, I thought, if he is Jim Olsen's replacement come here to study a local spy, watch who he gets close to.

Rather shyly I told Jock Oban-Smith about my addition to the bubble and he agreed that it was a good one.

So I watched. The young soldier was called Harry Trask, which seemed a good name for him, whether it was his own or not. He was a nice boy and I liked him. Back home he had a pretty little wife called Livia; he showed me her photograph but, of course, anyone can have a photograph and call it what they like. A solitary soul, he seemed to make few friends outside the ancient world. I used to meet him walking on the beach, face screwed up against the onslaught of wind and sand and spray. He was musical, too, so I let him come and listen to Vivaldi and Handel on my record player. He didn't seem to like anything written later than 1760. If I had had Bronze Age music, I expect he'd have chosen that.

I was very slow. It was spring before I took in that the only person he seemed interested in was *me*.

Me. Why me? I thought.

Ironically enough, it was just about the time this sank in that I became convinced my bubble was no bubble but the truth. Hard to say exactly how I arrived at this conclusion, perhaps things he let drop, perhaps his very evasions and discretions.

Why me? Why was he watching me? What had I got that he wanted?

Well, I knew what I had got, even in his absence, and that was a husband attached to a highly strategic airfield. Far away from me at this moment, of course, but it might be presumed that I had noticed things about his life and work, or had had secrets told me, as a wife. So if there was a leak, I was due for suspicion.

Or a further puff for my bubble (now getting rather unpleasant and hard, like some grotesque physical cyst) it might be thought that I was a spy.

Jock Oban-Smith was surprised that I no longer joined in our game. (Clara had never played.) How could I tell him that I seemed to be inside the bubble myself?

Jock liked immunity, you see. He liked to be the doctor identifying the disease, not the patient in fever with it. And he had all the right antigens to protect him from contemporary society, too, for he was rich and Clara was well born.

'You're getting dull, my dear girl,' he complained. 'I shall have to do something.'

'I don't know what, then,' I retorted.

'I'll ask Clara.'

Jock always asked Clara, although he didn't always do what Clara suggested. About me, for instance, I know she thought Jock shouldn't encourage me in our games. She thought he was in love with me, but he wasn't. Jock wasn't in love with anyone, not even Clara, only her family tree. He *did* love genealogy; it brought out the best in him. He would tell you about her descent quietly and gently, as a special privilege, when he felt you had earned the honour. Clara never mentioned it herself. She was above that sort of thing.

It was early summer when I learned, through the usual

devious routes by which such news came to me, that my husband's return from the Arctic was delayed. I had suspected it already, of course. I began to wonder if he would ever come back. There comes a time in any long absence (does there not?) when you feel that the loved one will not come back at all. This fear had a great deal to do with what happened. I was anxious. And there were no letters from him, you see. From where he was no letters could come.

I let Harry see me as often as he wished from that time on, get as close to me as he seemed to want, because I was watching him watch me.

I thought that way I could find out what I was supposed to have done.

Inside the bubble values get distorted like a reflection in a crooked mirror, so that my behaviour seemed acceptable and even good sense.

As Harry got closer, and we met more often, I thought: if he's watching me then I'll give him something to watch. So I went to the airfield often. I had a lot of contacts there, it was an easy thing for me to do. I entertained some of the young pilots; they were lonely and came willingly to drink coffee and listen to music. It was harmless enough, they expected little of me except companionship, but the bubble distorted everything, and I suppose I looked like a woman amusing herself in her husband's absence.

Jock Oban-Smith it was who acquainted me of the next development. He stopped me in the street one day, the usual keen wind was blowing.

'You're crying,' he accused.

'No, I'm not. My eyes are watering in the wind, that's all.'

'Have you had bad news from that husband of yours?'

'I tell you there's nothing wrong with me.'

'You've had no news, though.'

'I expected none,' I said tersely. I tried to move, but Jock wouldn't let me.

'That young man's in love with you.' He meant Harry.

'I think not.'

'He's very very interested,' said Jock.

'Oh, fascinated,' I said.

33

'You wouldn't go doing anything silly? Couldn't blame you, I suppose.' His kind face looked concerned. 'I always said it was a pity, your husband being away so much.' He wagged a finger. 'And I'm thinking of that young man, too, as well as you. You've got a hard heart, he hasn't.'

'I have? Is that what you think? But I'll have a word with him,' I promised. 'I've been meaning to, really.'

The next day I met Harry on the sands. He had a small dog with him, a stray mongrel he had befriended. Everyone in the town knew the dog. It was known as 'the little lame dog'. They stopped when they saw me.

'It must be lonely for your wife,' I said. 'With you away.'

Harry and the dog turned to look at me, moving their heads simultaneously as if the same string pulled them both.

'It was her choice,' he said defensively. He hadn't talked about his wife much lately and I had begun to wonder if she really existed. Now it looked as if she did. 'Her own choice,' he said again. 'It's her life back home, her pottery and the shop where she sells it. No, she couldn't leave it.'

'Hasn't she ever moved about with you? I mean, as the army has moved you from country to country?'

'Only sometimes.' He was always tight-mouthed about his army life. Then he countered : 'You must know all about loneliness, with your husband so long gone.'

'Only it wasn't my chọ ice I was left.'

He gave me a wary look, almost exactly like the stray dog's. 'What's your husband's name? You've never said.'

'Edward. Always Edward.'

'What a funny way of putting it : as if he could change names.'

Inside my bubble the sound of his words was magnified and distorted. Was I hearing true? Now it sounded as if he thought the spy he was watching was not me after all, but my husband, and that because he could not watch Edward he was watching *me*. It figured, as they say where he came from.

'I only meant that some people shorten it to Ted or Ed or Eddie; he's always Edward,' I said. 'Still, he's been a long time away.'

The dog pawed at my leg, he was a friendly fellow, and I bent down to pat his head.

Harry said : 'For me, it's been a lovely time, I've had a lovely time. Knowing you, our walks together, the music. A good time for me.' He spoke awkwardly, offering me the words like a shy present.

I was terrified. Is it then, not a spy story after all, but a tender love story between two lonely people? Had I made a terrible mistake?

'You do like me, don't you?' he said, still hesitantly.

'Oh, yes. I do.' I patted the dog's head again so that I need not meet his eyes. But instead I saw the dog's lambent gaze, and it was almost the same thing.

'I think you like Americans. There was another, wasn't there? Jim Olsen.'

'I wondered if you'd mention him.'

'He seems much missed. Everyone says how nice he was. I wish I'd known him.'

'You might meet him one day, I suppose.'

'America's a big country,' he observed mildly. 'He was from Boston and I'm from New York and never the twain shall meet. Oddly enough, though, I have sort of heard of him. My – ' and here he hesitated for a word, the right, the true, the telling word. He came up with it. 'My folk know his folk.'

'Ah,' I said. 'So there's a connection.'

'And he's never got back home yet. They're getting a bit worried.'

'As you say, America's a big country. I expect he's visiting somewhere. He loved the sands here,' I said. 'I often used to meet him walking here. Or he met me. I don't know which way round it was, which of us kept meeting the other. But he certainly loved it here. Perhaps he never got any further home than these sand dunes.'

'But that's a terrible thought,' he protested.

'What, not happy for him among all the little crabs and molluscs? But I was only joking.'

'I'll never get used to your British sense of humour.'

'What you really mean is that it was a joke in incredibly bad taste.'

'Well, it was rather.' He was stiff.

'I'm a bit on edge, one way and another, about absent friends.'

'Were you so close to Jim Olsen, then?'

'Not really,' I said after a pause.

'You have the reputation for letting people get so close to you and then no closer.'

'That's about it,' I said.

'You see, I'm being completely honest with you.'

I sat down on the sand, where it was dry, and the dog came and sat next to me. After a bit Harry sat down too.

The sky was a clear, pale blue, the sort of blue washed with silver that you only get in those northern days. Towards the west it was banded with pink and gold.

'It's coming towards the longest day,' he said, looking at the sky.

'Yes, so it is.' The season of the white nights, so the Russians called it. The further you got into the Arctic Circle, the longer the day.

'And the shortest night,' he went on. 'Hardly any night at all. Already the hours of darkness are shorter than I expected.'

'Yes.' I did not take my eyes off the sky. 'It's being so far north. Next week I am going to Norway, to take a trip on a small ship that goes round the fjords. It goes right through the Arctic Circle to Kirkenes. I shall leave the ship there and go right up to the Russian border. I'm going to study the birds and the flowers.' I did look at him then, and saw his eyes bright and hopeful. But who knew quite what the hope was for? 'Why don't you come too?'

'I could come,' he said slowly. 'I could get away.'

'I shall go right up to the Russian border. If you've never seen the tundra country you'll love it.' I spoke sweetly. I meant him to accept. I was punishing somebody and I wasn't quite sure who.

If any letters had come then from Edward, I believe I would have shown them to Harry, and said : 'Look, read them and see for yourself. Make up your own mind what he is and what I am. Is he just a nice, shy, inarticulate man who has gone away on a scientific trip, or is he something more devious?

And if he is, then what am I? An innocent victim or his assistant?' But no letters came.

'How do you get there?' he asked.

'Well, if you really don't know, and I'm sure you do, you fly to Bergen and get on the boat there. Then leave it at Kirkenes. The boat gets booked up well ahead, but I'm sure you will find a berth.'

He didn't rise to the implication of my remark, but said : 'Are you sure *you* will?'

'Oh, I have had mine booked for months.'

'I can see you plan ahead,' he said.

'You have to,' I answered briefly. 'Well, what about it?'

There was nothing explicitly sexual about my invitation. He could make what he liked of it. He had offered me a show of affection, love even, and I had replied in kind. He would have to come to Norway, I thought. If he was a C.I.A. agent, as postulated in my bubble, he would have to accept.

'I'll come.'

'What will you do about the dog?'

'You've got a cat, haven't you? What are you doing with her?'

'Clara Oban-Smith is looking after her. It's all arranged.'

'Will she take the dog too?'

'Clara always says yes to everything. It's what makes her such a good wife.'

'You can be a bitch sometimes, can't you?' he said coolly. Oddly enough, it was at that moment I believed that he might be in love with me.

I shrugged. 'Successful wife, then.'

'And you are not?'

'Manifestly, I am not. Successful wives are with their husbands, not left behind.'

'But that is due to an Arctic trip. Wives, women, can't go on such trips, can they?'

I paused. 'Well, I tell you : it was just a little bit more than that. The trip, I mean.'

'What?' The question was wrung from him.

'You don't sound surprised. I'm sure you've suspected. Jock

Oban-Smith has.' I thought for a moment. Yes, I was nearly sure that Jock's imaginings stretched that far.

'You mean he *has* left you? Your husband has left you?'

'Not quite that. I mean the Arctic trip had its secret side. As well as doing all the official scientific things.'

'You mean spying?'

'But of course you've already guessed it.'

He didn't answer, but stared at me with a completely blank expression. I suppose that's how you look when your cover is blown. That's what they call it, isn't it?

'If that is what the party including your husband is really up to, I don't believe you'd know it,' he said coolly.

'You mean that my husband wouldn't dare to tell me?' I said as coolly back. 'That would depend, wouldn't it?'

'On what?'

'On what sort of a husband he is, and what sort of a wife I am,' I said, still cool. 'I suppose you don't tell your wife anything. Poor Livia. I pity that girl.'

He stared hard for a minute, then suddenly burst out laughing. Loudly. 'What a girl you are for a joke,' he said. 'You almost had me believing you. Like the suggestion you'd got Jim Olsen buried here beside you.'

We walked back into the town, not talking much, and the dog loped beside us.

Over the next few days I got on with my arrangements for the voyage, and I presume he did the same. Jock Oban-Smith said he deplored my departure, but he did nothing to stop my going.

'I suppose you've dropped all that story about Harry Trask now?' he said.

'Oh, completely.'

'You've fallen in love with him, that's why.'

'Oh, rubbish.'

'It's true.' He sighed. 'And it was such a good game. "Bubbles", I mean. Of course, I can never play it now.'

'Yes, you can, Jock,' I said kindly. 'You'll never stop. You're playing it now : me in love with Harry Trask. That's a prime example of a good bubble.'

38

'I admit it,' he said after a bit. 'And in my bubble you're doing it to pay your husband back for something.'

'For what?'

'That I don't know. Leaving you alone so long – something like that. I'll give it thought.'

'You're quite cold-hearted under that friendly exterior, Jock,' I said.

'Never you mind. Remember I'm looking after your cat while you're away. Doesn't that show a kind heart?'

'I'll see you about that, Jock,' I said.

Jock Oban-Smith put on his spectacles; they were a tiny, round, steel-framed affair, an affectation which increased his likeness to a fluffy-haired owl. He was long-sighted, Clara short-sighted; they were a perfect match.

'And shall I see you tomorrow before you go?'

'Oh, probably. Yes, I'm sure, Jock,' which meant, as I knew he guessed, no, he wouldn't.

'And where are you off to now?'

'Just for a last look at the sands.'

'I'll say goodbye now, then.'

'Goodbye, Jock. Goodbye.'

He kissed my cheek. 'I see you've got your shopping bag with you,' he called after me.

It was lonely on the beach, with only the hungry cries of the seagulls, and I wanted it that way so that I could say goodbye.

I was kneeling on the sand in the shelter of a low range of dunes topped with rough sea grass, still thinking I was alone, when I heard my name. I looked round, trying to hide what I was doing.

'Oh, Harry, you?' I leaned back on my heels.

Quickly he said : 'I wasn't following you.'

'No, of course not.'

'I just wanted to take a look at the places where we've walked. You can understand that, can't you?'

I nodded; I wished he would go away. I knew he wouldn't, though.

'What have you got in your hand?' he asked. He was staring at me. 'It's a little spade. A children's spade.'

'I found it on the sands,' I lied.

But his eyes had wandered beyond me. 'You're burying something.' He moved to see better. 'It's your cat. Your own cat.'

'He was very old,' I said. 'He might have died while I was away. I wanted his last hours to be with me. Besides, I didn't quite trust Clara Oban-Smith's care of him. She's decent, of course, but she has no imagination. People with no imagination can't be really kind.'

'My God, you are ruthless,' he said.

'I couldn't help it. It really is much kinder this way.'

'But if it had to be so, couldn't you bury the creature in your own backyard?'

'Oh no, here is best,' I said swiftly. 'More natural, more beautiful. But I must bury him deep, because of the seagulls. You can help, if you like.'

'No, the job's nearly done. You'd better finish it yourself.'

He watched me sprinkle the last sand on the furry face. 'You did love the creature.'

'Oh, yes.'

'And yet you killed it.'

'I had to.' I stood up. 'Honestly, what I did was best.'

Both of us started to walk away, the town lay ahead of us; behind us the sea and the dunes.

'Clara's all right for your dog, though,' I said. 'As a matter of fact she's looked after him before. He's anyone's dog, really.'

'Don't tell me Jim Olsen had him before me,' he said.

'There was a relationship,' I admitted, not willing to meet his eye.

We walked on in silence for a few minutes. Then : 'Do you know what I'm wondering as I plod beside you?'

'No.' There was a strange note in his voice. I glanced at him quickly, there he was, shoulders hunched and head down.

'I'm wondering whose dog he will be next.'

'I think you will be his last owner,' I said seriously. 'But you needn't come with me. Stay here. Be his master.'

'No, I'm coming with you.'

We boarded the boat at Bergen and sailed slowly, and with

many stops at the Norwegian towns up the coast and down a fjord or two. Bergen, Trondheim, Tromso, Harstad lay behind us.

I think he enjoyed it. We went sightseeing at each port, and then ran to catch the *Arctic Queen* before, on the minute with Norwegian punctuality, she sailed.

There was an American couple on board not on good terms, I thought, for they bickered constantly. I thought that perhaps it was the way they liked to live, but it seems not, since they began to look more and more miserable. The wife said to me : 'Do you ever have a cold war with your husband?'

'Yes, and a hot one too sometimes,' I said.

I think she imagined Harry and I were husband and wife, and I suppose we did seem like a pair, which in a way we were, although, if she had bothered to observe, she would have seen we had separate cabins.

At Kirkenes we left the *Arctic Queen* and moved into rooms in the small modern hotel where it seemed as though only businessmen came briefly, to look at the open-cast iron mine. Or perhaps there was the occasional educator visiting the school.

One other class of visitor there was, and I was not surprised to see them : neatly dressed men with quiet faces and well-drilled shoulders, an air of discipline and quiet authority belying their unobtrusiveness.

We were two days at Kirkenes and several such men were there during that time. I knew why they were there. A few miles away ran the Russian border, and on their side of the frontier were red telephones in guard huts that rang for emergencies only. And beyond the line of demarcation, and on this side too, were who knew what bits of sensitive military equipment? One does not leave frontiers like this guarded only by fresh-faced militiamen.

I wondered what languages the unobtrusive men spoke when they called at the military H.Q. outside the town. Any one of the N.A.T.O. languages, I supposed.

Harry fitted into their background remarkably well, he looked just like one of them.

'I've enjoyed this trip so far,' he said on our first evening after dinner. 'And it has been perfectly educational.' I looked at him sharply. 'But I haven't seen any sign so far of your interest in the flora and fauna.'

'Tomorrow,' I said. 'We'll take a picnic and walk. It's marvellous country for walking.'

'You've got a map, have you? It's not the sort of country to wander in, I should say.'

'Oh, I have a map.'

The next day, early, we set off together. True to my word, I had a picnic lunch (thick smoked sausage and cheese sandwiches) in a bag hanging over my shoulder.

Until that moment I hadn't been quite sure that Harry would come. I thought that in the night he might have packed his bags and gone away. Or even had me arrested. I was sure he could have done either of those things and kept within his remit.

Instead, he walked beside me quietly. The further we had travelled inside the Arctic Circle, the better the weather had become. Behind us we had left a cold, windy Scotland, here it was warm and still. The landscape was golden, the grasses tall and the trees tiny and fragile. A small stream traced a winding path across the grassland.

'It's like the landscape of the moon, isn't it?' I said. 'Or what one used to imagine the moon might have been like before one knew it was covered with dust and dry boulders. This is timeless and quiet.'

'Lovely now, but it must be grim in winter,' said Harry.

'Snow and ice,' I said.

'I hope you know where we are.'

'The river follows the frontier,' I said, pointing. Distantly we could see the wooden watch-towers from which unseen Russian eyes might even now be watching us.

'The Norwegians presumably have something here also,' he said looking round.

'Bound to have. I expect we could find it if we wanted. But, of course, they wouldn't let us get too close.'

'To the frontier, you mean?'

'To anything,' I said lightly. 'And we won't even stare at the Russians in their turrets, in case it provokes them.'

'Could it?'

'I don't know. Depends how they're feeling, I suppose. But sometimes I believe the Russians and the Norwegians meet. Fishing in that river. It's a salmon river, you see.'

'So they catch salmon?'

'I suppose it's all there is to catch up here,' I said. 'You haven't got a camera on you, have you?'

He shook his head. 'No, no camera.'

'You must be hot in your jacket. Why don't you take it off?'

He mopped his brow. 'It *is* getting hot. Never thought of the Arctic Circle being so hot, somehow.' He didn't remove his jacket, however.

I looked up at the sun. 'Nearly noon. I suppose it's as hot now as it ever will be.'

By now I was deeply puzzled. We had come all this way together and so far he had offered me nothing but simple, un-questioning companionship. Perhaps my bubble was all wrong. Perhaps he was just what he seemed, a man who had abandoned the army for scholarship.

But no. Life could not be as innocuous as all that, and if it was, then he was not. There were lines about his mouth such as simple scholars never had.

We were quite close to the river bed now, and for a while we walked along a narrow track with birches and tall grasses on one hand and the silver river on the other. Then the river seemed to twist away out of sight.

A small hollow with a tree to lean against seemed to invite us to sit down. 'Let's have our lunch here. shall we?' I said.

I sat down. He remained on his feet, looking down at me. I held out my arms.

He knelt. 'I waited a long time for you to ask me to kiss you.'

'I think I've been asking all the time.'

'Ah, you don't know yourself.'

Even as I kissed him, I was experiencing a moment of shock. Not to know yourself, not to be sure what signals you are sending out is dangerous. So I had not given to him exactly the impression I thought I had?

As our hands explored each other, I thought : dammit, he's feeling me to see if I have a gun.

I drew away a little. 'No, I haven't got a camera, either,' I said.

'What do you mean?' He sounded puzzled.

'Never mind. Let's have our picnic now.' I unpacked my bag and spread the food out in front of us. I was hungry and ate quickly, keeping one eye on the countryside and another on Harry as I ate.

We leaned back against the tree in companionable silence. At least companionable on my part. I don't know what it was on his.

'Of course, I haven't got a camera,' I said. 'Neither have you. Neither of us would be silly enough to bring a camera right up to the Russian border.'

'If you say so.'

'Neither have I got a gun. You wondered about that, didn't you? I felt you wondering,' I said drily. 'We've been speculating about each other, haven't we? About what we are, and why we are both here. And if I haven't got a gun, *you* have. I felt it when you kissed me.'

'Yes, I have got a gun,' he said. 'Many Americans carry guns.'

'Oh, yes? On pleasure trips? Let me spin you a tale of what I imagined about you. I thought that you had come into my circle of friends to succeed Jim Olsen as a C.I.A. agent. Jim having gone – ' I hesitated, 'gone away. After a while, I decided that you were watching *me*. And it is certainly true that through, or because of, or even in spite of my husband, I could know secret matters. Jim had watched me. Jim had gone away. You had come in to take his place. That's what I thought. So I thought I'd lead you a dance.'

'You've certainly done that,' he said.

'Haven't I? And perhaps we're both innocent. Perhaps you're not what I think you are, nor am I a spy.'

'I suppose it's your sense of humour again,' he said. 'I reckon you ought to take it in hand. It spoils you, Elizabeth.'

'Never mind.' I settled myself comfortably against the tree.

44

'I know how we can work things out. I have a plan. And it depends on where we are.'

'I know where we are. Just this side of the Russian border.'

'No. I don't think you realised how the border winds. It does follow the river, roughly, but then the river loops too. We are now across the border. We are in Russia.'

'What?' He stood up quickly with alarm.

'Yes,' I said calmly, still sitting where I was. 'But dinna fash yourself, as they say where we have both come from, all may yet be well. We shall both be arrested, but if I am an innocent tourist and you are innocent also, then eventually we shall both go free. Probably not at the same time, and probably not together. But if I am guilty of what you suspect, and you are guilty of what I suspect...' I shrugged.

'Then what?' he said.

'We shall still be arrested, but only one of us will go free.'

'Is this another specimen of your sense of humour?'

I ignored the jibe. 'I have a plan : let's make an arrangement to meet for coffee in McVitie's in Prince's Street in six months' time.' I smiled. 'If we are both there, well then, we are both innocent of everything.'

'I wish I knew what to make of you.'

'Well, it doesn't matter now.' I had my eyes on the skyline. 'I can see two men approaching, and they are Russian soldiers.'

Then I too stood up, waiting.

Six months later I finished my drink. The coffee hadn't been bad. Not good, but not bad either. Considering.

I called out to the waiter. 'Can I pay for my coffee?'

The waiter bowed and smiled. 'You enjoyed it? A good cup, eh?' which was clever of him since he was not speaking his own language.

'Delicious,' I lied, speaking in his.

'And your companion?'

'He enjoyed it too,' I said.

My husband, comfortably out of his Arctic trip and suitably apologetic for not having written ('I really couldn't, Liz, circumstances, you know. I dare not communicate with you'), came into the café then and heard the conversation. 'Your

Russian's coming on,' he said. He sat down with us, making a third.

'I've worked at it.' I looked around me. 'I'm beginning to settle down. What about you, Jim?'

'Slowly, slowly,' said Jim Olsen. 'Give me time.'

'We did the only thing,' said my husband. 'Once we'd turned you, Jim, once you were one of *us*, people determined to upset the structure of society as we grew up in it, we all had to clear out. As much to protect you as anything, Jim.'

'I hope you're right,' said Jim.

'Oh, you're safe enough,' I said. 'Harry thinks I've killed you and buried you in the sands. I had to sacrifice my poor old cat to make sure. Still, I'd never have left him with Clara Oban-Smith anyway.'

My husband said uneasily : 'I suppose Harry was what you thought? We never really heard, you know.'

I shrugged. I didn't know. I was still wondering. For that matter, *he* may have been wondering about me. And that's what I mean about the bubble being dangerous. I may have ruined a perfectly innocent life.

Ivor Drummond

POTTERTON'S PARTICULAR

Potterton was a long time deciding to murder Webb, longer formulating his plan, and longer still waiting until all the pieces came together – waiting for, as he put it to himself, that precise conjunction of all the planets which the Plan required.

Webb had been an irritant from the first moment that he appeared on the river-bank. No more than an irritant, because he had no power. Then, over the seasons, he began to exert that baleful, that almost magical influence over the other members of the syndicate which, to Potterton's uniquely clear-seeing eye, was having the effect of destroying the best dry-fly fishing in England.

It *had* been the best. It had been the *best*. During the fifties, Potterton had accepted invitations to fish the Test, Itchen, Kennet, Wylye, Lambourn – all the most renowned chalk-streams where gin-clear water, fly-laden, gurgled over the weed-beds and the sharp gravel, and the speckled monsters dimpled the surface with the rings of their rises – ay, he had fished them all, and come back always rejoicing to his beloved Wych, little queen of rivers, most delicate and difficult of all, most lovely, most unspoiled . . .

Until Webb came.

When Potterton retired from the Museum in 1960, he bought himself full membership of the syndicate which had the fishing, instead of the weekend-only rod which had, save during his brief annual holiday, been all that his duties in London permitted. He gave a sort of huge sigh – a sigh of the soul – and promised himself a truly happy life for the rest of his days. He booked a bedroom at the White Swan – not twenty yards from the bank of his beloved river – from May to September. Year after year, every single year, he was there all summer; he went nowhere else, from the first cast of the Large Dark Olive on

47

May Day until the last cast of the Silver Sedge, when the evening had grown dark and cold, on the 30th of September; he went nowhere else – he wanted to go nowhere else; he did nothing else – he wanted to do nothing else. He was keen on his fishing.

In the winter, of course, he went back to his little flat in London. He went out very little. He had a fine library of fishing books, and he had his fly tying equipment – masses of it – cabinets full of it, meticulously neat, with which he conjured tiny miracles of delicate craftsmanship hardly to be distinguished from their frail exemplars. His eyesight, in bifocals, was good; his abstemious fingers did not tremble; he had no arthritis in his hands. He tied better flies than any brash lad of fifty. He knew it, and the fish he caught knew it.

He made himself strict rules on the river, did Arthur Potterton. He was the purest of purists. He scorned the furtive nymph, creeping low through the water, be it never so exact an imitation; he deplored, though he could not openly condemn, the grannom, hawthorn, gnat, beetle, caperer and such (as he termed them) *vulgar* insects; he did not really approve of the Mayfly; for him, fishing was the use of the Olive, each in its season, Dark, Medium, Pale Watery, Iron Blue, Blue Winged, dun and spinner, and all else was crudity and fraud.

He was aware that he was old-fashioned. He liked being old-fashioned. He was aware that, as he reached and passed the age of seventy, he was inclined to be intolerant. He had, he told himself, more and more to be intolerant about. (He told himself many things, because he seldom spoke to anybody else.) He held to his own line. He was what he was, all through, and he looked it – a little, skinny, scrawny, baldish man with bright blue eyes, bifocal spectacles, broken veins about his nose which looked dissipated but were (almost wholly) the effect of wind and sun; on the river he wore always the same misshapen tweed hat, chocolate-brown knickerbockers and green gumboots. The people at the White Swan became quite fond of him . . . well, they became used to having him there all summer. He gave no trouble, and paid his bills promptly.

Of course they knew his routine. He made sure they did, from his very first day there. An early call, regardless of the weather.

48

Tea and toast with the paper in his bedroom, enjoying the birdsong that fluted through the little wistaria-framed window, and, yet sweeter, the contented and contenting babble of the river at the bottom of the lawn. Up and away, in tweed hat and gumboots, with sandwiches in grease-proof paper in his pocket. Back when the last fish had at last stopped rising – no matter how late – to cold meat and salad left ready for him, under a plate, in the Residents' Lounge. He almost always had it to himself. When he had frugally eaten, he wrote up his fishing diary. Date. Weather conditions. Temperature. Direction of wind. Barometer. Fly observed on water and in air. Activity of fish. Methods. Patterns used. Success and failure. He was ruthless with himself. When he had bungled, he recorded the bungle, unsparing, trying always to learn from his mistakes. And after that he went upstairs to his bedroom and tied a fly or two, under the bright lamp on his dressing-table. That was to him as reading a last chapter in bed is to other men – a quiet closing of the day, a preparation for tranquil sleep.

His sleep was always tranquil. Though you would not have known it to look at him, he was a happy man.

Until Webb came.

It was in 1968. Webb, still employed in some contemptible and over-rewarded capacity, had only a weekend rod. He spent those weekends at the White Swan. It was there, rather than on the river, that Potterton first learned to fear and detest him.

Item : he had a wireless. He played it in the morning, when Potterton was trying to do the crossword puzzle. A fellow hectored and jabbered, reading the news or making jokes or the like. Then there was music. It was hard to decide – Potterton did not try to decide – whether voice or verse more bestially drowned the seemly piping of the birds, the yet-sweeter murmur of the running water.

Item : he used the Residents' Lounge after dinner. To be sure, he might lay claim to some sort of right to use the room, being ephemerally a resident, but Potterton had come to regard it as *his* sitting-room. Once there, Webb *talked*. He *smoked*. He *drank*. Legally, no doubt, he was allowed to do these things, but morally . . . Potterton had a word about it with Mr Abbott, the landlord. Mr Abbott seemed not to understand. The Abbotts *liked* Mr Webb. He was ever so jovial, said Mr Abbott, and a very generous gentleman.

He had bought them.

So on Friday and Saturday nights, and sometimes Sunday too, Potterton wrote up his fishing diary in his bedroom. It was not intolerable, but it was a damned imposition.

The most irritating thing about Webb, at this early stage, was that he so closely resembled Potterton himself – another little stringy man, tougher than he looked. And he was – or claimed to be – an equally devoted fisherman. And they were both bachelors. Potterton found that the two of them were bracketed together in people's minds – the White Swan servants, the water-keepers, the other rods of the syndicate. He, Potterton, was likened to Webb! Webb to himself! He might have been flattered, since Webb was ten years his junior. He was not flattered.

Webb revealed himself to be a competent enough angler. He threw a fair line. He caught his share of fish, using nymphs and all manner of sneaking ploys. Modern opinion – modern books – said that they were respectable : even that they demanded a high degree of skill. Pish, thought Potterton. Fie, fiddlesticks. These were the strongest words he used, even silently to himself.

A rule had long existed on the Wych, as on many other fisheries, that the nymph was not to be used before the middle of June. During the 1970 season, Potterton tried to influence his fellow-rods into barring the use of the nymph altogether. To his utter consternation Webb, the new boy, who should have kept his mouth shut, moved a counter-proposal. He urged the free use of the nymph *throughout the season.* A sunk fly in May! Potterton could scarcely believe his ears. He could still less credit the evidence of his senses when *the others supported Webb.* The Admiral. Dr Graves. Old Mrs Wisdom. Many of the rest. Potterton got up and left, in a pointed manner, without a word. He did not trust himself to speak.

Webb began to make other suggestions, at other meetings, always in a manner which skilfully combined good humour with modest hesitation. His political manoeuvres in the syndicate were as devious as the methods of his fishing. The suggestions were without exception odious to Potterton, and they were without exception adopted.

Item : more money spent on mowing the banks and cutting back the riverside trees. Potterton liked his river wild, unspoiled. He did not want his back-cast made easy. He was not interested in fishing from a shaven lawn. He was overruled. The place began to look like a suburban garden.

Item : dainty green wooden benches were dotted at intervals along the bank, to increase its resemblance to a municipal park.

Item : stock rainbow trout were introduced. Potterton liked the wild Wych trout, yellow-bellied, gloriously speckled. He hated the introduction of tame exotics. Webb, with bluff humour and becoming modesty, pointed out that rainbows were just as hard to catch, that they put on weight at three times the speed, and so forth . . .

Item : as a result of these follies, the subscription was increased.

Potterton began to be obsessed by Webb and his works. But he dissimulated. He hid his hatred. He was as friendly to Webb as he was to anyone else.

In 1972 Webb retired.

'I'm going to follow your precedent, Pot,' he said in the Residents' Lounge one evening at the very beginning of that black season. 'I've discussed it with the Abbotts, and they're going to fix me up just as you're fixed. Room next to yours. Put in a few sticks of my own furniture. Share your bathroom. May to September. Thank God for retirement. Now I'm going to be happy seven days a week.'

It was during that summer that the Admiral had his stroke, and Webb contrived to have himself made Secretary of the syndicate. Effectively, he managed the water. The others were delighted to hand all the bother to a keen man with time on his hands. He spent money lavishly on stock rainbow, on a perfectly needless fishing hut, on a new footbridge, on excessive weed-cutting. His whole approach was to meddle, to improve on Nature, never to leave well alone, to turn the Wych into an artificial fishery, over-barbered, too comfortable, too easy. He took the others with him !

And Potterton held his peace. But, by the end of the season, his decision was taken.

In 1973 the old keeper retired and Webb found a successor, a lout called Waghorn, whom he had known anciently on some commercialised drain of a so-called chalk-stream. Potterton disliked Waghorn on sight. He was cocky. He tried to get all the rods to use his flies. He specialised in nymphs. His flies looked like artificial shrimps to Potterton. They were no better than lures. The man belonged on a reservoir.

One of Waghorn's bestialities was the way he persecuted Old Bones. Old Bones was a local character, not of high moral reputation but not much trouble to anybody. He had been a poacher, and in and out of Winchester Prison a few times, but he had largely retired. He took a few fish out of the Wych, tickling or cross-lining. Nobody much minded. He only caught what he wanted to eat. In Potterton's view his methods were quite as sporting as Webb's. Potterton rather liked him than otherwise, a little wrinkled man of much his own size and build (of much Webb's size and build) with gentle manners and a sort of dignity : yes, Potterton liked Old Bones as much as he liked anybody, although they scarcely exchanged fifty words in a season. But Waghorn was a bully. He chivvied Old Bones. He spent far too much of his overpriced time trying to catch the old man red-handed with a fresh trout. He never did. It was, Potterton thought, Old Bones's dignified manner which enraged Waghorn to such a ridiculous frenzy. The poacher talked to the keeper like a bishop talking to a bad little boy. It made Potterton come as near to laughter as anything did.

In 1975 Webb put in two thousand rainbow trout, reduced the size limit, and increased the number limit. The Wych was going downhill, Potterton thought, at a speed which was becoming vertiginous. He at least felt vertigo. He felt sick with helpless anger.

Helpless? Not altogether. By the end of August 1975 Potterton's Plan was complete. During the winter he acquired a piece of lead piping, a small polythene bag, and a pair of field-glasses for bird-watching. It was all he needed. It was a matter simply of waiting now, and of seizing the chance when it came.

1976 saw another detestable innovation. Previously, always,

anybody could go where they liked on the water. If someone else was fishing, you kept decently clear of them. Good manners, goodwill, good sportsmanship, commonsense – you needed no more to provide plenty of room for everybody. That was not good enough for Webb. He must meddle, he must interfere and dictate. He proposed dividing the river into beats, and limiting each individual to a single beat on any particular day.

'It works very well on the Lodden,' he told the syndicate, his bifocals (identical to Potterton's) glinting amiably in the lamplight. 'It means we can rest the beats in rotation. It keeps other people out of your hair. Nobody puts your fish down or comes too close to you. I believe, on balance, people prefer it.'

On balance, people did prefer it. Potterton pretended to agree, fighting down his rage.

And then he saw that the new arrangement, nasty as it was, would help the Plan. The mechanism more perfectly interlocked. The margin of error was reduced to vanishing point. In the solitude of his bedroom at the White Swan, tying late at night a Pale Evening Dun, Potterton gave one of his rare chuckles. Webb had made his own execution easier, more certain, by his latest outrage. It was a pretty irony. Potterton almost wished he had a friend, to whom he could tell the story. He had none. He told it to the Pale Evening Dun.

Throughout the rest of 1976, throughout 1977, throughout most of 1978, Potterton waited his chance. He knew that the particular combination of circumstances he needed would form itself at last. His only fear was that he might become too enfeebled with age – might even die – before things came right for the Plan. He thought not. He was durable. The odds against his combination did not seem to him long.

On Monday, September 25th, Potterton had the Number Four Beat. It was a fine day. All September had been glorious. There was nothing doing on the river. There was no fly; no fish were moving. Webb, no doubt, was dragging a big artificial shrimp – practically a minnow – on spec under the rafts of cut weed, pricking more fish than he hooked, spoiling sport for honest men. Potterton fished only risers – authentically catchable fish authentically rising to the floating insect. When there were none, he watched the wagtails and chaffinches through his new field-glasses.

He saw one fly on the surface. He scooped it up with his fine-meshed entomologist's net, and inspected the tiny dead creature. It was one of the commonest and most useful of all flies, the adult female Medium Olive, with dark thorax and legs and tail, transparent wings of wonderful delicacy, and translucent crimson abdomen. Lunn, the great keeper at Stockbridge, had long before invented the classic imitation, Lunn's Particular, with peacock-quill body dyed to the proper crimson, and flat blue-dun hackle-tip wings. Potterton esteemed this pattern and used it often, But he was an inventive, a creative fisherman. He wondered if improvement was not, after all, possible to Lunn's masterpiece. Translucency was the key. A body of dyed quill was not translucent. But if a man were to spin a very little crimson seal's-fur on to pale silk, and perhaps rib the dubbing with fine gold wire . . .

Potterton recorded this idea in his fishing diary, and then set himself to tie Potterton's Particular. He set up his fly-tying vice on the dressing-table in his bedroom – a vertical rod, angled to the right, ending in tiny jaws tightened by a screw. With tweezers he selected an up-eyed hook of size oo (he disdained use of the modern American numbering) and fitted the bend of the hook into the jaws of the vice. He waxed a two-foot length of gossamer primrose silk, and whipped it on to the shank of the hook. From the spade-hackle of a blue-dun game-cock he snipped two long individual fibres, to which he added one fibre from a similar feather dyed red. He tied the three fibres to the hook with two turns of silk, to imitate the three slender *setae* of the natural insects. (The one red whisk, an invention of Potterton's own, he believed to give a naturalistic effect of iridescence.) He tied in a few inches of his finest gold wire, at the tail of the hook, just where the bend began. From an envelope he took a pinch – no more – of seal's-fur dyed a wonderful claret : the springy, shiny, resilient fur with which a sea-creature was naturally protected. With practised finger-tips, he teased the fur on to his waxed silk, then twisted it, so that the fur was held by the silk in a sort of glittering, furry rope. He tied this rope up the shank of the tiny hook, and examined the effect. Translucent. The effect was translucent. It must better imitate the natural than the opacity of quill.

He wound the gold wire up the body of his fly, four turns,

to hold the dub together and to increase the effect of translucency by virtue of its reflecting glitter. Wings? He decided
to give the fly wings, not through any real belief in the super-
iority of the winged over the hackled fly, but because winged
flies were traditional. A winged fly was a gentleman's fly. The
hackled object was a cad's lazy substitute. Wings, then – a
third of an inch of blue-dun hackle-tip, tied flat in Lunn's excellent fashion. And then a very springy, game-cocky hackle,
tied round the hook just behind the eye to make a sort of
miniature flue-brush. The fibres of the hackle were the insect's
legs; they also kept the fly afloat. The whip finish. The spot
of varnish on the head. Done.

Potterton tied three more, identical to the first : more than
he himself would need the next day, unless he had more accidents than was usual for so careful an angler : he would offer
them to other rods, to Major Cartwright or Dr Graves, as he
often did. They always took them. They probably used them.
He would not offer a fly to Webb.

The morning of Tuesday, September 26th, dawned as fine
as the rest of the month : a bland, bright day, boding delight
on the river-bank if not great fishing. It was the last day of the
season bar four. Potterton, eating his breakfast, thought that
Webb had got a reprieve. He struggled with the crossword
puzzle in spite of the almost unbearable distraction of Webb's
wireless set. Webb was getting a little deaf, and played his
wireless louder.

Potterton had Beat Three that day, Webb Beat Six. The Plan
required Webb to have Beat Five. Of course it required many
other things too.

Potterton got his rod, his beautiful Sharp's 'Eighty-Eight',
out of the rack in the hall. The fly at the tip of his three-yard
tapered cast was a Little Red Sedge, which he had been using
(rather shamefacedly) the previous evening. Wrong now : un-
seemly. He took it off, and tied on one of his new seal's-fur-
bodied spinners. It looked very fine. It looked both gentlemanly
and a killer, like Potterton himself.

As he came out of the garden door of the White Swan,
Potterton saw Dr Graves dressed not for fishing but for
doctoring.

55

' 'Morning, Pot. Not a bad day. Might try to come down later. Got to see Mildred Wisdom.'

'Ah. She is ill?'

'Can't tell you till I've seen her, can I?'

Potterton showed Dr Graves, who could appreciate these things, his new fly. They discussed translucency. Graves was impressed that Potterton could spin such springy, intractable stuff as seal's-fur on so tiny a hook. Potterton nodded, accepting the Doctor's admiration as his due.

Dr Graves, in turn, accepted a Potterton's Particular. He promised to try it the very next time he saw spent female Medium Olive on the water.

'I'd know this as your fly anywhere, Pot. Ha! I see your trademark, that one red whisk, you cunning old devil.'

Potterton walked up Beat Two, which began at the pub. Near the top he met Waghorn. It was a social morning, by his standards, too social. The keeper greeted him as cockily as usual, tilting back his black-and-white checked cap with a fore-finger to the peak.

'Beat Three today, Mr Potterton, sir? Ah! The Squire had a grand day there yesterday.'

'The Squire' was Waghorn's name for Webb. He used this absurd honorific because Webb was Secretary of the syndicate and responsible for Waghorn's appointment. It was an odious piece of toad-eating.

'Two and a half brace the Squire had,' went on Waghorn flatly, 'one over two pounds, lovely deep fish. Using one of my bugs, I do believe.'

'Bugs?' said Potterton with distaste.

'Do you try one, sir, for once in a way. I tied up a new batch las' evening, wi' a variation, so to call un, for to entice they fish wi' a gleam o' colour.'

Waghorn took a little box of clear plastic out of his mackin-tosh pocket, and rattled it under Potterton's nose. From it he took a great beast of a fly, fully three-quarters of an inch long, an imitation bug, a foul caterpillar, grey wool with a rib of fuse-wire and a scarlet tag at the tail. This tag, presumably, was the variation. Already an unsporting lure, the dot of red made it a grotesque, a plug, something for coarse fish.

Potterton took the great horror, suppressing a shudder, because it saved time to do so. Waghorn must have known he would not use it – seemed, indeed, surprised that he even accepted it. Usually he refused any such fly, which caused prolonged argument, boisterously patronising on Waghorn's part, feignedly affable on Potterton's.

The thought struck Potterton that three of the conditions of the Plan were today met – he had the right beat; he had a distinctive fly just invented and tied by Waghorn; and no one had seen him talking to Waghorn.

'Have you shown this fly to anybody else?' Potterton asked Waghorn.

'Yer! Showed un to Dr Graves, an hour ago. He wouldn't take un. Too big, says he. Just the right size for the job she do, I say, but he won't take un.'

Another condition met. There was an independent witness to the design of Waghorn's monstrosity, who would, because of his disapproval, remember it in detail.

Unfortunately there were other conditions, equally crucial, which were not met.

'The Squire,' said Waghorn, 'was to of 'ad Number Six to-day.'

'Yes,' said Potterton sadly.

'But Mrs Wisdom's took queer, what was to 'ave 'ad Number Five, so Squire's been an' moved hisself down to Number Five.'

Potterton struggled to conceal his sudden excitement.

'Major Cartwright, he'll switch from Number One up to Number Six. That way we'll rest Four an' Two, an' I can be mendin' that ol' hatch on Number One without disturbin' of nobody.'

'You'll be there all day?'

'Ay. There's a day's work in that ol' hatch.'

By a chance of Mrs Wisdom's indisposition (which Potterton sincerely hoped was not serious) Webb was on the right beat for the Plan. And Major Cartwright, the right man, would be going upstream to his beat, his new beat; he would see Potterton fishing, as the Plan required. And Waghorn would be out of the way, down at the hatch on Beat One, as the Plan required.

'Will you see Major Cartwright, Waghorn?' asked Potterton, making a titanic effort to speak normally, casually.

'Yer, to tell un to move up to Number Six. So's I can mend the ol' hatch, d'ye see.'

'To be sure. Well, be kind enough to ask him . . .' Potterton spoke slowly, using the long-rehearsed words, careful to get them exactly right. 'Be kind enough to tell him that I shall be trying for that big fish, the four-pounder, under the alder on the bend.'

'*Be* there a four-pounder under the alder on the bend?' asked Waghorn incredulously.

'I think so. I'm sure of it. I call him "Jaws".'

Waghorn laughed, shaking leaves from the September trees. He was amused and amazed that Potterton used so modern, so frivolous a reference.

'So I would be very much obliged to Major Cartwright,' said Potterton impressively, 'if he would very kindly take the path behind the copse, instead of walking up the bank.'

It was a reasonable request : just about a reasonable request. It was possible to walk up the right bank of the river, on Beat Three, without frightening fish under the far bank : but Major Cartwright was a man of nervous affability, an ingratiating fellow, who would die rather than risk offence to a peppery old curmudgeon like Potterton. He would undoubtedly take the path behind the copse. He would see Potterton in the distance, on the bank, by the bend, a little below the alder on the far bank. He would not go near him; he would not talk to him. Somebody else might – Webb easily might, or Dr Graves – but not Cartwright. Not Mrs Wisdom, either, but she was wrong for the Plan for a different reason. Major Cartwright was never an early bird on the water. He was an idle fellow, lolling at home over his breakfast well into the morning. He had never been seen on the river before eleven. Potterton had been at pains to build up a reliable statistical and behavioural picture, and he knew, empirically, that Cartwright would not pass Beat Three before eleven. Mrs Wisdom, on the other hand, *was* an early bird, as keen as Potterton to get out.

'What fly catches most fish?' she was fond of saying. 'The fly that's on the water most. *That's* the fly that catches most fish.'

So had she been the one moved up from Number One to Number Six, she might have been by Three at ten o'clock. Too early. No good for the Plan.

The position of the copse in relation to the river-bank, and the position of the path that ran behind it – that was what made Potterton's occupation of Beat Three right for the Plan. Major Cartwright's personality made him the right man to come upstream from below, at the right time, and Beat Six was the right place for him to be aiming at. Beat Five was the right place for Webb to be. Beat Two, between Potterton and Waghorn, was empty, which was right. Beat Four, between Potterton and Webb, was empty, which was right. Potterton had one of Waghorn's dreadful new flies, another of which Dr Graves had seen, which was extremely right.

One thing only was missing.

Potterton sketched a gesture of farewell, of dismissal, to Waghorn. He went on up the river to Beat Three. There was a heavy dew, and millions of cobwebs, dew-spangled, in the rough grass. The smooth, unhurried little river was beautiful in the morning sunlight. Potterton's heart thudded with love of the thing he was preserving.

The river he was saving from the Beast, from the Power of the Dog : if only the one remaining condition of the Plan was met. It was possible.

For the first time in thirty years, Potterton found himself praying : let Old Bones be on the river-bank.

For the first time in seventy-five years, Potterton's prayer was answered. Old Bones was on the bank. He was asleep under a thorn-tree, with his head on his rolled-up mackintosh. He wore a faded, dry-mud-coloured tweed coat, very much like Potterton's. This was useful to the Plan. His cap, a black-and-white check very like Waghorn's, had fallen off his head on to the grass. His thin white hair fluttered over his skull in the gentle breeze. He looked very old and frail in sleep, although he was not much older and certainly no frailer than Potterton.

With a feeling of compunction rare to him, Potterton woke Old Bones up. The poacher blinked, sat up quickly, looked round nervously. Potterton realised he had been up to no good during the night. Probably there was a brace of nice plump fish

59

hidden somewhere. Rainbows. That was all right with Potterton. The river was well rid of them.

Potterton took out a ten-pound note. This was so much part of the Plan that it was part of his fishing equipment, in a special pocket of his waistcoat, and had been for nearly three seasons. He tore the note across, and handed half to Old Bones. It disappeared as though by magic somewhere inside Old Bones's clothes. Old Bones looked at Potterton with dignified enquiry.

'You can have the other half later this morning,' Potterton said.

'That will be nice,' said Old Bones.

Potterton explained that he wanted Old Bones to sit on the river-bank, a few yards below the alder on the bend. He was to hold the rod, and to stare at the water under the alder. He was not to look in any other direction, but simply at the water under the alder. He was to wear Potterton's hat, all the time. He was on no account to take it off. He was not to smoke his pipe. He was not to try to use the rod, but simply to hold it.

Old Bones nodded intelligently. He asked no questions. He would pretend to be Potterton for an hour, for reasons which did not concern him, and afterwards say nothing about it to anybody, ever. Perhaps he thought Potterton had a girl he wanted to visit on the sly. He himself was still a menace to the village girls, and he was nearly eighty. There was a story about Old Bones and Waghorn's daughter, and the reason she took off to London suddenly in July . . .

Webb came by, going upstream towards Beat Five. He stopped for a chat, thick-skinned as ever, not caring that he might be frightening the fish on Potterton's beat. He was over-dressed, over-equipped, hung about with gadgets, his deer-stalker hat too new, his tie too regimental, his waders too shiny.

'Have you seen Waghorn this morning, Pot?' he asked, turning away finally from a conversation which he was enjoying because he was doing all the talking.

'No,' said Potterton.

'Nor have I, unfortunately. Expected to see him down at the hatch, but he wasn't there. He told me yesterday he was going to tie some more of his killer-bugs. Wanted a few. Great fly for the time of year. Don't expect *you* to agree.'

Of course a man like Webb did not tie his own flies. Even

a great bedsock with fuse wire wrapped round it was beyond him. An oaf as well as a cheat.

Webb's death warrant had long been signed. He himself now sealed it, by frightening Potterton's fish, and by yearning for thievish lures.

He stumped off upstream. He was out of sight in a few seconds. He would be out of sight of anybody as he walked up Beat Four, and while he fished (so to call what he did) Beat Five. At least, he would be out of sight of anybody on Beat Six. That was part of the Plan.

The time was a quarter to eleven.

Potterton waited. Old Bones already wore the tweed hat, and sat docilely on the bank where Potterton told him, the rod in his hand. At eleven, Potterton moved into the deep shadow of an oak-tree near the bank (the shadow was part of the Plan) and raised the field-glasses which (according to the Plan) people were so well used to see him carrying. From where he stood, he could see part of the bank near the bottom of Beat Two (which was part of the Plan).

Through the field-glasses, at seven minutes past eleven, Potterton saw Major Cartwright waddling upstream towards his re-allocated beat. That meant that he had seen Waghorn, that he knew Potterton was stalking an enormous and wary fish, that he would go by the path behind the copse. He would see only Old Bones's back, in tweed like Potterton's tweed, because Old Bones would be keeping his face turned towards the alder; he would see the tweed hat Potterton always wore, and the rod which was always in his hand.

As soon as he was sure Major Cartwright was coming up-river, Potterton himself started. He was wearing Old Bones's black-and-white checked cap, which made him look like Old Bones, or like Waghorn. He went fast – much faster than Cartwright, who was fat – but cautiously, in case Webb had stopped for any reason. He was out of sight of anybody except Old Bones, and of him after a few seconds. He was out of sight of anybody until he got to Beat Five and to Webb.

'Hullo, Pot,' said Webb, greatly surprised.

Potterton had about three minutes. After his hundreds of rehearsals he was sure it was enough.

'Done a stupid thing,' said Potterton. 'Left my fly-box in my room.'

'My dear chap, what a bore! You don't want to walk all the way back to the pub.'

'Not much.'

'Well, borrow what you like. Pheasant-tail? Tup? Black Gnat? This whitish thing? Nymphs under the flap there Sedges in this box.'

He was bursting with false goodwill, putting on a show of sportsmanlike generosity. Half his flies had been tied by his creature Waghorn, half bought in London shops. Potterton took the box of sedge-flies – great fuzzy things, vulgar objects – and immediately dropped it. Flies sprayed over the grass.

'Drat,' said Potterton.

'God damn it,' said Webb. 'At least they're easy to see.'

He fell to his knees to gather up his flies – knelt before Potterton, as though begging something from him. He was. He was begging for death.

Potterton drew from the bottom of his fishing-bag the object which had made it inconveniently heavy for nearly three seasons – the lead pipe in its polythene bag. He glanced down. At the level of his shins, Webb, hatless, was rootling about in the grass for his flies like a pig looking for truffles. Potterton hit him as hard as he could on the back of the head with the lead pipe. There was a good big crunch, a bit sickening to Potterton even though he warmly approved of what he was doing. Webb collapsed. Potterton, gritting his teeth, hit him twice more, as hard as he possibly could. Webb's head was a squashed mess, a bloody misshapen pudding. Potterton felt his pulse. He was dead. Potterton snipped the polythene bag with his fishing scissors, and let the lead pipe slide out of it on to the ground. It bore no fingerprints – he had wiped it with meticulous care on the day, long ago, when it had gone into the polythene bag. He lit a match (carried for three seasons, although he never smoked) and held it to the blood-smeared polythene. The stuff melted into gory shreds, destroying the fingerprints on it. He dropped it. He took from his flybox the grotesque big nymph Waghorn had given him. He removed the fly from Webb's cast, and tied on the nymph. He dropped

62

the fly he had removed. Neither it nor the nymph nor Webb's cast would carry usable fingerprints, he thought.

He glanced at his watch. Cartwright would be near. He trotted to the bottom of the beat and peeped through branches. Cartwright was two hundred yards away. Potterton went back to the body of his enemy. He filled his lungs and gave a great scream. This was the only part of the Plan which he actually enjoyed. The purpose of the scream was to time Webb's death exactly. Then he ran to the footbridge thirty yards upstream (Webb's needless new footbridge) and went quickly but cautiously across it, and deep into the woods on the other side. The blood on his gumboots smeared ferns and brambles. That was good. He trotted, wasting no time but not exhausting himself, downstream to the bottom of Beat Three, where there was another footbridge. He washed the blood off his gumboots. No one saw him. As he crossed the footbridge, he saw, downstream, a disappearing back in an old mackintosh. Old Bones. He wondered why. Well, the old man had done what was needful. He could have the other half of the ten-pound note when he liked.

Potterton's rod was on the bank, but the cast had no fly on the end. Odd. Perhaps, defying orders, Old Bones had tried to fish, and had left the fly in a tree. Perhaps that was why he had run away, embarrassed at the thought of Potterton's annoyance. Something like that. It was a small matter.

Cartwright panted downstream, and blurted out his dreadful news.

'You were in that position from ten-forty until Major Cartwright came downstream to find you, sir?' said the Detective Chief Superintendent.

'Yes.'

'You saw no one?'

'No.'

'Not Mr Webb? Not Major Cartwright? Not the man Waghorn?'

'No. I'm sorry. I was concentrating on the water, looking for a particular big fish.'

'I understand, sir. I'm an angler myself. Not what you'd

call game-fishing, but the best I can run to . . . You had not, earlier, seen Waghorn?'

'No.'

'On your way upstream?'

'No, I'm afraid I saw no one at all after I left Dr Graves.'

'Then you will not recognise this?'

It was the fly – the monstrous 'bug' with the red tag.

'What a horrible thing,' said Potterton, careful not to overdo his pretence of seeing it for the first time.

'Dr Graves identifies it as one which Waghorn devised and made only last night. Waghorn's wife confirms this. Dr Graves and Major Cartwright both saw Waghorn this morning, but neither of them took one of these things. He did make an error, didn't he? Oh dear, I do wonder why he did it. Such a brutal murder, too.'

'A sudden rage? A sort of brainstorm?'

'I'd like to think so, but it won't do. The whole thing stinks of premeditation. He must have crept upstream from the hatch at the bottom, avoiding Major Cartwright and yourself, and he must have had his weapon prepared. You don't carry a lump of lead about, wiped absolutely clean, without meaning to use it for something. Oh well, the motive will come out in the wash, I daresay. It's that fly that screws him, if you'll pardon the expression. He can swear black and blue that he was down by the hatch all morning, but how did poor Mr Webb come by a fly that didn't even exist until yesterday evening, unless Waghorn went up and gave it to him?'

'I don't know,' said Potterton.

'I'm afraid I must bother you again, sir.'

This time the Detective Chief Superintendent was accompanied by Dr Graves. Graves was looking oddly at Potterton.

'Go on,' said Potterton.

He was writing up his fishing diary, in the Residents' Lounge now blessedly and permanently free of Webb.

'I want to be quite clear about your movements. May we go through it again? You did say, didn't you, that you were at the bend in the river, where Major Cartwright saw you, from ten-forty or thereabouts – '

'Ten-forty exactly.'

'Yes. Until Major Cartwright came and found you.'

'Yes. I was there – I must have been there – when poor Webb . . .'

'Just so. Major Cartwright exactly confirms your own statement. And you did say that you saw no one?'

'No.'

'Not an old fellow they call Old Bones?'

'No.'

'Can you, Mr Potterton,' said the big grey policeman, 'identify this?'

In the palm of his hand lay, unmistakable, a Potterton's Particular. The lamplight glittered benignly on the seal's-fur and the gold twist, and on the distinctive single red whisk between the two blue-dun ones.

'This looks like a fly of mine,' said Potterton. He glanced at Graves. Graves was still staring at him oddly. 'Is this the one I gave you, Doctor?'

Graves took an envelope out of his pocket. He shook out of it the fly Potterton had given him, identical to the one in the policeman's palm.

'I understand, Mr Potterton, that you devised this fly and dressed these examples yesterday evening?'

'Yes.'

'How many?'

'Four.'

'How many have you now?'

'Two.'

'May I see them?'

'Yes.'

'It is impossible that this fly in my hand should have come from any other hands than yours, at any time before this morning?'

'Yes,' said Dr Graves unexpectedly.

Potterton had no idea what the policeman and the doctor were about; he knew only that he was tired, that he wanted to get his fishing diary written, that he wanted to be alone with his warm feelings of triumph and safety and cleverness.

'I did lose a fly this morning,' said Potterton, since they

65

seemed obsessed with the wretched thing. 'That must be it. Where did you find it?'

'Embedded in the cheek of a man called John Boneman,' said the Detective Chief Superintendent, 'known as Old Bones. He was murdered with some brutality this morning, with a knife which has not been found. His watch – identified as stolen, incidentally – was broken in the struggle, and shows eleven-ten, which confirms the provisional estimate of the time of death. The murder was committed, and the body found, in undergrowth close to the river-bank, near the bend in the middle of the part you call Beat Number Three. You have said that you were there, and you were seen there. You have said nobody else was there, and nobody else was seen there. As if that wasn't enough, nobody else in the world, except you and Dr Graves, had a fly quite like this one. Dr Graves at the time was with Mrs Wisdom in her house six miles away, with his fly in his pocket.'

Waghorn, thought Potterton. The business about his daughter. His back I saw, his dirty mackintosh.

They'd find the torn half of the ten-pound note.

'Come along,' said the policeman. 'I've got a nice car outside and we'll go down to the station and have a nice long talk.'

'But . . .'

'You caught the old villain poaching and had a fight, eh? Stabbed him with your fishing-knife, then threw that in the river. Yours or somebody else's, *that's* no difficulty. You might get away with manslaughter, but I can't see the court taking kindly to stabbing a man of nearly eighty.'

'But . . .'

'Come on, man. Waghorn's got a chance, because nobody actually saw him anywhere near that crime. You've got *no* chance. Funny, though, isn't it? Two murders on the same day, on the same bit of the same river, and the evidence that sends you both up, God willing, is a little bit of fluff tied round a fish-hook.'

'Not fluff,' said Potterton. 'Seal's-fur.'

He began to laugh. It was the first time anybody had ever heard him laugh. It was a horrible noise.

Sarah Gainham

BUSINESS HAZARD

'We shan't have long to wait,' said the younger man. 'His flight was due five minutes ago.'

'Good idea of yours, breakfast with Tremlett. We can get the flight at eleven.'

'That's what I thought,' said Henry modestly. 'Then, if we fill in Mr Tremlett now you won't have to come back here before Hanover.'

It was quiet in the wide-spaced entrance hall below them, as they stood at the rail of an inside terrace between Arrivals and Departures, able to oversee both comings and goings. The days of clanging loudspeakers battling with echoes of each other are long over in airports and the calm is grateful to the ears of those who once suffered them. Henry strolled over to the expanse of daylight on the other side of which, cut off into silence by invisible armour, the great birds circled and manoeuvred. Far off, others posed at rest, inquisitive beaks inclining to the tarmac, considering it seemed, the transcendental worms of future flight paths. Lance Petrie, who had proposed this elevation, remained at the railing to look down into the hall.

'Long to wait' hung on the cool, tempered air, a deep melancholy imparted to its cadence by refraction through his thoughts. He lounged on the railing, coatless in the English manner although outside was a sharp morning and the horizontal sunlight was only just beginning to disperse frosty mists. He had welcomed his assistant's suggestion of coming so early, pretending that it was practical, time-saving. So it was, but Lance's real reason was that it cut out the gap of waiting, of conscious time, by filling it with activity. Cut out the still veiled transference from night to day, from the short space of dark filled with living to the business of daytime; that gap of doing nothing in which thought and feeling waited. There was always this unreality of the transfer, echoing the physical transfer from her room in the hotel to his own to bath and order coffee in time to take the expected buzz of the telephone on the night table which was Henry reminding him of what they were to do that day.

And he did not have long to wait. Her flight would leave in forty minutes and there she was, beneath his gaze, crossing at an even stroll diagonally the early morning emptiness of the tiled floor to check in. Foreshortened the burnished hair was imposed on the dark furs, the pale overnight bag swung outwards from a pale-gloved hand. She loved her luxurious things, not for their value but for their prettiness and because she had earned them herself. She never mentioned this; indeed she rarely asserted anything or made direct statements. They were both practised at not saying things. But sometimes they would, one or other, say things in front of companions that had inner meanings for themselves, memories that gleamed softly like flesh under thin silk, exchanging scraps of memory gratefully without meaning looks or loaded emphases. As at dinner the previous evening Margaret commented on the absence of one of their number who preferred a Brecht play to their company; they saw that play together, twenty years before in another city, in the days when theatre or concert were sometimes more than half a way of getting through time when they could not go to bed. Nowadays, having money and influence, matters could be more easily arranged but now as then, as always, they were an illicit pair.

'His flight is late. Did you see?' Henry came up behind Lance, looking over the sloped tall shoulder. 'Look. There's Mrs Marshall. What an amusing woman! I was afraid she would be formidable but she was enchanting yesterday evening.'

From the checker's desk Margaret now moved to the newspaper kiosk.

'She said her flight was early,' said Lance. 'Should we get some papers too? How late will Tremlett be?'

'They said twenty minutes.'

'Fog somewhere, I suppose.' Twenty minutes, twenty years. 'I've got early-morning glooms.'

'I'll go down and get some papers then. Pass the time.'

She was moving again now and with a pang Lance saw that she was about to go through the barrier. A woman, shapeless in one of those tent-like overcoats, was just behind her, obscuring Lance's view. He felt an absurd anxiety that he would not see Margaret go through passport control, but the woman in sludge-coloured tweed went to the other desk and he saw the bright head tilt as Margaret spoke to the half-visible policeman in his glass box. She put up her hand and with a swift movement pushed the passport back into her handbag, retaining the bright green slip of cardboard in the light shape of her glove inside which he could almost feel the warm sense of her hand. She turned the angled bend and disappeared. She was gone.

'Henry!' Shout from the balustrade, yell for help as love went under for the hundredth time. 'Don't forget the local papers!'

Margaret trailed down the wide and empty corridors, past the extra Customs counter where she had never yet seen anyone exposing wares or invoices for inspection. The moving staircase slid her downwards to the blocks of seats, the coffee bar, the duty-free shops and the pairs and groups of international businessmen, those continual travellers who accompanied her journeys, so like each other that she sometimes thought she must know them all. Even in summer when shoals of tourists were drawn through here by tides of expectation turned to irritability, it was quiet in spite of the occasional disembodied voice; walls and ceiling were padded, glass reinforced, against noise as one might expect the walls of insane hospitals to be against the howls of inmates. Travelling in winter has the advantage that amateur travellers are not there to clutter up the machinery for the professionals whose measured, passionless routines are carried out without thought, from habit. Dimly the whine of a taxi-ing jet penetrated and Margaret wondered without interest how glass was made soundproof. A low, two-tone bell introduced a sexless muezzin calling its servants to board the Swissair flight for Rome and Damascus and two nordic blond men with document cases and wearing heavy coats and fur hats at identically jaunty angles, moved together in step to gate eight. Fur hats to Damascus, she thought, but perhaps they'll convert on the way too. That's not bad, I must tell Lance that. She lit a cigarette and it tasted dry and harsh so she put it out again. She was queasily hungry after an almost sleepless night and though the thick sheets of newsprint were comforting the words she scanned did not enter through the eyes into the brain except to register 'no news' for the headlines in both journals were of a Security Council meeting. Her hands turned and she looked below the fold. Another politician in trouble; this time sex and not speculation. Margaret's eyes wandered. A woman in a wide overcoat walked past, she seemed to be looking for someone. Surely Margaret did recognise something more than a general business type about that face? Unusually round, sulky mouth, the set of the eyes? Her thoughts slid to Lance, increasing the feeling of recognition, but that, she knew, connected to Lance and not to the passerby. Did you remember, he had asked her in the night, it seems like yesterday that Brecht play. How we argued about it then, it's more than twenty years ago.

That new young man of Lance's seemed competent and pleasant as well, she thought vaguely. Lance said he was recently married and his wife did not like living abroad; strange that the girl did not think of that when marrying a man already working for an international company. But probably she had thought only of marrying that man and not of his job and of finding herself here, among strangers. Who am I to find that odd, when my whole personal life has been ruled for over twenty years by the single chance of meeting the only love after marriage – and marriage to a man I believed I was in love with until Lance and I met. The neuter voice intoned a summons and without clearly hearing it Margaret recognised the name of her destination and rose unhurriedly, pulling her glove back on. Going through the electronic doorway the keys in her pocket pinged loudly as usual and she fished them out to be seen and laughed at. Margaret drifted to gate four, glanced at her watch and did not sit down. The apron bus drew up silently, ground staff chattered secrets into oblong black speakers, the doors slid back and noise entered with the cold push of wind. The few passengers clung to uprights and were swayed over to mount rectally into the belly of the jet where

Margaret, as always, took the back seat because it was nearest. The flight being less than half booked, she could shed her coat and bag on the middle seat and incline herself sideways into the window place. Something about the swivelling movement reminded her and she heard Lance's absorbed undertone clearly, as if he were still with her, saying 'Just a little this way . . . yes' and a stab of anguished pleasure made her close her eyes for an instant.

'You don't need a newspaper?' asked a bright voice and Margaret shook her head, smiling slightly and indicating those already reposing on her knees. The trundling whine increased to a roar, speed trembled, ceased and sank away as the great upward shove lifted steeply, pushing her back, aquiescent, into cushioning.

'Hullo, Mrs Marshall. May I join you for a moment?'

It was the woman in the voluminous tweed coat, now shed to reveal that she wore a suit of the same muddy brown cloth. Margaret knew now that she did recognise that voice, the insinuatingly modest manner, the round face with the dark skin, brown hair, eyes that seemed to flinch away. But she connected these features to no remembered name or circumstance, only to a slight disinclination for the whole person before her.

'You don't remember me.' Plaintive acceptance; so the acquaintance had not been fleeting. 'Of course you wouldn't. It's years since I left Marshall and Dexter.'

'Of course,' repeated Margaret with automatic friendliness. 'I was thinking of something else. How are you? Is it still Joan Willis?'

'So you do know me!' Flattering by being flattered. Tiresome creature; there was something bothersome about her departure from the managerial offices, Margaret thought. 'No, I married. We're in business too, the same sort of business but nothing like as big as yours, naturally.'

'I hope business is good? Where do you live now?'

'Near Lincoln. Do you still have your lovely house?'

'Yes, I'm going home now.'

'You must be lonely there sometimes. I was sorry to hear about Mr Marshall.'

'Thank you. But the two children and work keep me from being lonely.'

'I suppose so. I think it was wonderful, the way you took over. It's a great responsibility for a woman.'

'It was a going concern, you know. I'm just a co-ordinating figurehead really. The others do it all.'

'I'm sure that's not true.' The pretence of admiration sank into a sigh. 'I know too well the problems of running a business, even a small one. And everything is so difficult nowadays.'

Do people mean it when they make that automatic complaint, Margaret wondered, when the longest boom in history is only just flattening out?

'I have a lot of problems. My husband – he's a clever engineer but not much head for business. I have to do all that side and it's a struggle. Well, you know all that. After all, you have to do a great deal yourself, or you wouldn't be on this plane alone, would you?'

'Well, I wasn't alone, you know. And I'm not going back for business reasons. I wanted to get back early because Annabel is coming home today. And everything was settled so I ran off and left the others to cope.'

'How is Annabel? Such a pretty child, she was.'

'She still is. This was her first term at the University so I wanted to be there when she came back for a day or so.'

'It must be difficult to combine children with all the travelling . . .'

Every single thing she says is negative, Margaret thought.

'It just has to be organised,' she replied, suppressing a yawn. 'I'd have gone back last night if the flight had been convenient.'

'I saw you last night,' said the former Joan Willis quickly. 'In the restaurant at the Eden.'

'Did you? I didn't see you. You should have come over.'

'Oh I didn't like to interrupt. You were having such fun with old friends.' Mild wonder as to how Joan Willis would know about her friends made Margaret blink and after the pause of her finding no reply Joan continued. 'And I was being dined by my client. At least, I hoped he would be a client but it turned out the dinner was a consolation prize and we didn't land the contract.'

'I'm sorry about that,' said Margaret, wondering again at this unlikely tale and hoping that this chat was not going to last for the whole journey.

'I recognised you at once. And Mr Petrie, of course.'

'Ah yes, he was your boss when you were with the company, wasn't he?'

Joan Willis laughed. 'I had such a crush on him. But he always admired you, naturally. I wondered yesterday, seeing you all, why he ever left Marshall and Dexter.'

'Well, he didn't leave. But running the continental side – the company has a different name there because of their laws about directors and all that.'

'Oh, that's right, I didn't think. So you're still – really – partners, then?'

'Fortunately for us all.' Margaret ignored with now determined cheerfulness the curious turn the conversation was taking.

Joan Willis bent her head to watch her own fingers running round the rim of Margaret's cosmetic bag which was on the seat between them. 'You always had such lovely things,' she said softly at last. 'Perfect taste. In everything. Of course, it would make all the difference to us if we could get a contract with a big firm like Marshall and Dexter. To supply some small component, d'you think?'

'You'd have to talk to the engineers about that,' answered Margaret firmly. 'I don't even know what you make, you see, and I don't take decisions on the engineering side in any case. But if you'd like me to, I'll speak to Roddy Dexter. Why don't you ring up one day next week and make an appointment?'

'In London? Or at the plant?'

'Oh in London. Ask for Wilder. You'd better write it down. Have you a pen?' Joan Willis wrote busily for a moment and cards changed hands.

'If *you* would have a word with Mr Dexter, I'm sure it would work out,' she then said. 'How is Mrs Petrie? And the children?'

Margaret fixed the rather prominent brown eyes with a direct and ironical gaze. 'They were all in fine form a week ago.'

'I remember we were all so surprised in the office when Mr

Petrie married. I mean, rather an ordinary-looking girl, and him so attractive. But . . .'

'But?' asked Margaret, knowing now that she must face this out.

'I mean, they said . . .' And then, daunted by Margaret's smile, 'Her father had a lot of money, didn't he?'

'Yes, that's the sort of thing people say. In fact they are a most devoted family.'

'You know how malicious people are, but, of course, you would know.'

'I do know,' agreed Margaret. 'And now I think I'll have a little nap, if you won't mind.' She yawned and added very deliberately, 'We were late last night and I'm tired.'

'And I've been bothering you! Of course you must have a nice little rest.'

Margaret leaned back and closed her eyes but she did not doze. How determined was this try-on? She thought carefully; it must have been eight or nine years ago that Joan Willis left the company. That meant, presumably, that she was there during the time Margaret and Lance Petrie were making themselves and each other so unhappy; the time that ended in the Petrie wedding. They had both made a serious effort to end it and had not seen each other, or not alone, for almost two years. Then the chance of bad weather as well as an airline strike had isolated them together in Milan for two days. They had never been able to resist each other and they hadn't then. Since those two days in Milan they hadn't even tried to. But as for Joan Willis, then Lance's secretary, Margaret no longer recalled her leaving. That in itself, given her excellent memory, argued that it must have been about that time; after those days in Milan when Margaret and Lance were confused and overwrought over the complications, moral and practical, they had reintroduced into their lives. Had Lance perhaps given something away? Something a malicious eye noticed? Joan had said something about having a crush on Lance; if she had shown that feeling, Lance might easily have rejected it with tactless clearness? But even more than this deduction, Margaret was now sure that she felt a nagging half-memory of some fuss connected with the person of Joan Willis. Personnel

74

department, she thought, that is the obvious first step, to find out when, how and why she left us and where she went to. That may tell me something.

,The stewardess announced in three languages that the descent to earth would now commence. Before she left Heathrow, not neglecting to wave companionably at Joan Willis, Margaret telephoned the personnel manager. There was some question of doing business with these people she said, would he check back in his own records, and ask questions if possible, if there was someone he could chat with, at the company Joan Willis went to after leaving them. Just informally; perhaps she was being over-cautious but she seemed to remember some unpleasantness. Yes, it was fairly urgent because she had been talked into saying she would put in a word with Roddy and needed to know about Willis before she did so. He would call her back at home? Splendid.

Once out of the airport complex, the car humming quietly on the road towards Hampshire, Margaret could consider Joan Willis further. Supposing her memory was correct and Joan's departure from Marshall and Dexter had been unfriendly, that would still not be a convincing reason, after the lapse of time, for refusing to do business with her. Margaret would still have to speak to Roddy Dexter and then leave the matter to him. If she did not the Willis woman might discover the omission – she might ring up to check with Wilder or Roddy, for instance – and she would then know of Margaret's hostility, which meant Margaret's knowledge of her own vulnerability. A careful euphemism, she thought. Well, if Roddy made a contract with the Willis firm, then Joan Willis had the best of reasons to behave well. If that proved not possible perhaps something else might be put in her way to satisfy her without being openly said. If, on the other hand, there was a fresh, direct threat made, Margaret would have to think again. To give in to plain blackmail was unthinkable; a fatal mistake. She would then have to find some decisive means of showing Willis the error of her ways. But it was entirely possible that it could all be arranged without trouble, the Willis sting drawn so smoothly that nobody need know. It could be that this devious approach was dictated by Joan's temperament; some people did choose

75

negative methods of getting what they wanted – in this case work for her husband's firm – when a direct and friendly appeal would have been more effective as a first move and would not have aroused Margaret's formidable animosity. The use of such means before gentler ones had been tried showed a certain stupidity as well as deviousness and malice, a malice that certainly arose from envy. Granted that stupidity, it should not be too difficult to outwit Joan Willis, thought Margaret.

Still, it was worrying. The attack was a bit too urgent, too determined, to be shrugged off. It occurred to Margaret that there was an air of practice about Joan's manner. Was this perhaps not the first time she had threatened somebody? Was she, as it were, a professional blackmailer? This was a chilling thought and a worse one followed it. Ought Margaret to let Lance know? No, not at once. Unless the Willis woman was unhinged she would not go to Fiona Petrie because that would end all chance of success. Nor would she approach Lance himself until she was convinced that her attempt with Margaret was a definite failure; otherwise she would not have first tried Margaret. It was ten to one she would not risk that in any case; she wouldn't want two witnesses to her blackmail. That would be enough to send her down for several years. Just the same, whatever Joan's rational motive was, her real one was jealousy. A jealousy strong enough to last for years; it might be uncontrollable by her reasonable determination to get material solace for it. In that case Willis might ignore the danger and go to Lance in order to humiliate him and man-like, he would be more easily frightened than Margaret was. She must act fast enough to prevent that happening. No need to worry him yet and perhaps not at all.

'I've got what you wanted and it's not good,' said the personnel manager on the telephone. This was ten minutes after Annabel flung herself with cries of joy at her mother and brother, all legs and arms and flying hair. Her shoulder bag fell to the floor after a strange shaggy garment, where they lay, shed as it were, in flight through the house and out into the garden. There, mysteriously aware of her arrival, the neighbouring young already gathered and as Margaret put down the receiver she could hear the first bopping of tennis balls on racquets. 'No,' he had said quickly to her suggestion. 'Don't switch on your recorder. I'm only fifteen minutes away. I'll come over if that's all right.'

'Seems odd to hear tennis so early in the year,' said her old friend. 'But that, after all, is why you had the hard court put in.'

'You were awfully cautious on the phone. What is it all about?'

'Libellous,' he said tersely. 'If anyone is thinking of our doing business with these people, they can put it out of their heads. Miss Joan Willis was asked to go after a confusion in the funds of the staff Christmas Draw. But even that was an excuse. She caused constant trouble in Lance Petrie's office, intrigue, gossip *and* papers getting lost. He asked twice for her to be transferred and we were looking for a slot where she couldn't do so much harm when the Draw thing came up. But wait, that isn't all. A week later Roddy got a visit from the head engineer of Elphire in Liège. Miss Willis had offered him the whole set-up of one of our patents and suggested he should alter it slightly and use it, paying her a fee. Luckily Roddy made a note of this which is still in the Private file. When the man from Elphire declined her kind offer, she went and got a job with Bulstrode's.'

'Oh,' said Margaret, her eyes widening. 'She did, did she?'

'Yes. Fortunately again, I trained with the staff man at Bulstrode. I gave him a call and he looked for me. Willis was only with them six months. Then she married one of their junior engineers and left, taking with her as well as a husband, one or two useful little designs. This was only noticed after a small company in Lincoln began producing imitations of some of Bulstrode's parts. Bulstrode could not do much because enough changes had been made for the new firm to be chancy to catch. It would have meant a long lawsuit and costs higher than their estimated loss. But, as he said, no need for anyone else to make the same mistake over Miss Willis, who is now Patterson, by the way. I promised to keep all this absolutely mum, needless to say.'

'Generous of him,' said Margaret, considering.

'Do you want me to let Roddy Dexter know? Quietly, of course.'

'Very quietly, please. We don't want to make an enemy.'

'Absolutely not,' he weightily agreed. 'She must have thought we'd got rid of the papers by now.'

'It just shows, doesn't it. Was Willis, in fact, fired by us?'

'No. It was put to her and she gave notice and was paid off. Including her Christmas bonus, by the way.'

Margaret laughed at that, but she did not feel like laughing.

'That part I remember because I had to do it and she cried. Embarrassing.'

'Yes indeed. Horrid. Well, so much for Miss Joan Willis. Now let's have a drink. Or would you rather join the tennis?'

'God, no. I get enough exercise with my own tribe.'

A few minutes later, staring out at the garden, he said, 'How did the contract go this week? Pretty, the snowdrops under the yew hedge there.'

'Very well. It's all wrapped up and we shall sign next week at the Industrial Fair.'

'Splendid. Lance and his new boy in good form?'

'Marvellous. We had a hilarious dinner last night at the Eden. You'll see them the week after next, after the Hanover Fair.'

'I say, how did this affair with Miss Willis come up?'

'She came and sat with me on the flight back today and suggested we might find some work for her husband's firm.'

'Did she now? I wouldn't have thought she'd pick on Marshall and Dexter. I wonder if she's still up to the sort of tricks she played with Elphire that time?'

'She's probably gone straight long ago. People do, don't you think?'

'If they have sense, yes. It's years ago, after all. Well, we can leave that to Roddy.'

But Miss Willis, as Margaret still thought of her, had not changed. On the evening of her interview with the buying department of Marshall and Dexter she telephoned Margaret at home.

'They were very offhand,' she complained in her soft, modest

78

voice. 'I almost got the impression that they didn't want to do business with me.'

'Oh surely not,' said Margaret with practised calm. 'Why shouldn't they want to? You are too sensitive. But I'm sorry it didn't work out.'

'So am I. I'm really very worried. I did hope you would ask them to be helpful.'

'And I did. But, naturally, it's a question of what products they need to sub-contract at this moment. You could try again in a month or so, perhaps.'

'Months! I can't wait for weeks, let alone months.'

'What you need is a marketing agent, don't you agree? Had you thought of that?'

'No. No, I hadn't.' The voice became still softer, more self-pitying. 'I was so sure you would help me, you see. Of course, I could ask Mr Petrie. He'll be at the Hanover Fair.'

'You could do that,' agreed Margaret. 'He knows a lot of the continental firms. He might be able to suggest something.'

'Suggestions won't be much help. I need help now. And if I don't get it, there will be trouble.'

'Oh dear, are things as bad as that? I'm afraid there's not much I can do directly. With us, I mean. But I'll see if I can think of something.'

'Yes, do try. Because I didn't mean trouble for me, you know.'

'No, it would be your husband, I suppose.' Margaret's voice was vague.

'Well, more likely you. And Mrs Petrie's husband. And then, there are the children, aren't there? And all the company complications.'

'Perhaps you had better put all this in a letter?' Margaret replied so swiftly, losing her head for a moment, that her words took on the tone of hilarity.

'So that you could go to the police with it? But that wouldn't really help you, would it? And naturally I should send copies to the Board and to Mrs Petrie. After all, scandal is scandal and children are children. The police could only make things worse, if anything, wouldn't you say?'

'I'm not at all sure what you're talking about, you know. You spoke of the police, not me. And what is all this about scandal and children? I thought we were speaking of sub-contracts and things.'

'So we were.'

'And I'm afraid, as I told you, that I can't interfere in engineering decisions. That is Roddy Dexter's affair and his word goes.'

'In that case it will have to be a straight money transaction.'

'A what?' asked Margaret, as if she were startled.

'Oh, come off it,' said Joan Willis with sudden coarseness. 'Let's say five thousand pounds in cash, for a start.'

'You must be mad. You need a doctor, not a marketing agent. Goodbye.'

Margaret found that her hands were trembling so that she nearly dropped the telephone as she put it back on its rest. She held them up before her, willing them to stop shaking. They were well-formed hands, graceful, competent. This lacquer is too bright, she thought. The stones in her rings winked as she turned her wrists to make sure the tremor was gone. Then she heard the insistent faint hum of the recorder and switched it off. Unless she really is mad she will guess and take fright as soon as she has time to think that conversation over. Just the same, I shall have to go to the police as soon as the Fair is safely over. If I put it off and Willis hasn't been frightened off – and who can tell about that? – then it will be too late. Too late to save Lance. The children. Don't think of that. Shall I tell Lance? I shall see him tomorrow. At the thought, the familiar, never satiated shot of desire pierced her. That won't be possible, she told herself and was at once transfixed by the anguished fear of losing him again, and this time for ever. No, she thought with violence, no! Useless to tell oneself that one ought not to want more than one has, that to want more is to tempt providence. Especially, as she did not fail to remind herself, if one has everything. Everything but Lance. We can never live together, never know the comfort and depth of companionship. But just the little we have together is more important than anything else. That wasn't what you said years ago, when he tried to persuade you to run away with him. You refused then, because the children were babies still. So he married and tried to forget you and by the time you were free, his children were there. And he loves his children as you love yours. He will never leave them. They will leave him one day but by then it will be too late. You will both be old by then.

No, I can't lose him, she thought, and the prospect was so dreadful that she rose abruptly from her chair, clasping her hands and turning sharply away from the silent telephone, as if not seeing it might undo what that few minutes had done.

'Mummy!' called Annabel's voice, 'can we go and get some pizzas for supper? Potts will drive, if I can take your car keys?' The presence of Annabel, a whirl of long-limbed energy, seemed to fill the charming room into which she now erupted. 'And some money?'

'No, not the big car, darling. Potts can take the Mini if he promises to drive carefully.'

'Are you all right, Mummy? You look all pale and wan.'

'Slight headache. I'm fine. Potts! Potts, where are you? Listen, Potts, not more than twenty-five. Promise?'

'If you insist,' said the boy gloomily and Margaret gave him the keys.

'You've only had a licence for a few weeks,' she urged crossly. 'So be a good Potts. If you aren't I shall call you Caspar.'

'Oh God, anything but that,' they cried together.

'Well, I didn't have the christening of him. I'd have given him a nice, sensible name. Henry, perhaps.'

'Yes, Henry's all right. Not as good as William, but not nearly as bad as Caspar.'

'Are you talking about me?' asked her brother, putting his head round the door.

'No, only comparing names. You coming to the pizza place?'

'No, I haven't finished with the bike yet. Bring a whole one for me, yes?'

'Look at your hands,' cried Margaret. 'Get out of here, you lout.'

'Don't worry, I'm going. Wouldn't stay in this dump anyway. Like a museum.'

'Does Mrs Betts know you're bringing pizzas?' Margaret called after them.

'Yes, we warned her,' they yelled back.

The door of the room slammed and then the front door. 'Will you never learn to close doors quietly?' said Margaret to the now empty room, and began to laugh. She sat down again suddenly and gave a quiet, wailing sob, tears blinding her. That woman won't be frightened off. She's too stupid to be scared. Terrorists everywhere, but nobody manages to kill people like her. If only somebody would shoot *her*. The shock of her own wicked thought sobered Margaret, and she sat quite still, staring in front of her but seeing nothing, until she heard the children's voices again.

Somehow Margaret had supposed that Joan Willis would be on the same flight as herself to Hanover; but she was not. That her enemy was not visible was irrationally unnerving and Margaret felt more worried at the thought of what the woman might be doing than she had before over the problem of maintaining her outward calm if Miss Willis should accost her in the group of her colleagues. It was essential to keep a normal and neutral manner towards her whether Joan wanted to convey that she understood the exact meaning of that telephone conversation or whether she intended to continue her threats. If she realised that she had been induced to make an open demand for money, which could only mean that the conversation was recorded, it was still vital that this should not become a declared threat which could cause her to lose her head before Margaret discovered what concrete evidence Willis possessed. If she still did not grasp that fact it was equally necessary that nothing should be shown by either of the antagonists that could expose the existence of a crisis to Margaret's friends and partners. If Margaret's ruse had succeeded in frightening the blackmailer into retreat, whatever evidence there was could then be bought off quietly by Margaret's lawyers. On the whole, Margaret forced herself to consider reasonably, that would be a preferable outcome to the discovery that Willis had no definite evidence, for a bluff would remain a threat to Lance; anonymous letters to Fiona Petrie would be just as disastrous as an open scandal. Only as long as the duel was confined to Joan Willis and Margaret could Margaret win it.

The moment she saw Lance's tense face as the group from London greeted him and Henry in the hotel hall, Margaret knew the vanity of that hope. The anxiety in Lance was so much there that she felt it as something almost palpable. They often knew each other's thoughts and Margaret knew now that Joan Willis had already spoken to Lance and in a way that had frightened him. The intuition of Lance's humiliation drove the blood from her heart like an onset of physical pain and Margaret felt dizzy for a moment as she said to herself with intense hatred, she shall pay for this.

'The people from Marburger's will be here at seven,' he now said, addressing the group in general. 'Is it agreed that we all meet in Margaret's suite at five to? Drinks and so on have been ordered and we shall sign. We have dinner with them tomorrow. Tonight we go to the official reception which they've put at nine o'clock this year – sensible because we're all up to our eyes at the usual cocktail time. But it does mean Margaret and Caroline having to change. You might get a rest after lunch,' he added with raised eyebrows at Margaret and she nodded.

'I'd better,' she agreed. She looked at the diary held by her secretary. 'Lunch with Ileanu?'

'That's the Rumanian second man for light industry,' Roddy Dexter explained. 'They are, as always, being awkward, I gather?' This to Lance.

'That's right. Usual thing. They want the formal estimate before going further. But we're sticking to it. If they insist, they pay the costs of the estimate if either side withdraws. It's the only way to make them wait until we're more or less agreed on specifications and terms. But don't bother with Ileanu beyond civilities. I've put you next to Nitevi who has the know-how and the say-so. Margaret will keep Ileanu busy.' He smiled his sudden taut grin at her and to the others it probably looked natural. 'You won't enjoy that but he'll foul up everything if he gets into Nitevi's act. Okay?'

'Of course,' said Margaret. 'What would the bill be, for the estimate?'

'Certainly ten, could be fifteen.' Lance meant ten to fifteen thousand pounds. 'For the whole unit. Production side is ours direct, but Nitevi agrees that we get the right to subcontract the buildings this time, after they made such a mess of them with that other affair. Ileanu's language is French, by the way, and bad at that.'

'What fun,' said Margaret, pulling her mouth in joke. 'I bet he has bad breath as well.'

'No. No, he's the scented type.' Lance looked at Margaret's pretty secretary. 'You'll be on his other side, Caroline, and if his hand wanders, don't squeak. Just keep him off Margaret. These Party apparatchiks are accustomed to any attractive woman being instantly available within their own set-up, and Ileanu has been known to get out of hand. He would then be resentful. You see?'

'I must go,' said Roddy Dexter, looking at his watch, 'if I'm to call on old Scarface before luncheon.' Old Scarface was a former university fencing champion, now a Federal Minister, with whom Roddy had spent a happy and somewhat piratical year at Krupps, years before in the occupation time.

'Give him my love,' said Margaret. 'I hope we're seeing him?'

'If that's all for the moment,' said Lance, 'we could go and have a look at the Marburger papers?' This to Margeret, who put out a hand into which her secretary put a red folder.

'Can I skive off?' Caroline asked. 'I'd like to see the Jap exhibit before the Fair opens. I can just make it if I fly.'

'Don't be late for lunch,' warned Margaret affectionately. 'I know you and your Harimito boyfriend.'

'You must have been up before dawn again,' said Lance as they went up in the lift. 'How d'you feel?'

'I'm fine,' she lied. 'Why? Do I look awful?'

'You look marvellous,' he answered brusquely. 'Got your key?'

As the door closed on the sitting-room, Margaret said quietly, 'What did Joan Willis say to you?' He was not in the least surprised that she knew.

They did not touch each other. Margaret began to hang up dresses and suits and Lance lounged against the upright of the connecting door.

'She wants five thousand quid in cash,' he said. 'Or else.'

84

'Just like that?'

'Just like that.'

'Any details of the "or else"?'

'Letters with pictures to all Board members and Fiona. She also claims to know a couple of newspaper city-reporters, but that I don't believe.'

'What has she got?'

'More than enough. She showed me two photographs to which dates and places can be definitely attached. Simple and unanswerable. For instance. Picture of you getting into my car in front of the Four Seasons – you remember? – me tipping the porter, your and my bags visible on the back seat. Behind the porter the hotel announcement board showing clearly a Labillard fashion show of the spring models 1969. That was October 1968. I checked, though I didn't need to. And you were supposed to be in the Bahamas, having missed your summer break that year.'

'Right. And the reason for the spoiled summer was Dick's sudden death.'

'Just to push the point home, as you might say.' He waited, not looking at her. 'Another picture of us both leaving your room – it must have been the Excelsior at Lausanne that time – broad daylight, corridor clock shows half past eight, waiter with breakfast tray down the hall but coffee pot and orange juice quite clear, and your room number on the door, just past my head. You're going to ask how she got them? I did, too. She says the Four Seasons one she took herself when she saw us, and that's what gave her the whole idea. We, of course, didn't notice her. The Lausanne one she paid the lift-boy to get.'

'She didn't show these works of art to me.'

'No. So she said. Wanted to try the velvet glove first.'

'She's lying there. She didn't give me time enough to be sure I wouldn't come through.'

'She may be desperate for money.'

'So it's a long-planned thing.'

'Evidently. Of course, it's possible that the pictures are faked, but they looked genuine to me.'

'Even fake mud would stick.'

'And there's also the point that the mud is not faked, even if the photos are.'

'The Board doesn't worry me,' said Margaret. 'They all know in any case. It's . . .'

They stood silent, seeing Fiona's pinched face, the children on both sides with their young features rigid with embarrassment, the gestures of turning away, the forced jokes with contemporaries. Annabel 'knew' something; William did not and his feeling for his mother would make him unforgiving. Lance's children were still too young to be anything but bewildered, frightened, lost in such a disaster, and their mother could be relied upon to make the most of her jealousy and grief with them as with the outside world. She adored Lance and had never been sure of his feelings. She was only sure that they were not adoration and when at last Lance did marry he picked a girl who would always be emotionally dependent on him. Only gradually did the debt become clear that was owed to her stubborn, blind love.

'The public, too. The Board, all right. But it could never be kept inside the circle.'

'It always has been?'

'Yes. But as an open secret which included Dick himself. Once on the table, in words, it has to spread. If only because Betsy Dexter is very thick with Fiona.'

'You're right. Such things spread of themselves once they're – what's the word?'

'Explicit.'

That word released in Margaret an unadmitted fear always there and now as real as a third creature in the room with them. It entered by way of their admission, never before put into words, of their long and deliberate deception of Fiona. They both knew without Lance having said so at any time, that the real choice had not been given to Fiona either before her marriage or since. And this misshapen little monster of a thought was alive and there with them. Over twenty years of tormenting and fulfilling love turned during that conversation into the dusty banality of an adulterous affair. They had been 'we' from the first moment; now 'we' was his family. Whatever happened, Joan Willis had divided them.

Margaret blundered, eyes closed, towards him and he took her in his arms. The familiar, unfailing physical longing was at once there; but the long kiss was a farewell.

They released each other and the silence continued until Lance said very quietly, his voice not quite steady, 'We ought to look through those papers.'

'Yes,' she admitted, and they returned to work, friends but no longer lovers.

It was after midnight when Margaret closed the door of her room and was alone. She could not bear to turn the key and lock him out but she knew he would not come. The process continuing in her mind all day issued now in the decision to go to the police as soon as she arrived back in London. She would tell the whole story; the name of her lover would be known but not mentioned between the policemen and herself. The usual agreement ruling cases of blackmail would ensure that however many people thought they knew something, only those who already knew the facts would really know; this was the only course which offered the least chance of rescuing Lance's family life. William, still at school, would perhaps be spared; Annabel who read the papers would have to be told in case she should guess. Lance would take his family to a Greek island for a month when the case of Joan Willis threatening Mrs X came up.

Somehow they got through the next busy days. Twice Margaret saw Joan Willis and nodded, smiling at her. There was a condescension now in Joan Willis's smile; she felt herself the victor, not only looking forward to money but enjoying the humiliation of Lance and Margaret. Over and over Margaret regretted bitterly the custom of quietly getting rid of unsatisfactory staff rather than go to the trouble of having matters out. If Joan Willis had been openly sacked for dishonesty years before, this could hardly have happened to threaten not only private lives but the whole stability of a large concern with all its dependent people. She blamed herself, too, for handling Willis carelessly and arrogantly at the start; incredible that she should have underestimated the woman's malice and determination. For it was plain that Joan meant to enjoy ruining them. The sum demanded as a first instalment proved that.

The flight home was fairly full but Joan Willis sat with an empty seat beside her and after a few minutes with Roddy Dexter, Margaret left him to flirt with her secretary and went to join her enemy.

'This time you come to me,' said Joan. 'I seem to have lost my lighter. Have you got a light?'

Margaret took out the lighter Lance had given her and lit the other woman's cigarette. Joan did not thank her. She quite deliberately blew her smoke into Margaret's face. She is stupid, thought Margaret. I was right about that, anyway.

'You will get your money,' she said. 'But from me. And for the future I can arrange through a subsidiary for your company to be supplied with orders. On one condition.'

'Mm-mm. No conditions.'

'Yes. And you will keep it. You will keep away from Petrie and his family. I shall know at once if you approach them. Now. When and where shall we meet?'

'You know Taliani in Greek Street? Next Friday at twelve-thirty.'

'Good,' said Margaret, slid out of the narrow space and went back to her friends.

'This is your captain speaking,' said a flattened, metallic voice. 'We have just heard that a lightning strike by twenty-five computer staff at Heathrow has made it necessary for us to land at a freight runway where this airline company has reserved emergency facilities for the convenience of our pasengers. There is no danger. We hope to provide buses right away to remove you and your baggage to Terminal Two. It would be a great help and would speed things up if the gentle-men passengers would lend a hand to the crew in handling baggage. We apologise for this little difficulty, which is beyond our control. Thank you for your attention.'

'Odd how foreign airlines captains always have strong American accents,' said Roddy Dexter. 'I'll go up front and see if I can find out any more.' He strolled away with his air of being effortlessly in command and presently returned with the news that some electricians and some bus drivers had come

88

out in support of the strikers. 'That means we shall probably have to walk miles to the Terminal. There will be a long wait for our bags.'

'We could leave ours and get them collected tomorrow,' suggested Caroline.

'Good idea. We'll do that. You're a clever girl.'

'Brutes,' complained Margaret. 'Just when I have a thousand things to do. They would.'

She leaned back, trying to relax. The delay meant that she could not now go to the police today. That left only three clear days to arrange for someone to be at the next table when she met Joan Willis at Taliani on Friday. She would have to get through the whole weekend in this state of desperate and impotent resolve. As for the future without Lance, she dared not think of that. She heard Roddy explaining to Caroline the complicated internal struggles between various trade unions and between union administrations and local shop-stewards. Evidently the shop-steward of the computer staff, in pursuit of some ambition, had called a meeting to which unionists representing various other skills felt obliged to go to protect their own interests or simply to know what was happening. This quite small group of men, in order to attend the strikers' meeting, would have left their own posts and abandoned machines and other staff so that immobility was bound to spread quickly through the highly co-ordinated technical processes of getting aircraft and passengers, mails and goods, on to and off the ground.

'You mean they just leave their machines? Including aircraft?'

'Sure. The meeting is on now. And other union men, which means everybody, down tools until they know what's going on, for fear of reprisals or because the electrician has turned a switch off.'

'But isn't that frightfully dangerous?' asked Caroline, opening large eyes at Roddy in pretended ignorance.

'You mean to us? Of course. But, you see, these technicians handle the machines and switches all the time; they don't think of it like that.'

'But they do turn things off? Lock things up, before they go away, surely?'

'Not necessarily. Only last week it happened in one of our shops. An argument developed about some detail and the men on the control bank both went off to report to their shop-floor man, leaving several million quids' worth of automated equipment running free.'

'I can't help feeling,' Caroline decided, 'that there must be a better way of settling arguments.'

'But, you see, they don't *want* a better way,' Roddy smiled.

Once landed, in the lowering late afternoon, the emergency lighting made everything more obscure than complete darkness, which was falling fast, would have been. Two women with small children and a very old man remained in the aeroplane to await the arrival of a car. The able-bodied passengers helped the crew to remove and pile the luggage. Others stood about in groups until the stewardesses were free to lead them.

'But I know where we are,' said Joan Willis, looking up at the huge neon sign of a freight company that was still half-lit. 'I've been over here before about a damaged crate. We can cut across the tarmac and save at least half the distance.'

'Oh no,' demurred the middle-aged woman to whom she spoke. 'I'd be afraid to go out there in the dark.'

'There's no danger.' Joan Willis was derisive. 'Nothing else will land now it's dark and the lights are still on over there. That's Terminal One,' and she raised an arm to point but the other woman was not to be persuaded. Margaret, overhearing, wondered how Joan Willis could know with such certainty where she was pointing. Margaret herself had been through the great airport at least a hundred times over the course of years but it being of its nature in a state of continuous change and alteration, she found the whole complex almost as confusing as the first time she used it. But she isn't sure at all, she then thought; it is just her nature to be sure she does know. Not only where Terminal One lies from here. She is just as sure that Lance and I are so afraid of her that between now and a week today I shall do nothing but draw cash from the bank.

'Ah well, if one *knows*,' drawled Margaret as if to Caroline and putting just enough suggestion of sarcasm into her tone to make it sting. She saw that both Caroline, surprised at a so untypical rudeness, and Joan Willis turned their heads quickly at her gibe.

'Well, I have business to take care of, if nobody else has. I'm off.' The voice was now sharply aggressive, but the thought of a future revenge, no doubt, made Miss Willis prudent. 'I'll be seeing you.'

There was much meaning in the slang phrase and Margaret clenched her teeth on it. Yes, and I hope you break your neck, she thought with a savagery that made the words seem almost audible. But they were not and Joan at once put her decision into action, making off diagonally into the wide interim of the dark.

'All very well,' grumbled the housewife, much offended. 'I think it's too risky.'

'You are right, ma'am,' the Captain's precise foreign voice praised her. 'It is unwise to wander about out there. It is almost dark, the weather is not good, the apron is always greasy in parts. And we do not know what is happening. Everybody could return to work while we are out there and things would get rolling.' The modern idiom made his seriousness, wholly admirable, sound ridiculous. 'It is better we all stay here until our own bus comes.'

Someone objected to a possibly long delay. He too had affairs to take care of and a train to catch to the north. This reminded the Captain of another argument. He raised his voice so that it could reach any stragglers.

'The delay is not our responsibility, sir, but I regret it. And once we have all left the craft I have no authority, but that lady who went has done so at her own risk and if anything should happen my company would not be liable.'

In spite of the faulty grammar he was impressively orderly and sensible. If Joan Willis could still hear him, however, he did not convince her and she continued on her own way. She will never stick to the rules, thought Margaret, that's why she gets away with things. Not like Lance and me, tamely abiding by the unwritten rules, going to the police when we are in trouble and allowing our lives to be wrecked. If either of us had half her nerve, we'd find some way of removing her.

Several other people were now conferring with the man who needed to catch a train, and they then moved off in a group; not venturing out on to the tarmac but cautiously skirting the buildings.

'Why don't we risk it?' suggested Caroline. 'It's only a slight chance of danger and we might stand about here for ages.' She sounded as if she were enjoying the adventure and Margaret's strained nerves agreed with her secretary's impatience of passivity. She turned to ask Roddy for his opinion, but he was going back up the landing steps with the Captain.

'If that other woman can manage, I don't see why we can't,' said Caroline.

'All right, let's.' Margaret made up her mind. 'I'm quite good at seeing in the dark. And anything is better than hanging about here now it is starting to rain.' She could see Joan Willis in the obscurity as a moving shape and had for a second a curious sensation of being led. To counteract it she said quickly to Caroline, 'Don't follow anything but the lights over there, and don't lose me, will you?'

'No, we'll stick close together.'

They were well out on the apron when the distant bank of lights began to flicker and go out in patches. There was a slight wind, or draught, that blew the rain into their faces. All about them at varying distances were objects which must be lifting and moving equipment. They went past a standing truck, its back open by a stacked fork-lift. Stationary freight aircraft were less of a hazard, being much higher off the ground which was not quite even. These all loomed out of the murk, some half-lighted, some humming with electronic sounds, some dark and still, just bulks without form. If there was anyone inside them they gave no sign.

'Are you nervous?' asked Caroline softly.

'Yes. Mind that.' It was a wheeled stair so well balanced that when Caroline knocked it changing her cosmetic bag from one hand to the other, it shifted.

They advanced, step by step as the lights gradually failed, removing their goal. By concentrating on what lights were still showing they still knew their direction but the surroundings were correspondingly invisible. Ahead and to the left there was a muffled sound. Then a blunt smack and an exclamation :

'God, that was a trolley,' said the voice of Joan Willis. It sounded some way off. There was the bumbling noise of something heavy rolling. 'There's a kerb here,' said the voice, rising nervously. 'Hey! Is anyone there? I've dropped my bag.'

'Wait. Keep still until that trolley stops rolling,' said Caroline. The two women stood close, almost touching. 'I can't see you,' called Caroline.

'Over here,' called back the voice uselessly. They heard a muffled thud and the sound of heavy wheels ceased.

'Don't move yet,' said Margaret sharply. 'The trolley's stopped but I can hear something else moving.'

'Perhaps it bumped something. That's what it sounded like. She's started the whole lot moving.' Caroline giggled to relieve taut nerves. 'Over here!' she called 'To your right!' Margaret turned round and instantly lost her sense of where she was.

'I'm sure I can hear something moving,' she said urgently. 'We must go back, Caroline.'

Caroline must have moved. Margaret put out a hand to catch her arm and found empty space.

'Where are you? I can hear voices,' wailed Joan Willis.

'I'm coming,' answered Caroline's voice. With her dark coat, black boots, long dark hair she was quite invisible.

'Caroline!' cried Margaret.

'Keep still. Don't move. I can see you against the lights. It's all right.'

'But you're going in the wrong direction!' Margaret thought she shouted and then realised that she was muttering to herself. Out of the corner of her eye she took in that the whole block of illumination was suddenly black. From childhood came the long-forgotten sensation of everything being out of control, of things happening above, around, outside her. There was a sense of something huge, imminently close to her and threatening but above her. Disoriented, she swayed slightly and shifted her feet to restore balance; it was like the feeling of those screaming rows before her parents separated. That was one of the bonds between herself and Lance, for they had both been almost destroyed in childhood by the wilfulness of their elders and that was where the dominating concern to protect their

93

own children came from, now menaced by Joan Willis and her stupid greed. Lance, she thought, my darling. She heard Caroline's voice swearing at some obstacle, quite a long way over to the left. On the right a distant truck turned up some slope and its headlights lifted and swerved across the space, leaving vision imprinted on Margaret's blinded eyes. Like a photograph she saw Joan Willis about ten yards away as she lifted her head from searching at her feet for the lost handbag; she seemed to be bundling at her voluminous overcoat as if she could have lost the bag in its folds. Margaret could still hear a slight but increasing bumbling and hissing sound which was not the trundling of the loaded trolley of a few moments before. It was at once quieter and much, much larger, more portentous, spacious. Somewhere she had heard that sound before. Then with a shock that stopped a heartbeat and flooded over all her nerves she recalled a journey when the aircraft had for some reason to be towed into its bay, without motors, towed by an electric tug that was almost soundless. It made just that sound of quiet, huge padded wheels, hissing slightly over wet tarmac, a whisper and sensation of some great body moving as it were stealthily.

Then she saw it loom up as a density against the bulks and shadows of the dark. Its form cut off the corner of a distant hangar outlined on the comparatively luminous sky of piled clouds. It moved. One of the man-made monsters, abandoned by its keepers, was rolling forward. Connections were made without thought in Margaret's mind. Caroline was well out of its path. How high were its wings? She must scream a warning. Some force like a hand restraining her struck her dumb and rigid for the immeasurable moment left to her. She dropped to the ground just as Joan Willis saw or felt the mass looming over her and howled in terror. As Margaret's body hit the tarmac, knocking the breath from her lungs and splintering lights through her head, she half saw the figure fling itself out of the path of one immense wheel and run straight under its pair. Half stunned by the impact of the ground, gasping for air, Margaret shut her eyes tightly. She saw nothing, she had seen nothing. Fear gripped her throat and her first cry was only a groan. Then she screamed loudly. She felt the passage of a wide sweep quite near before her as the enormous machine ran past over the trembling ground, without the slightest check in its almost silent progress. There was not a sound from over there, not a single moan or cry. All she had done was keep silent in that instant, her voice strangled in her throat. Margaret distinctly heard the spatter of rain before the voices began calling, Caroline's, a foreigner's, Roddy's yell. People were running. Lights stretched out, cautiously a car approached, headlights spraying the gleaming black. Margaret lay still, outstretched. I couldn't have saved her. I screamed but I saw it too late. Having kept quiet in that instant, there was nothing more to be done.

Jonathan Gash

EYES FOR OFFA REX

Councillor Ash waited in the silent darkness, watching the road. A clear night with stars tingling overhead, the sort which made you remember. He pondered seriously for a moment, worried by the possibility of an untidy detail, before memory flooded in to clear his irritation away. That phrase, Tennyson wasn't it? *Shivered to the tingling stars.* You had to learn by heart once. Too bloody idle to learn anything at all these days, he thought in some annoyance. Look at the way kids come slouching in for jobs, thinking everybody owed them a living. And the state of some of them.

The lonely spot was ideal. Bright moon, blind bend, frosted white skeletal trees, and a road covered with black ice. A night worth waiting half a year for, since that summer evening when Gordon had refused to sell the Offa Rex – and thereby had condemned himself to death.

Ash congratulated himself for choosing well. Short of unforeseen calamities – like that drunken sot parking for a snog with his tart last Friday night and spoiling the plan – he would kill tonight. He found himself sweating heavily despite the subzero temperature. Concentration did that, made a man sweat. Concentration and sex.

His watch said tennish. Gordon would be saying his farewells in the *Goat and Compass* before driving this way. Luckily Gordon was no mechanic, never had been since a kid. Too reflective, too indrawn. Ash desperately wanted a fag. Gordon of course never smoked. How the hell a cold fish like him ever won Janey . . . In other circumstances Ash would have made a contest of it. As it was there were bigger things at stake than a mere bird, though once Gordon was dead . . . Even if Janey did have a good job in the local hospital laboratory, well, widows were known to be receptive to consolation from some body attentive in just the right way. He found himself grinning without humour and switched his face off. Discipline.

The poem came back for a fleeting second. It was where that knight was carrying the dying Arthur through those icy caves, his clashing harness echoes among the stalactites. An eerie funeral scene. Appropriate to remember that, in a way.

The exciting part would come in a month's time, when Janey disposed of Gordon's estate and sold the Offa Rex. Ash realised his hands were trembling. Concentration to lift a man's temperature, he thought wrily, and lust to quiver him like a pointer.

Ice was beautiful. No real snow to speak of for several days then persistent fog all yesterday, a faint suggestion of a thaw early this morning and a snap frost at dusk. Black ice warnings were out on the motorways with the radio ominous with warnings all day. Ash knew this stretch of country road like his own hand, but then so did Gordon. They had cycled along it often enough. No lights of course in these ancient curling East Anglian village roads. Near the river black ice tended to form faster, almost heaven-sent.

Before settling in to wait Ash had examined the surface beyond the medieval humpback bridge. Lovely. Worse than a skating-rink. Tyres needed chains for grip on a night like this. Gordon's never had even a trace of tread on them. Ash knew because he had looked. Served the fool right. The iron-hard frozen roadside would hold no imprints so Ash had selected a slight recess to the right of the road. Gordon would come over the bridge on to the black ice which covered the road for almost a hundred yards – only to find a strange car cutting across suddenly from his right, where there should only be trees . . . Gordon's sudden instinctive braking on black ice would cause his death. Not really murder. You couldn't call it that. It would be a sort of suicide, or an accident. The narrow road doglegged left where the oxbow river curved again, and the parapet was too low, always had been. Ash himself had complained in council meetings about the possibility of cars crashing through at that point into the slow deep river so far below . . .

Black ice was essential. The more usual pale stuff was always easier. And it shone white in moonlight, giving ample warning to change gear before taking the bridge. That was the bewitchingly sinister beauty of black ice. Roads always looked innocent and bone dry, innocently black as the tar beneath but more slippery than any mirror. Ash found himself grinning despite his nervousness. If only he'd allowed himself the radio, perhaps a nip in a flask to keep the cold out, or a cigarette. But no. Discipline always paid well.

A beam lit the sky, waved once and was gone. A car was coming. 'Good old Gordon,' Ash growled.

He fired the engine, a first time start. Keep a cool head. The Jaguar would be reported missing fairly soon. Surprising how easy it had been. Ash's own car was waiting in the same pub yard. Pinching the Jag to do the job was probably over-cautious but had actually proved very little risk. Unpleasantly simple, in fact. And it was vital for Gordon not to recognise Ash's select green Humber, should things go wrong.

The headlights swathed the sky again. The oncoming car was at the Dragonswell turn-off. Sure enough the lights flickered on to the sideroad. It had to be him. Ash gunned the engine into a deep sustained roar. Three hundred yards. Ash clenched his hands a few times to loosen them, the way the army made you prepare for action. Then into first gear with the throttle slightly dipped and the ·lutch slammed flat. At the last minute he decided the powerful engine could cope and snicked into second, a simple modification to his plan proving complete adaptability and control, something he would be able to look back on with justifiable pride.

The oncoming car lurched, its lights jerking skywards once then dipping to silhouette the humped bridge's ancient stones. *Now.*

Ash rolled the Jaguar on to the road. A horn sounded, already despair in the note. A faint squeal, then Ash was trundling among the trees on the opposite side of the road, quickly turning with some difficulty and having to reverse to make the road again. Pinching a car with chained tyres really had been a brainwave, he complimented himself. He managed the turn without difficulty. Six seconds and he was off in the direction from which Gordon had been driving.

Ash put the headlights on after two hundred yards. One glance in his mirror showed only darkness over the river valley. No lights shone there at all. Poor Gordon. He reached now for a cigarette. Soon the Offa Rex would be his.

Hardwick, the golf club secretary, approved of the doctor and the policeman even if they hadn't played a round in years. He expressed it best to Mrs Aspern when going over her catering accounts. 'Without the quack and the local C.I.D. a golf club's missing something – tone, perhaps.'

Mrs Aspern would have none of it. 'A lady doctor lays herself open to scandal,' she shot back, 'coming in bold as brass – '

Hardwick sighed. 'Times have changed, Mrs Aspern.' They had the same argument every Saturday. 'And lunch in a crowded clubroom's hardly the height of depravity.' It was hopeless. Mrs Aspern had a trick of exclaiming, lips tight shut, which discredited any innocent explanation.

Across the restaurant Dr Baxter was trying to reason with Inspector Young. 'You're reading too much into it, George,' she was saying, about his disappointingly simple road crash case. 'The dead man's wife has every right to feel aggrieved with the police.'

'Why?' George Young found to his surprise he was losing the argument. 'The bloody woman drove me mad.'

'Well, was she irrational?'

'No. Calm but uptight, if you know what I mean. My point is there's no such thing as murder without trace, Clare.'

'But any theory's possible, George – '

'That's her very argument!' George realised he had raised his voice and caused some heads to turn. He smiled to show all was well. Clare grinned and passed the salt to give him time. 'But surely you can see how illogical the statement is?' He salted his veal unnecessarily. 'A so-called "murder" without evidence of murder *is* an accident. By definition.'

Clare was becoming interested. 'There's another way of putting that, George.'

'Go on, then.'

99

'The way the woman did. Her husband might have been killed deliberately. Your people failed to elicit any evidence for what she *knows* to be true.'

George growled, 'We've combed the river-bank, the bridge, the roadside –'

'Here.' Clare was looking thoughtful. 'Is it that case in today's local rag? Black ice, the car?'

'That's it. Summerston.'

'I read it,' Clare said. 'Doesn't ice leave marks?'

'Not after it melts, love,' the inspector said drily. 'Mrs Summerston believes another car lay in wait, pulled out, causing her husband to lose control.'

'It's quite possible.'

'Not to a local man,' said the inspector doggedly. 'He knew the road in all weathers.'

'I've driven over the bridge several times,' Clare cut in. 'With ice around you put both feet on the floor so the car slows without braking.'

'So he'd had a few drinks and forgot.'

'Or was made to brake suddenly, instinctively.' Clare put her knife and fork down. 'Another car hidden in the dip by the old bridge . . . You'd slam the brake down by reflex action.'

'Only if there *was* another car, Clare. You're as daft as his wife.' George waited in silence for a moment.

The doctor tilted her head enquiringly. 'Come on, out with it. There's something you haven't admitted.'

George shrugged uncomfortably. 'She says she knows whose car it was.'

Clare gasped audibly. 'And you've done nothing?'

'Of course we did.' George refilled their glasses. Clare had chosen the wine this Saturday, a German *spätlese*, somewhat too sweet but ripe enough. 'We checked every damned thing. The suspect's own car was parked until well after closing time at a tavern several miles away.'

'Vouched for?' Clare must have touched a nerve. George's reply sounded bitter.

'You think I'd forget to check on that, too?'

'Sorry,' Clare said meekly. 'But only most of the evening, not all?'

'He hinted that he has this bird . . .' George admitted sheepishly as Clare smiled with understanding. 'But Janey Summerston claims that's all a front. She said it's the sort of thing the other chap would do.'

'Was he rich?'

'The deceased? Far from it. And there seems no funny business, nothing we hang action on. The only rum point is they were friends, grew up together.'

'How terrible!' Clare sipped at her chilled glass. 'Bitter friends lifelong?'

George was beginning to feel uncomfortable for some reason. 'Look, Clare. Can I make my original point?'

'What was it, George, dear?' Clare fluttered her eyes disarmingly to make him laugh.

'Be serious. It's that some people are incapable of accepting the truth, even if it's there before their very eyes. They'll lie, make accusations, go demented – even pillory a best friend to disprove reality.'

'Well, distressed people do behave irrationally.'

'More than that.' George now felt he was winning. 'There's guilt. *Her* guilt. A twenty-six-year-old husband who prefers to spend his evening drinking with the lads in a pub rather than go home . . . *She*'s guilty, see? Needs a scapegoat. So she picks on the only person she can think of, a bloke whose name was probably often heard around the house. Comes along to the cop shop and accuses him.'

'Did she have a motive as rational as the rest of her story?'

'As *ir*rational, Clare,' George reproved, catching her smile.

Mrs Aspern also caught the smile and the inspector's sudden seriousness as he decided to tell Clare Janey Summerston's account of Ash's motive in killing Gordon. Her lips thinned. She closed the office hatch thinking of Mr Hardwick's gullibility and that all men are fools. Like children.

Inspector Young would have enjoyed meeting Janey Summerston on practically any other occasion than just before her deceased husband was subjected to inquest. She was pleasantly slender, neat without seeming obsessional and even wore colourful clothes. Her twin set matched the pleated skirt and the shoes showed sense instead of flamboyance. The only indications of grief were the dark rings beneath her eyes. Other than that she seemed composed but full of conviction.

'I know what you're thinking, Inspector,' she had said. 'That I'm deranged, and that in another week or two I'll come to my senses. That is not the case. I'm in earnest.'

George Young kept his calm. That was a familiar reaction and you had to make allowances. He said mildly, 'Mrs Summerston, we need something more than supposition.'

'It is not supposition,' Janey Summerston said evenly. 'I'm sure it's true.'

'But Councillor Ash is a well respected man – '

'So was Dr Crippen.'

' – and was known to be a friend of . . . of your husband.'

'They grew up together, went to the same school.' Janey Summerston nodded as if acknowledging something to herself. 'Their paths diverged.'

'They didn't see each other much?' The inspector found himself drawn in despite exasperation at the uselessness of it all.

'No, not for the past few years. Except at occasional meetings.'

'A club?'

'No. The coin-collectors' circle.'

'So they were no longer well acquainted,' Young said firmly. 'So neither evidence nor motive.'

'There *is* motive,' Janey said. 'Gordon's collection.'

Inspector Young heard Sergeant Brent cough twice, his signal for some additional information on the subject. He clicked his pencil to show the hint was taken.

'Is Gordon's collection valuable, Mrs Summerston?'

'Not really.'

'Does any agreement exist that will allow Councillor Ash, or any other named person, to take possession of the collection in the event of your husband's death?'

'No.'

'Is there anything in that collection which they own jointly?'

'No.'

The interview had ended only after an hour's arguing.

Janey Summerston insisted that Ash had somehow engineered her husband's accident. As George told Clare Baxter when describing Janey, there was simply no reason to believe a single word the grieving woman uttered.

' – though everything's possible, Doctor,' he concluded with mock formality, making Clare pull a face at him. She had won a telling point the previous week using the selfsame words.

'I still have a funny feeling she may have something, George.'

'Look,' he threatened. 'If you're going to claim woman's intuition . . .'

'I shan't,' Clare laughed. 'We've both agreed there's no such thing.'

Mrs Aspern watched them rise and go through into the club lounge.

Clare drove to the surgery straight from the golf club though she was off duty call until midnight. Anderson, only one year her partner in the practice, looked up with surprise from the notes he was completing.

'Hello, Clare,' he said, taking in her appearance. 'I thought it was boutique and a hairdo on Saturdays.'

Clare quickly crossed the surgery to shut the door which communicated with Nurse Hargreaves' domain. The younger doctor's casually modern manner still rankled with her, though they had had this out several times and he remained as amused as ever at her propriety.

'Gordon Summerston's one of ours, isn't he, Derek?' she asked, moving behind him to the record files.

'From Dragonswell? Yes; did an insurance medical on him last month. Fit as a flea.'

'Dead,' Clare said. 'Accident.'

Anderson stopped writing and grimaced round at her. 'Hell fire. Third this month. It's a bloody epidemic.' He saw Clare hesitate before speaking. 'What's up?'

She flipped through the envelopes and found Gordon Summerston's. 'I don't know. Something really rather odd. Nothing important in his records, though.'

'Road accidents aren't mysterious, Clare. They're just an utterly stupid waste of people.'

'I suppose you're right, Derek.' She dropped the envelope on Anderson's desk and opened the side door to let herself out. 'Have fun.'

'You know,' her younger colleague said, eyeing her legs and grinning, 'for a geriatric bird you're not at all bad. If you play your cards right you could have me.'

'Get on with you.'

Nurse Hargreaves overheard as the door went and lifted her head, interested, wondering about Dr Baxter and Derek Anderson. You could never tell with some women, she told herself, especially ones like Clare Baxter. Except sometimes.

Inspector Young sat at his desk leafing through sales catalogues. Sergeant Brent had got them for him from Constable Mac-Andrews, the station's one avid collector. It had been interesting just to see MacAndrews, normally rather taciturn, come alive when asked about his hobby. Rather than look down on his inspector's transparent ignorance about numismatics, the lad obviously had been delighted to explain the inner politics of local collecting circles. Collectors of hammered coinage evidently were the P. and O. line among numismatologists, it seemed. Summerston and Ash were even more specialised than this, having focussed in a modest sort of way on royal coinage of the pre-Conquest period. And MacAndrews had even been moved to wax lyrical when enlarging on the greatest yet the most obscure of the ancient kings. George Young had never heard of him, but to hear the young constable talk there should have been no such era as the Dark Ages. That whole period was apparently illuminated by the blinding brilliance of the mighty but mysterious Offa Rex.

Afterwards Young had thanked MacAndrews and sent him back to his point duty. He flipped the catalogues over curiously, looking at the photograph of the old coins. 'Bloody lunatics,' he muttered. 'An old penny's an old penny, no matter how rare.' He stared at the pictures so long he began to imagine things. 'Bloody lunatics,' he said again, and shoved them aside. He would have to see Ash. He'd put it off long enough.

Ash watched the inspector's car leave, and turned back towards the house conscious now of the immensity of his success. He'd done it, achieved the impossible. Murder that even the Law agreed was an accident.

Janey was too impoverished to keep Gordon's collection. The Offa would be sold with the rest of it at auction, seeing she knew nothing about numismatics herself. And guess who would be at the auction? He chuckled. Probably within the month the Offa silver would be his, in his hand. Unique and glowing, with its frontal portrait and those pellet eyes staring from the surface. Clever of her to spot the way he had killed Gordon, though. The interesting thought came that only a woman who knew a man really well could have sensed the truth like Janey had done. But *how* well did she know him? Maybe she too had felt that flicker of desire. Maybe she sometimes found herself thinking of the aggressive Councillor Ash instead of her drippy husband. He found it an erotic idea. Janey *and* the Offa Rex? Maybe.

Funny to think that soon he would be able to look into the eyes of Offa, the greatest hero king between Alexander and the Conqueror. Unless, he thought wrily, this bloody welfare state increases the widow subsidy. He chuckled inwardly at the idea. Maybe he should propose that to the Council. He was still smiling an hour later over a brandy.

Early the following day Janey Summerston faced Mr Watkins in his office. The shoddiness of the place contrasted sharply with the sleek auction premises next door, but this was as the elderly auctioneer liked it. What is traditional is best, his favourite saying. The old man was less embarrassed by Janey's tragedy than her obvious courage.

'Are you sure you wouldn't rather take Gordon's things somewhere else, Janey?'

'No, Mr Watkins.'

'I mean, because I am an old friend of your father's I can't guarantee a higher percentage. There are rules about auctions. You know that?'

'I understand.'

'Very well. Think about it a few days and – '

'No.' Her surprising firmness took him aback. 'Before the end of the month, please.'

Janey Summerston herself had met widows sentimentally clinging to outmoded belongings, unsuitable houses and even whole life styles in obedience to some inner compulsion they assumed was loyalty. To her they always seemed pathetic. It was something she would not do. She explained this attitude while her father's erstwhile bowling companion listened gravely.

'And are you going to include that Offa piece Gordon bought here some years ago?'

'That too.'

'It may cause quite a stir among local collectors.'

'So I believe.'

'You have quite decided not to sell it privately?' Mr Watkins fiddled with his spectacles to give her an opportunity of replying before launching his rather Edwardian sales talk. 'I am certain that an auction is the proper place, and will produce at least the yield which any private sale would.'

'Thank you, Mr Watkins.' Janey Summerston rose to go, pausing a moment to add, 'I am sure you will achieve the best result, only . . .'

'Yes?'

'Can . . . can I lay down conditions?'

'Why, yes, within limits. A reserve price, that sort of thing?'

'Nothing like that. But . . . I would like the best piece from Gordon's collection to be quite safe.'

'I assure you, Janey, that –'

'Please.' She drew breath and confronted him with that almost belligerent decisiveness. 'I want one piece to stay enclosed, in a separate container until the buyer takes possession.'

'We must allow proper inspection, Janey.'

Janey was shaking her head. 'That will be all right. Two sides of its case will be glass. Free inspection will be quite in order, but it must not be removed at any time.'

'Very well.' Mr Watkins made a note. 'Er, which piece is it, my dear?'

Something flashed in Janey's eyes as she spoke. Even before the words fell the old man knew the answer.

'The Offa Rex,' she said.

A few moments later he watched the door close behind Janey. He felt uneasy, conscious that something was wrong. Not a mere clerical error which could be traced and accounted for, but a gross violation in his way of life. Something irrevocable.

In the town library Gillanders was being distrait. 'Nobody borrowed that book in a twelvemonth,' he was complaining to his deputy in the library office. 'Then we have four simultaneous demands for the wretched thing. It's just too much. Has there been some exhibition we haven't heard about?'

'We must ask for an extra copy, sir.' Miss Mortimer loved any excuse to increase the library's stock.

'We certainly must not,' Gillanders snapped at her. She didn't have to face the town's sour finance committee. 'We'll no sooner get ourselves fitted out with extra copies of J. J. North and of Dolley and nobody will want them. It happened before. Remember that stupid flute-maker's biography? A sheer waste of money. Anglo-Saxon coins indeed.'

Miss Mortimer knuckled under. 'Yes, Mr Gillanders.' She knew a tantrum when she saw one.

The auction sale went off with surprising simplicity. Mac-Andrews was excited at the idea of being seconded from point duty to attend in plain clothes. Inspector Young thought it dull as ditchwater. The previous week he had spent some time with Mr Watkins, who had gone over the auction procedure for his benefit. A careful record would be kept of all buyers. Surely nothing could go wrong.

The Offa looked so ordinary to George Young. It was in a grey metal box, heavy as lead, with glass top and bottom. Even the glass was heavy, so thick and dark he only saw through to the piece with difficulty.

'Lovely, isn't it?' some enthusiast said as the auctioneer droned away on the rostrum.

'Er, aye,' the inspector said doubtfully. A strip light showed the contents of the box. One coin, goldish in appearance, somehow set suspended in a sheet of grey metal. That must be the Offa Rex, though MacAndrews had said it was silver, not gold. The metal container was like a small safe. 'Can we open it and look, please?' he asked an attendant.

'No, sir. Instructions,' the man said.

So Janey Summerston's demands were being met. Young glanced round the throng and saw Charles Ash seated in the third row. Item two hundred and nine. At the rate the auctioneer was going it would be well into the afternoon before the Offa coin was sold. As he turned to go he noticed the metal sides of the container were engraved. He bent and read, 'The Property of Gordon Summerston, deceased twelfth of December.' The same legend was inscribed on all four of the metal sides and, he observed with puzzlement, even on the glass surfaces. Odd. The engraving looked new. Maybe the case had been made specifically for this auction?

At the door he bumped into Janey Summerston. He said hello but she avoided his gaze and determinedly swept past. Come to see how high a price her husband's precious Offa fetched, no doubt. As he stepped outside on to the pavement he gave a barely imperceptible nod in MacAndrews' direction but the bloody man was listening rapturously to the bids. He told himself it was stupid to worry. The annoying part was this irritating feeling of having arrived at a football match where nobody would tell you the score.

Ash drove home faster than usual and was in his study almost before the engine had silenced. He lifted the heavy box out on to a piece of felt as soon as he could tear off his coat. He opened the windows, though he knew his wife would play hell about draughts. Cigar smoke was death to a coin's patina. That and the acids which oak gave off into the atmosphere, hence the preponderance of mahogany and teak in his study.

Lamp, magnifying glass, a glass of brandy and he practically fell on the heavy box. He had waited years.

'Not yet,' he shouted when his wife called for him to come down for supper.

It had been a cinch. Old Watkins had looked disappointed at the low price. Maybe he'd expected a Christie's level. The thought made Ash laugh aloud. If Janey hadn't been so foolish as to try the cheap trick of washing a gilt paint over the Offa

Rex the price might have soared. As it was, her pathetically obvious device of gilding had brought the price down to within easy reach of his pocket. At least two London dealers had shone their beam quartzes at the Offa through the thick glass and then drifted across to the pub in disgust and not returned. Gordon should have taught her better, Ash thought contentedly. No numismatist wants a precious surface tinkered with. Still, it would only take a few minutes and the right chemical solvents to get that muck off – and then he could gaze serenely at the tiny eyes on the coin portrait of the great Offa Rex. Eye to eye. It would need care, though, and the daylight of morning which was so essential for proper numismatic work.

He looked for a moment at Gordon's engraved name on the case. Quite well made and solid lead, but Ash wasn't having somebody else's name labelling *his* prize item at any price. No sir. The box had to go. His own cabinet would display the Offa to the fullest possible advantage. And a small side lamp, perhaps opposite his desk . . .

It took a moment's work with a screwdriver to unscrew the interlocked edges of the box's sides. Ash smiled triumphantly as he finally lifted out the middle section holding the Offa piece and placed it gently down on the felt.

He brushed the surface using a small painter's brush. Typical of women, always wanting to gild the gingerbread. If she'd left it untouched it possibly would have gone for a fortune. He turned the Offa over and bent closer, enthralled. He stared at the portrait so long his eyes began to prickle.

He looked up eventually after what seemed only mere minutes, and was surprised to notice it had started snowing ouside. Strange, he thought, there had been no such forecast. Then he blinked to clear his eyes and saw the late afternoon skies were only dulled and grey. Not snowing after all. He smiled. It must be the strain of peering at his new acquisition for too long, that and the excitement. After all, you could count the owners of an Offa Rex on one hand these days.

Upstairs that night the organism was sleeping beside its mate. Its component cells were synchronized, bathed in homeostatically controlled fluids. Its organs were subordinated to autonomic feedbacks beyond the main organism's conscious awareness as its vagal impulses rhythmically modulated the respiration. Yet it slept disturbed. Epithelial cells were starting to replicate out of time along the margins of the organism's eyelids. The exquisitely beautiful polarised membranes hugging each nucleus were now punctured and leaking, the semi-permeability which protected and sustained the delicate internal genome's *milieu* already starting to bleed translucent fluids inwards to stifle the shimmering opalescent chains of cistrons. Deeper still in the organism's eye the vital ganglion cells were dying. The retinal structure appeared intact, but the ganglion cells themselves had been deformed some hours. Tomorrow the retinal rods would still be aligned, but the cones would begin to show the gross deformities revealing their spreading metabolic doom.

Councillor Ash groaned in his sleep, once.

Downstairs in the darkness of the study the Offa Rex was concealed under a layer of green felt, a covering which failed to impede the steady emission radiating from the coin's surface. The lifeless silver moulding the face of the great king beat with silent vigour. The open pellet eyes, pressed directly against the felt covering, stared blindly upwards as if to follow the unseen rays streaming out through the cloth and piercing the very substance of the elegant cabinet's solid wood beating outwards and filling the air of the silent room.

Three days later a freezing fog came over the sea marshes. The dark hawthorns and the thin sloe hedges showed no whitening frost. Instead the chill remained hanging in the air, coating paths and trees and surfaces with an ominously transparent coating of ice. On the main coast roads the streams of night traffic dwindled to a trickle, and finally ended. By the sixth day every one of the low Hundreds was overlaid with black ice and the small fishing fleets were back, closely staithed in the silent estuaries. The town quietened. The villages recovered their lost medieval pace. Wise travellers chained their tyres and hoped for snow or thaw. Wiser people stayed at home.

On that sixth day Janey Summerston phoned Charles Ash.

'Charles? Janey Summerston.'

Ash tried to perk up on hearing her voice, though he'd been terrible just lately. The wife was in bed though it was only nine. No reason to stay up on such a lousy night, and she had telly up there. She had been useless lately anyway; always was, when he felt unwell.

'That you, Janey? How good to hear you.' He modulated his voice, politically trained to instant solicitude. It had gone hoarse at the weekend, probably part of this illness. Maybe a bug going round. 'I haven't really had a chance to express my sincere condolences about poor Gordon.'

She cut in quite briskly. 'Never mind that, Charles. How are you?'

'Quite well,' he said, puzzled.

'Are you sure?' Janey's voice paused then went on, 'No sickness, Charles? No loss of appetite? Eyes as good as ever?' He could almost hear her smile. She surely hadn't rung just to ask after his wellbeing . . . had she? 'Your voice is hoarser than it was at the auction, Charles.'

Ash felt the blood drain from his face, the vessels prickling and tightening. 'How did you know I've been off colour?' He doubled at a sudden gripe.

She went on, her voice cooing, 'Tired these days, Charles? Listless?'

'What's the meaning of this, Janey?' He needed to suck moisture into his tongue to get the words out. 'How – ?'

'Listen carefully, Charles. You'd better sit down while I explain, seeing you are so ill. It might prove a shock.' She surely had no way of knowing anything about his illness, not having seen him since the auction. 'For the past six days, Charles,' she coursed on, 'your eyesight has deteriorated quite drastically. You can no longer see to read. There are sores round your eyelids and mouth.'

It was true. He had seen Smithson at the clinic only the previous day. The best eye man in the county, Smithson had made a number of tests. He had obviously been puzzled.

'You are too tired to bother with anything.' Janey might have been reading from a list. 'Ulcers on your face, Charles.

You've developed a cough. I'll bet your wife has said how pale you've gone. Soon you will vomit after every meal.'

Ash, thinking fast, said nothing.

'I do hope you are paying attention, Charles, because this is really rather important. Your blood cells have begun to decrease, Charles. Your count will fall and fall – '

He began shaking. His arm quivered uncontrollably. He held the receiver away to silence the woman's brisk professional voice. Twice he brought a handkerchief to his mouth to stifle a sudden retching. The bitch had done something, got at him somehow.

'How do you know this? What have you done to me?' He knew she would still be there, listening and waiting.

'A little preliminary explanation, Charles,' Janey reprimanded. 'You ought to know that there are some sixteen thousand effective and available poisons – '

'Poison?' And he knew. 'In the gilding on the – '

The crisp detached voice called him back. 'Please don't interrupt. I was about to say that if you call the police I shall deny any allegations you make. And calling a doctor will not help you. I've been careful enough to select a combination of poisons that produce a very complex symptomatology, as you now know.' So she knew he had been to the clinic. Of course, she worked at the hospital. 'By the time they work out the antidotes it will be impossibly late.'

'Janey,' Ash said brokenly. 'I swear to God I had nothing to do with Gordon's accident. Please. That inspector came by and told me what you'd said – '

'There's not really time for blustering, Charles,' Janey cooed. 'You've begun to *die*, Charles. Don't you understand?'

She was insane. There could be no other explanation. 'I'll give you anything, Janey. Honest to God. If it's money – '

'To tell you the antidote?' Janey's laughing tapped against his eardrum. 'I've got it here, waiting.'

'Waiting?'

'Don't be so mistrustful, Charles. I know your motive in getting rid of Gordon. It was me, wasn't it, dear?'

Her? Ash was sweating heavily. He rubbed his free hand along his thigh in an attempt to dry the palm. Of course he fancied her, always had, but *kill* for the lunatic? Yet he had to agree with whatever the mad bitch said. Once he'd got the antidote he'd streak over to Dr Baxter and get her to inject it . . .

'You guessed,' he managed to get out, somewhat too carefully.

'And now I'm making sure, Charles. Of you.'

Ash hesitated. 'What do you want me to do?' Instinctively he was more guarded on the instant. Begging had been new to him, but bargaining was something he understood. The main thing was to get that antidote.

'Charles? Come here. Now.'

'In this fog? There's fog, black ice.' She made no answer, the bitch, knowing he had to obey. 'I'll come, Janey. I can hire a car.'

'No. You come alone, Charles.'

She was asking the impossible. 'But my eyes. For Christ's sake. And it's atrocious on the roads.'

'Very well,' she said sweetly. 'Let's leave it a few days, shall we?'

'No! No! I'll . . . I'll come, of course.' He cleared his throat. 'Darling.'

'I'll be waiting,' she replied. 'Darling.'

Click. Brrr. Ash replaced his receiver, still shaky but conscious there was a way out. The bitch. Sussing him out like that. And putting the poison in the gilt, washing it over the Offa Rex, guessing he would be unable to resist examining it. Some stuff that needed only a trace to produce its effects. No wonder the eye consultant had been puzzled. He must get over there. Fast. And everything would be all fine again soon. She *had* felt the pull between them both. He rose to get his car keys and his coat, almost grinning with relief though he felt rotten. That old fatal Ash charm. Women like a man who's aggressive, bit of a show-off. If she would go to these lengths to get him, maybe more than a little care was called for. She would need careful handling, careful yet firm. The old sex game, at which he'd always been permanent winner.

His car started first time. Beautiful smooth movement. He moved at a crawl out on to the drive, never hearing his wife's voice calling. The ice-filled fog was everywhere. Its density froze the car lights a few feet ahead. He had to sit perched forwards on the edge of the seat to peer with his fading eyes. The bloody specialist had wanted to admit him to hospital immediately, as if anyone with a councillor's responsibilities can drop everything just like that. Ash suddenly remembered his eyedrops but they'd be useless now after what Janey had told him. He decided to press on with his ulcerated and blood-shot eyes straining into the fog. It had to be the antidote.

Luckily there were few cars out, and he managed a steady crawl. But by the time he reached the Dragonswell turn-off he was driving about five miles an hour, with the side windows wound down so as to see the blur of the grass verge. The largest of the ulcers along his upper lids were bleeding now from the cold. Every few yards he was having to stop to dab inexpertly at the blood and pus. He had used three handkerchiefs. Twice he stopped and tried squeezing his eyes tight shut for a moment, hoping the vision would improve. It was definitely fading. His inner rage surfaced momentarily and even overcame his fear, making him groan aloud. As soon as he'd got that antidote he'd see she suffered for giving him this fright, by God he would. Play her along, then put the boot in. That's all some women could understand, the sadistic cow. If she'd wanted him, for Christ's sake, why hadn't she just phoned and said so when Gordon was out? She had more than sex coming to her. He'd see to that. By God . . .

He approached the humpbacked bridge gingerly. The thought had crossed his mind that this was all a ruse, a come-on, to get him out here in these appalling conditions. But if so, she was foiled. He was hardly going fast enough to skid down-hill, let alone on a comparatively level road. And his tyres would stay chained until April. Still, it was with relief he saw his head beams regain the road, dipping from the hump to follow the few feet of the hedgerow remaining visible. The next danger would be the end of this straight bit where the road doglegged from the river parapet. It would be more dan-gerous than usual because the bloody council roadmen had stayed at home on account of the weather. And there was no parapet. Gordon had demolished it. Thankfully, Ash saw four orange roadlights blipping ahead indicating where the road bent. At least the road-safety man had earned his pence. Ash leant further from his car and, craning to see, accelerated slightly but thankfully towards the orange lights.

On the far side of the river Janey watched his shrouded lights approach. In silhouette she could just make out the gap in the parapet. Beside her on the bank the four lights blinked their warning, popping faintly with every flash. They even looked quite pretty spaced out like that. She stood quite proudly among them, in line on the wrong side of the river.

Ash only realised when his car tilted, hesitated, then slid elegantly forward into the river ice with a loud crack. Its onward motion caused it to slip quite a distance from the bank and away from the hole it had made on entry. His head, projecting from the side window, was jerked forward with a snap and flipped against the door margin. The last thing he knew was the gruesome, sordid nature of the act of dying. Janey was unable to see most of the events. And, regretfully, she could not stay to listen to the bubbling and sucking beneath the ice where the car lights were fading deep in the water. She had a job to do. She took four cloth covers from a shoulder-bag and hooded each warning light into darkness. Being on trestles they weighed heavily so she could only carry two at a time. And she had to go all the way round, along this bank to the humpback bridge, and then walk all the way along the road to replace the warning lights by the gap in the parapet.

Thirty minutes later Janey somewhat breathlessly unhooded the last of the trestled lights spaced out along the road, in place again to warn drivers about the parapet. Just as they should be, she thought, pleased. Of course, it would have been easier to carry them across on the ice, but she'd decided against that. She hadn't wanted to risk an accident.

Inspector Young knew the county pathologist vaguely from his attendances at coroners' courts. Henderson was one of those slender, rather creaky, bespectacled men who must have looked elderly even as a gangly lad. His twinkly yet detached manner always impressed and conveyed confidence. Only once had the inspector seen him flustered, and that had been over a minute typographical error most men would hardly have noticed. He seated himself in the chair Dr Henderson indicated, trying to avoid looking at the specimens on the low bookcase behind the pathologist.

'Ash, I presume?' Henderson's reedy voice matched his frame.

Young nodded, wondering if his own personality was as entire as Henderson's appeared to be. 'Question of foul play,' he said.

'You surprise me.' Henderson turned the pages of the file. 'Typical road-accident injuries. Death due to multiple injuries. Even if he had survived the trauma he would probably have drowned. Shock, that temperature, bewildered under the ice, concussed. As it was his broken neck did the job a fraction speedier, that's all.'

'I viewed the deceased,' the inspector said. 'What was all that round his eyes?'

'Odd ulceration. He'd been to the ophthalmology clinic recently. Our surgeon was unsure. Extensive ulceration, possibly chemical or toxic. And his vision.'

'Could he not see properly?'

'No. The eye surgeon found massive retinal scarring, atrophy – '

'He was going blind.' It was intended as a question but emerged as a flat statement.

'Yes. Dr Smithson wanted to admit him.'

'Why?'

'Well.' Henderson paused to consider the confidentiality issue before conceding. 'I spoke to Smithson after the post mortem. He too had seen nothing like it, except once. And that was a case of irradiation burns from dangerous emitters. Some military job.'

The inspector thought hard. Lead boxes are used for carrying radioactive stuff. That heavy lead box, its dark glass top – dark because lead-containing glass is basically darker than the modern colourless kind?

A faint nausea came which he recognised as fear. He, like

others, had bent to squint at the Offa Rex for a moment. Maybe some irradiation had got at him too.

'Are you all right, Inspector?' the pathologist was asking.

'Just suppose, Doctor,' he said slowly, 'I wanted to display something, a coin, say, covered in an irradiation chemical, yet wanted to avoid injuring people. How could I do it?'

'Depends. A lead box, with a thick window of lead glass,' Henderson said. 'And stopping people getting near. The inverse square law operates.' He drummed his fingers on the notes. 'Of course, for this degree of eye damage you'd need to be pretty close.'

'What quantity would be needed? The amount you could get on to, say, a penny?'

'Easily.'

Inspector Young drew breath. 'Can you examine a house for traces of a radioactive chemical?'

Henderson smiled thinly. 'Again, just supposing, Inspector?'

The C.I.D. man thought over the sombre joke for a moment. 'No,' he said. 'Real.'

'What's it all about, or am I not to ask?'

The C.I.D. man did not reply immediately. There was a faint risk that Janey Summerston was friendly with one of Henderson's own people, maybe from some shared training course at a technical college. A small chance, but why take it? 'A private worry,' he said at last. 'Nothing much.'

'Loose ends?'

They agreed that Dr Henderson would arrange for the dead man's car to be monitored for radiation with a minimum of fuss. Samples would be taken from the house drains, the contents of Ash's study and the garden examined for the presence of radioactive isotopes and reports sent direct.

'We want this done absolutely confidentially, please,' Inspector Young said.

'If you wish,' Dr Henderson assured him, eyeing him quizzically.

'Are the tests for radiation really, er, good, efficient?'

Dr Henderson smiled thinly. 'If there's a trace we'll find it.'

On the way out of the building he stopped at the porter's desk to ask if he knew a technician called Janey Summerston.

'Not here, guv,' the grey-haired man said. 'Probably over at the hospital. They have hundreds. Overpaid and underworked.'

Inspector Young left, satisfied there was now no chance that Janey might hear of Henderson's forthcoming investigations for radioactivity at Ash's home. No harm making sure. For the first time he felt one move ahead of Janey.

They met at the golf club the following Saturday under Mrs Aspern's disapproving gaze. Neither Clare nor George made any pretence that they were lunching to chat over the weather.

'I've put two and two together, George,' Clare announced as soon as they had ordered.

'And made five?'

'Stop it.' She watched the wine being poured, knowing the instant he spoke that he was more than a little depressed. 'We may be only a rural village practice, but we do get the news-papers. And there's gossip.'

'Shall I start?'

Clare was in no doubt. 'No. Me. See how close I get to the truth.' She fortified herself with a sip of wine and waved absently to friends who tried to beckon her over. 'Mrs Summerston somehow persuaded Ash to drive to Dragonswell that evening. Maybe she phoned him. Despite the terrible deterior-ation in his sight he drove that way and suffered the same consequences Gordon Summerston had. Right?'

'In a way, Clare.'

She looked at him blankly. 'Well? What do you think?'

'All right so far. Go on.'

'That's as far as I've got,' she said, pleased.

George recounted the tale of the Offa Rex piece and the auction.

'It only occurred to me too late,' he admitted. 'I think Janey put some chemical on the Offa Rex, some gold-coloured cor-rosive which would blind anyone coming too close. It certainly was in a hell of a box.'

'Which nobody was allowed to open except the purchaser?'

'Correct.'

'There's a way of finding out, George,' Clare observed. 'You'll have to get your forensic experts to search the box and Janey's home for whatever chemical – ' She halted as George shook his head. 'What's wrong with that?'

'It won't work, Clare. In fact it didn't.'

'You must ask Henderson, the county pathologist. He's a good man.'

'We did. The traces have all gone. Janey knew that Ash would buy the Offa Rex. No traces at the Ash house, in the car, Ash's office, his study. Everything negative, clean as a whistle. The Offa piece as well. Every bloody place and thing we could think of.'

Clare was intrigued. 'If you suspected all this, George, you should have at least *some* evidence to catch her.'

'The pathologist was very helpful,' George continued miserably. 'We talked it over. He got the very best technologist to do all those things. In absolute confidence. Sampled everything.'

'And he found not even a trace – ?'

'*She* found sod all,' George was unable to resist the vulgarity. 'Nothing.'

'Radiation.' Light dawned and Clare grasped George's arm vehemently. 'It really must have been radiation, George! That's it! She put – '

'Shhh. Keep your voice down.'

Clare sank her voice to an excited whisper. 'Janey put some radioactive isotope, perhaps cobalt, into a gilt wash. Safely shielded, so only Ash himself got the full effects on opening the case.' She shuddered. 'How really horrid. It's well, almost snakelike. If we're right.'

'Oh, we're right. She'd learned enough about coin collectors to know that a gilt wash would bring the price down to something Ash could afford, and that only the actual purchaser would have the right to handle it afterwards.' And stare affectionately, he thought with his spine tingling, into those sinister little pellet eyes of Offa Rex, eyes which would beam an unseen but lethal irradiation into the retinas of the observer. As inevitable as night following day. He shivered at the unpleasant analogy.

'I don't understand. You can easily detect radioactive iso-topes, George,' Clare breathed. 'The hospital has a good radio-active isotope laboratory, best in the eastern counties. Why not use it?'

'I know.' George watched her carefully. 'It's the one Hender-son calls in when he needs help of this kind. He hasn't a radiation lab of his own. The only point I forgot to check.'

'Then let's phone the radiation lab now,' Clare suggested, still eager.

'No. Because Janey Summerston would answer.' George did not look at her as he said this. 'That's why, love.' He felt her aghast silence for a moment before continuing. 'She's the head technician in the radio-isotope section at the hospital. Natur-ally, Henderson got them to do the job – in strictest confidence, of course. I was being so bloody cautious I didn't even tell Henderson all my suspicions, in case Janey somehow got word.'

'And *she* was the technician sent out to examine – ?'

'I believed I'd thought of everything.'

' – Giving her the opportunity to clean up every single trace of radiation,' Clare cried softly.

'Bloody marvellous,' George said bitterly, 'letting ourselves fall for it. Practically arranging for a murderer to examine in private every possible clue.'

'Crime?' Clare asked. 'Are we sure it was a crime?'

'Well, wasn't it?' George asked, honestly seeking an opinion now.

'Maybe not,' Clare offered. 'After all, we're only guessing.' They both recognised her kindness but George persisted.

'But maybe? You still admit it might be?'

Clare hesitated. 'I don't know. There's no way of knowing any more, is there?'

George bit back his irritation. Sometimes Clare made him furious. She seemed to have an innate skill at escaping the point.

'A crime's a crime, Clare. Ash may subconsciously have guessed how Janey was blinding him. He wasn't humbly accept-ing his punishment. A man doesn't do that. He was driving to Janey to ask her to undo the damage she'd inflicted on him. Maybe he had bribery in mind, perhaps even a confession.'

'Did you call on Janey Summerston?' Clare could not avoid asking.

'Of course we did. She claimed ignorance of the whole thing.'

They sat in silence for a minute.

'*Would* she have helped him, Clare?' George asked eventually.

Clare shrugged. 'Who knows? A woman can be very touched when faced with the harm she's done.'

'Or she can put the boot in,' George countered. 'Worse than any man.'

'Women don't do that sort of thing,' Clare said primly. 'Anyhow, George,' she finished, 'maybe he just lost the road in the fog.'

'Maybe,' George said.

'Like Summerston.'

The remark came almost under her breath.

As the soup arrived George looked carefully at her expression, wondering if a woman really could be so vengeful as he guessed Janey Summerston had been. Clare was half-smiling, the way she sometimes did when making a joke, but in the moderate light of the club restaurant he couldn't quite tell.

Anthony Lejeune

SOMETHING ON EVERYONE

John Deakin's voice, normally a controlled and confident instrument for speech-making, trembled on the verge of a stammer. 'As I told you on the telephone,' he said, 'I'm in rather a jam.'

'All right,' said Lord Frane, 'let's have the story.' It was lucky, he thought, that the Great British Public – the voting public – couldn't see Deakin now. The man was shaken and scared in a way that Frane had seen several times before in his long political experience; the way of hitherto unblemished success which suddenly hits trouble; the way of a much-praised rising politician before whose feet a gulf has opened which threatens to swallow up everything he has achieved and hoped to achieve.

Deakin's fears, whatever they were, might be exaggerated. People generally did manage to get out of their troubles somehow, particularly if they had sophisticated and powerful friends. But, of course, not always. Frane could remember one or two sad cases . . . He didn't really like John Deakin very much, but the Party had great hopes of him. He looked good on television – which is what mattered nowadays. If he came unstuck, it would be not only a personal tragedy but damaging : and Frane's job was to see that the Party didn't get damaged.

The other two people in his drawing-room were very old friends : George Liddle and Sir Peter Farmiloe, sound Party men both, who knew the world and knew Westminster. Frane had asked Deakin if he minded their being present; their advice might be useful, he'd said.

Deakin swallowed a little more whisky. 'I got this letter a month ago,' he said. 'It was from a man I once knew, called Derek Shee. You might have come across him. He was interested

122

in politics. I think he was on the Candidates' List for a while. Anyway, this letter referred to something which once happened to me, and said that, if I wanted to talk about it, I was to put an advertisement in the personal column of *The Times*, consisting of just one word – 1968, the year 1968, which is when the thing happened.

'So I did that. I put the advertisement in. And late on the afternoon, when it appeared, Shee telephoned me at my office in the City. He wanted me to meet him at a pub that evening. I went there. And he asked me for money – to keep quiet, though I'm not sure he ever put it so crudely. But the implication was that, if I didn't pay, he would sell the story to a newspaper. He didn't ask for a great deal, only the equivalent, he said, of what a newspaper might pay him. Five hundred pounds. I agreed. I got the money out of the bank next morning, and delivered it to him at another pub.

'It's odd. I knew as well as anyone else that when you pay off a blackmailer you don't get rid of him. He's likely to come back for more. I've heard that, and read it, a dozen times. And yet I believed, or I convinced myself, that I was getting rid of him. He telephoned again this morning, wanting another five hundred. When I hesitated, he began putting on the pressure, hinting at what would happen to my career if the facts became known. Only hinting. He was obviously being careful not to say anything too explicit on the telephone. He told me to be at the same pub tomorrow evening at six-thirty. I said I'd think about it, and hung up.'

Deakin paused, and looked at the others for their reaction.

'Did you consider going to the police?' asked Frane.

'Of course I did. But I can't.'

'Because you don't want to tell them – whatever it is that Shee knows?'

'Partly that. And partly because it wouldn't be safe, would it? That's one of the things I wanted to ask your advice about. I mean, if there was a prosecution, I might appear as "Mr X", but surely the chances are it would leak? There would be gossip in the Temple or in Fleet Street, and then in the City and at Westminster. And I'd be done. Isn't that likely?'

Frane nodded. 'I must admit it is. At least, there would be a

123

danger. And this is something you absolutely can't risk?'

Deakin took another drink of whisky. The only sound in the room was the soft ticking of a handsome clock on the chimney-piece and a faint murmur of traffic, deadened by good double glazing and heavy velvet curtains. At last Deakin said : 'I think I'd better tell you.' He glanced at Farmiloe and Liddle. 'I know I can trust all of you to keep quiet about it.'

From his inside pocket he produced an envelope. 'First,' he said, 'here's the original letter.'

The address on the envelope and the letter inside were type-written, rather badly. Frane read it in silence, and then handed it to the others.

It said : *Dear Mr Deakin, It's a long time since you heard from me, but I've been hearing about you. As one of your supporters, I've been shocked by what I heard. It's about the poor little girl and the cover-up. At the moment I'm the only one who knows, apart from those who were involved. But if the facts were ever published, it would do great harm to the Cause we both believe in, and it would ruin you. I need reassurance. If you are willing to talk about it, please insert a small ad in* The Times, *just saying '1968'. Meanwhile I don't think you should tell anyone else about this letter. Yours very sincerely, Derek Shee.* There was no address or date.

Having read it, Farmiloe handed the letter back to Deakin. 'Quite clever,' Frane said. 'You couldn't exactly call it a black-mailing letter.'

'While making the intention fairly plain,' added Farmiloe.

Deakin took a deep breath. 'What he's referring to happened in my last year at London University. There was a girl. Not a student, just a girl I met at a party. She became pregnant – and that's when I found out she was only fifteen. Only fifteen! My God, in many ways she was far more sophisticated than me. My father and her father fixed it up between them. My father paid, quite a lot. I lived in a nightmare for several months, in case something went wrong. But nothing did, and the girl kept quiet. I never saw her again, but a few years later I read about her in the papers. She'd killed herself. Sleeping pills and drink.

'I'm not proud of that story, but, looking back, I can't see myself as a villain. If it hadn't been me, it would have been someone else. The father was a drunk. Her mother was dead, and there were no brothers or sisters. That's how we were able to hush it up. Eventually I really had almost forgotten about it. It seems like something which happened to someone else.'

'How did Shee come to learn about it?' asked Liddle.

'From the girl's father, when he was in a maudlin condition one night. He swore Shee to secrecy, and said he was going to tell him a family secret he'd never told anyone before. Well, that's the size of it. What do you think?'

Frane poured whisky. 'It's not good. I've no idea if the police would prosecute after so long. Probably not, and I could make discreet enquiries about that. They might feel they had to if it became very public. But that's not entirely the point, is it? How do you think your Constituency Association would react?'

'Some of them might be sympathetic. But they'd sling me out. And then my job, which is really just a way for the bank to sponsor an M.P., would go too.'

'So at all costs it must not become public. I think I agree; it would be too risky to go to the police. John, I'd like to mull this one over. Could you bear to go home now, and let Peter and George and me talk it out and see what we can come up with?'

Two hours later they hadn't come up with much. Farmiloe had begun by wondering if the matter was actually as serious as Deakin thought. 'It's a long time ago, and he wasn't responsible for the girl's death.'

'If that's all there is to it, I'm inclined to agree with you,' said Liddle. 'But is that all there is to it?'

Frane shook his head. 'I doubt it. You know Deakin's reputation. You've seen the gossip columns. He likes girls, and very young girls too. If once this can of worms is opened, who knows what may crawl out?'

'So you think that's really what's worrying him? Nice man, our promising young colleague.'

'We don't *know* there's anything else,' said Farmiloe.

'There's always something else,' replied Frane. 'He's not

my favourite man, but nor am I inclined to throw first stones. The remarkable thing, surely, isn't when somebody gets found out but that most of us never do. If our lives and careers were extended indefinitely, we should all come a cropper sooner or later.'

'Speak for yourself.'

'Oh I am, I am. But the point is, we've all seen political scandals. Several in the past few years. And once they start to unravel, it's very difficult to stop them – particularly if the press has got wind of the story.'

'In most of the cases you're talking about, the best policy would have been to make a clean breast of it straight away. Trying to cover up was what did the real harm.'

'Making a clean breast of it might have been a very fine gesture,' said Liddle, 'but it usually wouldn't have saved the chap's career.'

'The art of covering up has always seemed to me an essential part of politics,' said Frane. 'The problem is to make the covering up stick. In Deakin's case, how do we persuade Mr Derek Shee to keep quiet permanently?'

'Threaten him with the police? I agree that an actual prosecution would be risky, but perhaps we could scare him.'

'We might scare him off demanding any more money, but that wouldn't prevent him from sending an anonymous letter to some newspaper. Rather the contrary indeed. He'd probably want to get his revenge.'

'Just think what Fearsome Fred would do with it in the *Daily News*,' said Farmiloe.

'I must confess I take that rag purely for Fred Mandeville's column,' said Liddle. 'He can be bloody funny.'

' "Scurrilous" is the old-fashioned word,' Farmiloe retorted.

'Well, a power in the land anyway,' agreed Frane. 'So we must keep his nose out of young Mr Deakin's past if we can. Any suggestions?'

'A private detective,' said Liddle, 'who might get something on Shee?'

'It's a thought, but I'm not very keen on bringing in someone else. We know where that sort of thing can lead, don't we?'

Frane knocked the ash off his cigar, then said slowly : 'I think I might talk to Mr Shee myself.'

'Is that wise?' asked Farmiloe. 'Wouldn't it be exposing the Party, an admission of vulnerability?'

'Oh,' said Frane cheerfully, 'I'll go in disguise.'

And so, in a sense, he did. He arranged to go with Deakin to the rendezvous in the pub. 'Just introduce me as a friend. I can be Mr Robinson.'

'He's not going to say anything in front of a witness,' objected Deakin. 'He'll probably think you're a polceman.'

'If he believes that, he'll believe anything. My grey hairs should convince him I'm not. But let's see what happens. I want to size the fellow up myself.'

He indulged himself in the agreeable notion of disguise to the extent of wearing glasses, which he never normally did except for reading, wrapping a muffler round his neck and pulling an old tweed hat down over his eyes. 'Pretty sinister,' he said to his image in the looking-glass.

The pub was quite sinister too, in an alley off the Strand. Shee had probably chosen it because nobody could be watching the entrance without being seen, and the bar, at that time of the evening, contained only a couple of regulars – the stage doorkeeper from an adjacent theatre and a newspaper-seller who had just finished peddling his wares. Later there would be some theatregoers, fortifying themselves before the curtain went up and restoring themselves in the interval : but not yet.

Arriving at exactly six-thirty, Frane and Deakin bought drinks and took them to a table in the corner. Five minutes later Shee pushed open the door. He froze for a moment when he saw Frane, but then walked over to them grinning. Neatly dressed, podgy, somehow too confident – Frane wondered if it was only knowing that he was a slippery villain which made him look like one.

'This is a friend of mine,' said Deakin, 'George Robinson.'

'I'm honoured,' said Shee. 'Don't I remember your friend from my political days? Not that we ever met. I was much too unimportant. But, of course, I've seen his picture in the papers. "George Robinson" – that's a good one.'

'I've heard about you too, Mr Shee,' replied Frane. 'Let me get you a drink.'

While he did so, Deakin and Shee sat in silence. When Frane had rejoined them, Shee said to Deakin : 'You decided to come then.'

'You asked me to.'

'So I did. Just for a friendly chat – since we have so many interests in common.'

'May I ask what those interests are?' said Frane.

'Oh, the good of the Party. And old times. I'm still very keen on politics, you know. I read the newspapers and I've a lot of friends in Fleet Street. I was thinking only today that I ought to get in touch with my friends in Fleet Street. Perhaps I will. Very soon.'

Deakin had already emptied his glass and was looking at it fiercely. 'For God's sake, man,' he muttered, 'say what you mean.'

'Mean? I don't mean anything in particular. But I had hoped for a quiet talk, just you and me. If you'd like that, per-haps you'd get in touch with me. The same way you did before. Shall we say within the next week? Now, if you gentlemen will excuse me. I'm afraid I can't afford to buy you a drink. I'm a little short of funds – temporarily : but that's a condition I hope to relieve. One way or another. Good night, Mr Deakin. Good night, Lord Frane.'

He grinned at them, and was gone.

'He thinks he's very clever,' said Lord Frane.

'Slimy bastard !'

'Oh yes. But a dangerous slimy bastard. I think we'll have to buy some more time.'

'You mean I'll have to buy some more time.'

'Insert that notice in the paper again. Say, two days from now. Then he'll presumably telephone you to arrange another meeting. Let me know. Meanwhile, I'll put my thinking cap back on, now that I've met him. Give me your glass. We need another drink.'

'Oh, let me,' said Deakin bitterly. 'It is my round.'

Frane was still sitting at his breakfast table, surrounded by newspapers, opened envelopes, coffee cup, marmalade and toast crumbs, when Liddle marched in, three days later.

'Richard,' he said, 'here's a turn-up for the book. I got a letter this morning.'

'Somebody loves you.'

'Somebody doesn't. Here, you'd better read it.'

Frane took the letter, examined the envelope, then the single sheet of paper inside. It was typewritten, rather badly. There was no address.

Dear Mr Lid 'le, it said. You don't know me, but I have followed your political career with admiration for many years. It would be tragic – for you and for the Party – if anything were to damage your reputation now. I've recently learned certain facts which worry me very much, and if they were published I feel sure they would worry other people too. Need I say more than that they concern a house in St John's Wood? If you are willing to discuss this matter with me, please insert a small ad. in The Times, *just saying 'Thanks to St John'. Meanwhile I don't think you should tell anyone else about this letter. Yours very sincerely, A Well-wisher.*

'The style seems familiar,' observed Frane.

'Doesn't it? You know what he's talking about – the house in St John's Wood?'

'I remember there were rumours . . .'

'The point is, they were wrong. The Special Branch were watching that house, for reasons we all know, and they saw my car parked outside. But I was actually visiting a lady next door. I explained that to the Prime Minister at the time. I couldn't deny the rumours publicly without bringing her name into it, so we agreed to make no statement and just let the rumours die down. Which they did. But if any paper trotted that old story out now, I'd slap a writ on them quicker than you could say knife. The lady in question is divorced now, and it doesn't matter anyway. What Mr Shee seems to be doing is relying on out-of-date political gossip. With Deakin it worked. But he's picked the wrong man this time.'

'Two wrong men.' Frane picked up one of the opened letters from beside his plate and tossed it over to Liddle. 'Snap.'

Liddle glanced at it. 'You too?' he said with astonishment.

Frane nodded. 'Mr Shee appears to have launched on a new career. Or perhaps – more probably, come to think of it – Deakin wasn't the first, just the first we've heard of. Now he seems to be trawling, to see what he can catch. But I'm glad to say he's got my little affair slightly wrong too. I was used by those whizz-kids in the City, and the ice was thin. My fault; one shouldn't stray too far outside one's own territory. Anyway, I'm not worried now about what he's hinting at. The ice held, that's what matters.'

'So he hasn't really got anything on you either?'

'Not really. I can see why he might think he had, and I wouldn't be specially pleased to see the story revived in the City pages – or in Fearless Fred's column. But, like you, I wouldn't mind waving a few writs in the air.' He chuckled. 'Come to think of it, I wouldn't mind collecting some tax-free damages. At my time of life I'm quite willing to be libelled if the price is right.'

'It shouldn't come to that,' said Liddle. 'We're not as vulnerable as Deakin, so we should be able to nail Mr Shee. Shall we go to the police?'

'Not yet. We couldn't explain about Shee without telling them about Deakin. And the reasons for not doing that still apply. I'll tell you what – you give me a photostat of that letter, and I'll have a private word with my friend, the Assistant Commissioner. Then we'll see what we'll see.'

Later the same day, Deakin telephoned Frane to say that Shee had called, and that a new meeting had been arranged for the following evening in a different pub. 'He said I'd bloody well better not bring anyone with me this time. And he said – or rather implied – that I had better bring the money.'

'I'm afraid you'll have to pay him again,' said Frane. 'But cheer up. The U.S. Marines may be on the way.'

'It's no joke to me,' said Deakin. 'And I can't say you've been much help so far.' He hung up.

Frane grimaced. No, decidedly he didn't like Deakin. He had made a note of the time and place of the new meeting with Shee. For a minute he was tempted by the notion of disguising himself properly – perhaps even a false beard? – and watching from a distance. Reluctantly he abandoned the idea and buzzed for his secretary. Her name was Carole. She was an inconspicuous sort of girl at first sight, but, Frane thought, distinctly attractive at second or third glance. He wouldn't have employed her otherwise.

The pub this time was in Earls Court. Again Shee arrived a few minutes after Deakin. He looked round suspiciously, making sure Deakin was alone before joining him.

'Left your friend at home?' he said.

'I came alone. That's what you told me to do. I've got some money.'

They both spoke quietly, and the room was noisy. No one could have overheard them. But Shee was wary. His eyes kept running round the room. 'How much?'

'Five hundred pounds.'

'In cash?'

'In ten-pound notes.'

'All right. This is what I want you to do. In a minute I'm going over to the bar to buy a drink. I'll leave this copy of the *Evening Standard* on the seat beside you. Slip the notes inside it and fold them in tightly. After I've come back, wait a minute, then say goodbye naturally and leave. Take the paper with you. There's a litter basket attached to the lamp-post immediately outside the door. Put the paper in that. Then go away.'

'I haven't told the police,' said Deakin. 'There's no one watching.'

'Just do it.'

He's nervous, thought Deakin while Shee was at the bar. I only wish he had more reason to be. He doesn't want anyone to be able to testify that he saw something pass between us.

His hand concealed by the table, Deakin carefully folded the paper so that the notes couldn't slip out. Shee returned. For a couple of minutes they made desultory conversation about the weather.

'All right,' said Shee. 'That's enough.' Obediently Deakin rose, nodded goodbye and went out, taking the paper with him. Shee watched through the window as Deakin deposited the folded paper in the litter-basket. He forced himself to wait another full minute, fearful that some passing tramp might fish the paper out of the basket. He felt reasonably sure, though, that Deakin had been speaking the truth, and that there was no one in the room who seemed in the least likely to be a detective.

Finally he put down his glass, left the pub and retrieved the newspaper, going through a little pantomime as though something in the headline which protruded from the basket had caught his eye. He walked away reading it.

He didn't notice the girl and her young man who came out of the pub almost on his heels. He had, after all, been quite right. They weren't detectives. But they followed him.

It was just about twenty-four hours later when Peter Farmiloe arived at Frane's house in a state of some excitement. 'I've been at the club,' he said. 'Bill Broughton was there and that rather pompous City fellow, Wysard. They were talking to each other in the bar, and I gathered from what they were saying that they'd both received blackmailing letters during the past few days. Almost identical letters. And they sounded to me very like the letter which Shee sent to Deakin.'

'Oh really? Well, if they were talking about it in loud voices, they must have been rather less scared than Deakin was.'

'They were. Wysard had already been to the police. Actually, they were being slightly cagey about just what was in the letters – though I bet you I could guess in Wysard's case – but they both said that whoever wrote the letters seemed to know something about them but got his facts all wrong. You don't seem very surprised. Had you heard about this?'

'I know that George Liddle received a letter like that a couple of days ago. And so did I.'

'My God! The fellow's running amok. Has he got something on everyone?'

'Almost everyone. He's nothing on you, has he?'

'Certainly not.'

At that moment Frane's Filipino butler came in. 'Mr Mandeville here, sir.'

Farmiloe practically shot out of his seat. 'Fred Mandeville? Fearsome Fred? He's on to us. What are you going to say?'

'Calm yourself. I asked Fred Mandeville to come and see me.'

'You asked him? Why?'

'I thought I could put him straight about one or two things. A pre-emptive strike, you might say.'

'He'll bite your fingers off.'

'No, he won't. Journalists very rarely bite the hand that feeds them. Anyway, he's rather a nice boy. He was at school with my son. Do you want to meet him?'

Farmiloe didn't, though he glanced curiously at the soberly suited, bespectacled young man who was waiting in the hall.

Frane and Fred Mandeville were closeted together for nearly an hour. When Mandeville had gone, Frane looked at his watch and thought that, with a bit of luck, his friend the Assistant Commissioner (Crime) should be at home by now. He telephoned him there, and they had a very private conversation. Afterwards he made another telephone call, no less private.

'Carole,' said Lord Frane around teatime the following day, 'I am now going to call on Mr Shee at that address to which you so kindly followed him. I shall take my swordstick.'

He didn't really think Shee was the dangerous type, but the swordstick made Lord Frane feel dangerous, which appealed to his romantic – or melodramatic – soul. A taxi deposited him outside a rather shabby Victorian house in South Kensington, which had been converted into flats. He pressed the buzzer beside the Entryphone.

Shee's voice said : 'Who is it?'

'Lord Frane. I want a word with you.'

'What about? I've nothing to say to you.' Frane was pleased to detect a note of panic.

'I've something to say to you. Let me in, unless you want another visit from the police.'

Silence. Then the door clicked open.

Frane walked up three flights of stairs. The door at the top was open. Shee was waiting there in his shirtsleeves, tie loose, hair unkempt, obviously a shaken man. Frane brushed past him into the sitting-room, then turned on him, standing rock-firm in front of the fireplace as though he owned the house.

Shee started to say something, but Frane cut him short. 'When the police came here this morning they took away a typewriter. Certain letters were typed on that machine.'

'That typewriter wasn't mine. And I never wrote the letters they were talking about. I'd never seen them before.'

'Of course you didn't,' said Frane cheerfully. 'I wrote them. And you might – I say you *might* – be able, eventually, to convince the police that you are innocent. Innocent of writing those letters. But in the process your little transaction with John Deakin is going to emerge, don't you think? And how are you going to explain that away? Are you with me so far?'

Shee tried to speak but proved literally speechless. Frane grasped his swordstick more tightly for a moment. It wasn't necessary, though. Morally and even physically he felt in command, dominating the wretch who now sat down, almost collapsed, on to the sofa.

Frane was enjoying himself. He went on : 'The police came here today at my suggestion. They are presumably now examining the typewriter and the letters. The type-face will match. They will also examine them for fingerprints. They won't find your fingerprints, but I can assure you they won't find mine either. They haven't – yet – seen your letter to Mr Deakin, which of course was written on a different machine. But you can hardly tell them that, can you? There will, therefore, be an element of doubt. Further investigation will be needed. Somebody, I imagine, will come round again tomorrow to interview you. Very nasty, that sort of interview, very embarrassing. Now I might – mind you, I say I might – be able to persuade my friends at Scotland Yard to take the matter no further, if, when the detectives come here tomorrow, they find that you've gone. Really gone. Left the country, without making any further nuisance of yourself. You've got funds – a thousand pounds which Mr Deakin gave you. I'm not asking for that back. You have a passport, I hope? Otherwise it'll have to be Ireland, to begin with. What do you say?'

'I really think we deserve this,' said Lord Frane, easing the cork out of the champagne bottle. He filled three glasses.

'How did you manage to plant the typewriter?' Liddle asked.

'I have useful friends in low places. I met this one long ago in the army. Locks speak to him : or rather he speaks to locks – and they open. It's his *métier*.'

'You mean he burgled Shee's flat?' said Farmiloe.

'I'm afraid so. Are you shocked? I've been wondering – purely as an academic question, you understand – whether I have actually committed any grave crimes. I caused that flat to be broken into – yes : but we didn't take anything, on the contrary we added something – *viz*, one typewriter. I issued a number of letters containing nasty insinuations : but I didn't demand any money. All round, I reckon I'm innocent. Pure as the driven snow.'

'While you were inventing nasty insinuations about me,' said Liddle, 'you might have invented something I could have let leak out publicly to please my constituents. You could have said I was the father of sixteen illegitimate children or something like that. I'd have increased my majority at the next election by thousands.'

'I hope some of your other victims don't find out who wrote those letters,' said Farmiloe, 'or you won't be at all popular.'

Frane chuckled. 'It was great fun. I'm tempted to go on and touch a few more of our friends and colleagues on sensitive spots – just to see them jump. One can do it to almost anybody. Except you, dear Peter. You're the unblackmailable man.'

'Hm. I wish I felt you intended that as a compliment. But what were you doing with Fred Mandeville the other day?'

'I was giving him a friendly tip. I told him that there was this man with a grudge against the Party who had been trying to blackmail several of its senior members. You may hear rumours, I said, about some of the stories he's got hold of. Somebody may even show you one of the letters. But be careful, I said. You'll be walking into a minefield of libel actions. This jolly blackmailer gets all his facts wrong. I suggested that, if Fearless Fred wanted a story, he might do one about The Incompetent Blackmailer.'

'You hid the leaf in the forest,' said Liddle. 'I hope friend Deakin is grateful.'

'I telephoned him. I just told him we'd got Shee off his back. He was moderately grateful. You know,' said Frane, emptying the bottle and starting to remove the wire from another, 'he really won't do. Not the right type at all. I must drop a word in a few ears . . .'

Michael Levey

POLICE FEEL CONFIDENT

'So,' Burgess said with such self-relishing slowness that I longed to kick him – like a jammed clockwork toy – into brisker motion, 'you're keen to see a piece of the action?'

He was miming judicial thoughtfulness as he solemnly rotated in his big fist the second glass of whisky I had paid for. I felt too hot, too close physically to him, impatient even while I coolly twisted my own glass before taking a quick gulp of lager. He rather wanted to see me sweat – metaphorically, anyway. I recognised the technique, though in fact it was he who was sweating in the throes of an incipient cold. Only too vividly could I see the dampness breaking out over his pink, puddingy features as if they were being slowly steamed.

'That's it,' I said cheerfully. 'I'm really keen.'

He let silence build up round my claim, listening perhaps for an echo of its truthfulness – and it was true enough – or just combating the somnolence induced by his state.

'Of course,' I added carefully, 'it's really up to Superintendent Cosgrove, I know. But I'm keen to be involved. If I can be useful . . . and I'm someone on the spot.'

'We're all on the spot now,' Burgess replied morosely, looking round as if constricted by the snugness of the miniature, cabin-like room. The first paper chains of Christmas hung already from the copper ship's lantern in the ceiling, and there were blobs of cotton-wool snow on threads at the porthole window-panes, vibrating in their own blizzard on the rare occasions the outer door opened. The pub was never very full in the evenings – one reason why I had brought Burgess to it. It was one of the few I could bear in the so-called village, though it must have been quite unlike Burgess's South London local.

'Not been here long yourself, have you?' he asked. 'Takes time to know a community, even a small one like this lot. Shouldn't think there is much to know, is there? Still – '

He paused and stiffened, patently seized on the brink of a sneeze, and began laboriously unfolding a large white handkerchief with a sky-blue border. Tensely, I waited to see if it would be ready in time, but somehow the process had had its own calming effect. Only by a blinking of Burgess's round pale eyes – almost the match, I noticed, of his handkerchief's border – was the passing strain apparent.

'Still,' he repeated, subsiding now into a relaxed, almost kindly tone, 'we could probably find you some leg-work. And believe you me, you'd learn something from working with us. Cosgrove may seem a bit old-fashioned, a bit of a bumbler, to young blokes like you, but he's thorough.'

'And very friendly to us all at the station.'

'Not so friendly where your Chief Constable's concerned.'

Burgess blinked again. He swallowed down the remains of his whisky and stared across the rickety table at me. It seemed as if he had decided to loosen a plank or two in the barriers of age and experience between us.

'The mon's a jackass, och aye,' he said in an excruciatingly broad imitation of Cosgrove's soft accent. We both laughed, and briefly might have passed for a couple of pub cronies.

'You meet all sorts in the job,' Burgess went on, faintly marking the replacement of the barrier as he put his glass back on the table. 'The bastards, the bent, at the top too – and a few as straight as Jim Cosgrove. Maybe he never took any of your fancy exams. And he's not one for psychology and all that. But you know where you are with Jim. The press know it too, though he's never been one for doing them favours.'

There was a pause in which I could almost hear the Burgess mechanism whirring towards getting up and leaving.

'Will he be seeing the press tomorrow?' I asked quickly.

'Local press,' Burgess said heavily. 'What you've got can turn up. There's no TV station nearby, is there? Funny thing; Jim's not averse to a bit of TV. Still, you can't expect much coverage when one old lady gets pushed over in her greenhouse or glasshouse or whatever – pushed or stumbled. I bloody nearly fell over myself in the rotten place. Shocking condition she let her property get into.'

'It's partly the sea air,' I heard myself saying absurdly as if in extenuation. 'But the case isn't closed, is it? If you'd have a word with Cosgrove about me, I'd appreciate it. Nothing much happens here.'

'I can see that.'

Burgess got ponderously to his feet and began buttoning up the stiff front of his surprisingly ostentatious furred black leather coat. 'Well, thanks for the Scotch.'

I knew I must detain him. Into that literally thick head I must drive the nail of my desperate need to be involved in Cosgrove's enquiry. Sometimes I had thought my mind was turning as rusty in the sea air of the suffocating pseudo-village as the tin signs I passed on my way back each evening to the blank warm room waiting for me at Mrs Jelf's.

'Another?' I almost pleaded. 'Help that cold.'

It was too familiar a remark, I saw at once. Decisively he shook his head and drew on his big black gauntlets, as though armouring his personality against all further contact with me. I felt the rising, accustomed taste of momentary depression – even with Burgess – at being left alone.

Once he had gone I could sit there no longer, though I disliked the ordeal of crossing the room by myself under the barmaid's demurely quizzical eye. I always meant to invite her to have a drink, and I always failed. Her soft, oddly teasing 'Good night, Sergeant', echoed behind me. An abrupt gust of salty wet wind confirmed how flushed my face was as I got the door open and turned the corner past the pub's amber gleaming portholes and the deserted sea-front.

The night was frosty and clear, like a foretaste of the traditional Christmas Eve. I climbed the East Cliff road, away from the sprawling lines of bungalows whose ranks blurred what coherence as a village Steyndean had once possessed. With the poignancy of a distant carol there came the obscene chanting of some local youths waiting impatiently in the high street for the fish and chip shop to open.

From the day of my arrival, I had hated the animation and noise in the summer months, the bus queues and the aimless, drifting visitors. But in winter I liked to see the glow behind the lowered orange blinds of the Sunkist café. Just at the crest of the cliff was the shuttered ice-cream parlour, The Smuggler's Haunt, closed until the spring. Only its rusting metal silhouette of a smuggler – with peeling paint and hunched tiptoe pose – stood out on the pavement, embedded in a lump of concrete. 'Do someone a dirty injury on a dark night' was the station cliché, but I always welcomed the outstretched hand holding an ice-cream cone which signalled my last steps to the security of the Jelfs' slightly isolated, sprucely shingled bungalow.

Yet recently this spell had failed. I was irritated now, even while bending to the toy-like, low, scrolled gate (over which I could easily have stepped), at the minute garden with its pocket-mirror pond, white-washed paving stones and rockery on which sat a large, vividly green frog in plaster. By the pond stood a red-billed stork which Mr Jelf claimed to repaint every year. On the darkest evenings it loomed still visible in the blueish light of the television filtering through the net curtains in the front room where the Jelfs settled from the late afternoon until their early bedtime.

With no children and no animals, they had retired to the coast after both working – as Mr Jelf told me – in a London club. They needed a lodger who would be, as were they, unobtrusive. I was their first; and it was a first for me too, since I had come to Steyndean only on promotion.

To my mother I wrote cheerfully about it all. She liked the sound of my large, mushroom-toned room at the back of the bungalow and was sure that the Jelfs must be proud of their lodger and feel specially protected. Even though Mrs Jelf provided no meals, it was something, she agreed, that I might use the kitchen. Although I told her details of cases I was working on (borrowing facts usually from stories I heard about crime in towns nearby like Brighton), I never described the spotless surgery which was Mrs Jelf's kitchen, with its rose-pink plastic container labelled 'Rubbish', its array of bottle-brushes, strainers and glinting instruments incised with names like 'kit-majig', and its stiff bunch of multi-coloured spontex sponges blooming in a jug beside the stainless steel draining-board.

139

When I stood there I often thought of my mother in her grubby kitchen in Darlington. Like Mrs Jelf she had always wanted everything – including me – to be nice. Already as a child, I understood that her efforts were always going to be defeated. The newest possessions soon grew tarnished in our home, and secretly I blamed my father, ailing, idle and ever-present. I shared my mother's determination that I should be different. 'Be a credit to me,' she had frequently said when I was growing up. She used to repeat it when I asked what she wanted for Christmas or her birthday. 'That'll be the best present.'

For this Christmas I wanted to give her the reality : my working on an unusually interesting local case, for which police in London had been called in. Far more than the fact of my being on the spot was the fact that I had a gift of observation. It had often been commented on and commended. It served me well. Even my father had grudgingly admitted it, calling me as a child 'old sharp-eyes' – a name I detested. All I needed was an opportunity to show just how sharp – how clever, really – I was. And the Rainier case offered me that.

I had not been on duty when the report came in late one evening of the death of a Miss Marietta Rainier. Her house-keeper had found her body in the conservatory, adjoining the big house they shared in the old, once exclusive part of the original village, well away from the sea-front. Quite how she had died was not clear at first, and the circumstances remained puzzling. She had somehow, it seemed, slipped or been pushed – anyway had fallen – and had fractured her skull on the loose tiles of the stone floor. There were scarcely any signs of a struggle, though I knew the pathologist's report mentioned some bruising round her wrists.

A possible motive might have been theft, for Miss Rainier was presumed to be wealthy. Her handbag had disappeared, though not the jewellery she was wearing; the housekeeper declared that she never kept much money in the house but that her rings were meant to be very valuable. Miss Rainier kept a locked desk in the conservatory, a room which no longer contained plants but where, apparently, she liked to sit by her-self in the evenings. It had its own door on to the rambling, neglected, large garden, and that was shut but not bolted. The desk had definitely been forced and the few papers it contained had been gone through, but it was difficult to establish if anything relevant or valuable was missing.

'Petty criminal from Brighton,' said one of my station colleagues who had known the village since childhood. 'Tried to pinch something, got a fright when the old lady caught him, shoved her over, snatched her handbag and ran.'

'Not a local man,' I'd heard the Chief Constable inform Cosgrove authoritatively on the day he arrived, as they walked down the corridor to the office set aside for him and Burgess. 'You can be pretty sure of that. Robbery with violence just doesn't fit in here. Your man – '

'Or woman,' Cosgrove interpolated, with a dryness emphasised by the long vowel he gave the first syllable.

The Chief Constable had halted, staring in amazement and unnoticing of my presence flattened against the wall. His beautifully waved white hair nearly but not quite rested on the collar of his smooth tweed coat, a little yellowed, as if cured where it curled round his ears. Abruptly his shoulders began to shake with noisy, wheezing laughter ('Humourless bastard,' the oldest constable had once muttered to me when we'd heard a comparable volley at the desk in the hall). Beside the heaving figure Cosgrove looked slight and very still, and incongruously jaunty in a bright blue mac, still wearing a round, oddly hairy blue hat which I could see had a speckled feather in its band.

'Cherchez la femme, eh?'

Another burst of laughter came from the Chief Constable as he moved on. He and Cosgrove disappeared into the office, and the corridor was suddenly hushed.

At first I had expected there would be a lot of talk in Steyndean about Miss Rainier's death. Perhaps there was, and I knew too few people to realise it. The Jelfs, I had feared, might waylay me – if only to lament that such things could happen in such a quiet place.

But the few large old-fashioned houses inland and detached from the nucleus of the village were hardly thought of any longer as part of it. I suppose the Jelfs had never seen Miss Rainier. Her housekeeper did her shopping. She would have had nothing to do with the East Cliff Bowling Club, which was their sole interest outside the bungalow. Besides, although at the police station we felt that the circumstances of her death were suspicious, many people probably preferred to think it had somehow been an accident, more sad than shocking : especially since they mostly did not know her. Even the arrival of Chief Superintendent Cosgrove and Sergeant Burgess appeared in their local newspaper as a thoroughly soothing event. When I bought that week's issue I had difficulty in locating the item about a wealthy spinster's demise. The front page was full of impending scandal over the washing away during November gales of the recently set up railings along the seafront, under the heading 'Names to be named in concrete cover-up, declares Councillor'.

For us at the station Cosgrove was obviously more interesting than Miss Rainier, though I noticed that the others hardly shared my concern with the case. The routine of existence at Steyndean suited them. It bored me and made me impatient. I had recently begun to feel restless, unrelaxed, almost sinking sometimes in the evenings amid the soft furnishings of my soft-coloured, luxurious yet neutral room at the Jelfs'. It was what my father would have called 'a cushy billet' : strange words I remembered asking my mother about in my childhood, hearing them repeated so often as we moved, without our ever finding the home that could justify the term.

At the Jelfs' I had apparently found it for myself. Yet I now returned to it tired and irritated : irritated even by the always discreet bubbling of their television set, a familiar sound as I stepped quietly down the thick-carpeted hall to my room. Something in me suddenly longed to hurl the bottle-brushes and scourers over the kitchen and leave the spontex mops gory with traces of ketchup and baked beans.

I felt savagely that it would be just my luck if Burgess's cold prevented him from turning up the next morning or if he was too stupefied by it to remember to say anything to Cosgrove about me. All night, it seemed, I lay sleepless worrying about that, and I woke late. I had to hurry down the hill, to find the station far more animated than I'd seen it before.

Burgess had already arrived; and there was a message that Cosgrove wanted to see me.

'Can't solve the case without you, Sarge,' the duty constable, Jenkins, added, grinning. I hesitated over a rebuke, flustered by Cosgrove's summons and conscious that not only was Jenkins virtually my own age but also one of the few people in the station whom I liked. I walked away hastily, saying nothing, and knocked on Cosgrove's door.

He was seated at a desk ringed by chairs, in preparation for the press briefing, and it was easy to obey his rather abstracted 'Sit down, laddie'.

I sat there, seeing him properly for the first time and listening, more than seeing, Burgess bulking large in the corner, breathing with great sighs and intermittent sniffs. Cosgrove was older than I had realised. Without a hat, his head was brownish and balding, peppered with freckles and sparsely covered with cropped-looking sandy fair hair. When he looked up I saw his eyes were much bluer than Burgess's and his expression almost simple in its friendly directness.

'Bill Burgess here tells me you're keen to lend a hand on this Rainier case.'

'Yes, sir.'

'That's good, though it's not much of a case so far. And I'm not expecting any revelations that Miss Marietta Rainier was queen of a spy ring, you know, or peddled dope. A wee bit of a mystery woman to her neighbours, maybe. But the worst we've learnt is that she dyed her hair and didn't always tell the truth about her age.'

'But she was killed, sir?'

'Aye, she was. I think we can be sure of that.'

'Unless she tripped on the rotten ruddy tiles of that blasted glasshouse,' Burgess interpolated. 'Perishing place.'

'Two ladies getting on in years, living in a house too big for them, Bill, mightn't take the care of it you or I would,' Cosgrove answered mildly. 'Two ladies who don't seem always to have hit it off either, from what we hear. The housekeeper – Mrs Praed – was quite open over that.'

'Not much sorrow about her, was there?' Burgess muttered. He gave a sharp, snort-like sniff so explosive in the cramped office that Cosgrove started. ' "Lived our own lives . . . never discussed each other's private affairs." Old rat bag.'

'Well,' said Cosgrove, looking rather prim, 'we can assume they weren't living in what used to be called sin. Now, laddie. It's a nice brisk morning for a stroll. I'd like you to go up there and see if you can find out anything more from the people with houses around. Make yourself agreeable. Just have a chat.'

'Should I check their original statements, sir?'

'You should not. And there's precious little to check anyway. Nobody saw anything or anyone. Mrs Praed discovered the body at about six o'clock in the morning – '

'She says,' Burgess interpolated from his corner.

'And she had last seen Miss Rainier at half past eight the previous evening, when she took her her supper on a tray in the conservatory. Then she went to her own sitting-room, watched television and had a bath before going to bed. Miss Rainier ate that meal. After that we don't know, except that by about eleven o'clock she was dead. Oh, and it was normally Miss Rainier who did the locking up, as she stayed up late most nights.'

'I went there once before, to *Las Pampas* – Miss Rainier's house,' I explained, 'when I first came here. She reported the theft of some money and suspected a window-cleaner. But there didn't seem anything in it.'

'Is that so?' Cosgrove said absently, clipping some papers together on his desk, while Burgess shifted and panted as if resenting the isolation in which Cosgrove had placed him.

There was a knock on the door, and the grinning face of Jenkins appeared round it. 'Excuse me, sir. The Chief Constable's just arrived. He thinks the press will be on us quite soon – and the television may be coming, sir, after all.'

'They must be desperate,' Burgess grumbled as the door closed. Cosgrove looked at his watch. I stood up reluctantly.

'I'd hoped to attend your conference, sir. Perhaps I could go along to Miss Rainier's after lunch ...'

He shook his head. 'You'll miss nothing. It'll be routine stuff. The investigation is proceeding. We're confident there's no mass murderer at large. So you cut along, laddie, and see what you can find out. Go and see Mrs Praed if you like. She might tell you something.'

'To sod off, probably,' said Burgess with a nasal laugh.

As I left the station I saw the stooping figure of the editor of the local paper hurriedly enter, adjusting his glasses and looking around anxiously, perhaps afraid he was late. There was no sign of other journalists or of any television crew.

Cosgrove was right : I would miss nothing. Instead, I felt a pricking of excitement in turning inland, away from the High Street and the shops, towards the despised area of those few large, red-brick, turreted villas shrouded from each other by now overgrown shrubbery, with dark gardens dominated by monkey-puzzle trees and intersected by paths winding away to tradesmen entrances no longer visited by tradesmen.

I remembered my first sight of *Las Pampas*, on the morning I had gone on my assignment to see Miss Rainier ('some silly old trout feeling lonely, I expect,' had been Jenkins' comment on receiving her call). It occupied a corner site, with at least three gateways over which I had hesitated. On that bright late summer morning the pinkish glass of what I thought must be the porch caught the light, obscured from the road not by trees but by two rings of giant, silvery grasses bleached and slightly waving in a distinct breeze which was the only hint of the not distant sea. I found myself approaching the house from the side on which was built what turned out to be the conservatory. It was from that glass doorway that Miss Rainier had abruptly appeared, asking, 'Are you from the police?'

She was very thin, and dressed in a long mauve-flowered robe, rather like a kimono. Her hair was an intense, glossy black, making her pale face look even whiter; and her narrow black eyes made me wonder briefly if she really was Japanese, though she seemed too tall – about as tall as I was. I had followed her inside the sun-warmed conservatory, where a pot of coffee and two mugs stood waiting on a long shelf against the wall. Unsmiling, she had gestured to me to sit in one of the faded basket-chairs which were the chief furniture.

'This is a serious matter,' she began, standing there, scrutinising me. 'Are you an inspector? You seem very young.'

Now, as I decided to leave *Las Pampas* and Mrs Praed to the end of my morning's enquiry, I felt how far away all that seemed, though it was only eighteen months ago. How awkwardly I had lowered myself into the creaking chair, conscious of being at a disadvantage while Miss Rainier interrogated me. And when eventually I started questioning her, how vague she had been about what sum of money exactly was missing – waving her thin hands around almost impatiently, with swooping gestures that set the rings she wore glittering brilliantly between us. She accused nobody. She had perhaps momentarily mislaid the money and first suspected the milkman, though he never entered the house, and then she had naturally thought of the window-cleaner. There was no need whatsoever for me to see Mrs Praed, who was totally trustworthy. And anyway she could not swear the money might not turn up. Possibly she had acted impulsively, but she was grateful to me for coming; and almost as some form of faint apology she had at last offered me a cup of by then rather cool coffee.

Las Pampas stood between two houses vaguely similar, though smaller – I found – once I got within their grounds. At neither did I learn much to report to Cosgrove, though I lingered in a sort of reverie before their bold turrets and balconies, conscious of the strong, privileged privacy these houses exuded. At *Mellerstain* fir trees grew close to the house, itself of grey stone, increasing the not unpleasant gloominess. Nobody answered the doorbell in the arched, pillared porch, and when finally I looked through the windows of what must have been the dining-room, I realised the place was empty.

'The last of the old ladies died in June,' the charwoman at *Abercorn Lodge* told me a few minutes later, as I skirted *Las Pampas* and walked up the well-kept, drive-like approach to the third house. She was busy in the chilly air burnishing the red-tiled steps to the gleaming lustre of lipstick, but seemed quite glad to stop and talk. Her employers, Colonel and Mrs Witherington, were away for the day, visiting their married daughter near Eastbourne. Anyway, they would have known nothing, she added firmly. They never spoke to Miss Rainier, as far as she knew. They were elderly people – marvellous for their age though – and the Colonel still played golf, often with the Chief Constable.

I glanced at her sharply, though she seemed innocent of trying to snub me. The old ladies at *Mellerstain* had been three sisters, only one of whom had married; Colonel and Mrs Witherington certainly knew them, though they weren't exactly neighbourly, but then it wasn't an area for anything like that.

I thanked her and walked down the drive, pausing at the gate for a last look at the extent of neat, trimmed lawn, suggestive now of a golf-links in the crisp winter light. As I paused there, I felt my reluctance growing to face Mrs Praed – and an almost panic sense of having nothing to question her about. She had made her statement. She would not welcome going over it once again. Although I had never met her, I saw her very much in Burgess's terms and certainly different from the plump, cheerful charwoman at *Abercorn Lodge*, who might even have asked me in for a cup of tea had I shown more interest in her gossip.

Opposite the houses was an open fence and a field divided into what looked like allotments. Where the allotments dwindled away at one side there was a high garden wall and above it the flat roof of another, whitish house I did not recall noticing before. I turned in that direction.

The house itself was very plain, almost square, of shabby stucco with symmetrical square windows and a central porch over which the name *Belmont* was written in faded capital letters. The door had been painted, freshly, a bright lemon yellow, against which its heavy knocker hung blackly. Even while I waited, having knocked, I wondered what I hoped to discover here; and when eventually the door opened, I was disconcerted to be confronted by a girl of about eight or nine, in a nightgown-like dress, with fluffy fair hair. Vaguely, behind her in the hall, there hovered a similar, younger girl.

'What is it?' the elder one asked in clear, clipped, surprisingly tart tones, keeping the door grasped in one hand.

I felt I must smile. 'Is your Mummy at home, dear?'

'Who?'

147

'Your mother. Might I have a word with her, if she's not busy?'

'What about?'

'Well, it's an official matter really,' I began rather awkwardly, glad that there was no one to see me wilting under the child's hard gaze and poised manner, so much at variance with her cloudy clothes and appearance. 'You see,' I went on, 'we're making some enquiries – '

'Are you fuzz?'

I paused. 'From the police, dear, yes. Now . . .'

Her sudden smile, directed over my shoulder, made me break off. A third girl, as fair and with a zebra-striped fur coat over her long dress, had appeared beside me, carrying a vast straw bag of groceries.

'Samantha,' the one at the door said, speaking with theatrical clarity, 'he's fuzz. I've told him nothing.'

'Super, darling. Clever you. I'll cope, if you and Portia could be angels and lug this into the kitchen.'

She passed the laden bag through the doorway and then swung round on me, asking 'What is it?' in exactly the same tone of voice as had the child. She was very young but clearly the mother.

'Mrs . . . ?' I countered, taking out my warrant card. She barely looked at it.

'My name's Samantha Buckle. I'm not married, as it happens, and I don't care much for policemen. That's one reason why I've come down here.'

She pulled a packet of cigarettes from somewhere out of the fur and lit one calmly, as if deciding that I should not be allowed inside the house.

'I'm investigating a death in suspicious circumstances,' I told her. 'A neighbour of yours, a Miss Rainier, was found dead on the sixth of December. You might have noticed someone or seen something suspicious the previous evening. We're questioning people in the neighbourhood.'

'Do you mean she was murdered?'

'We are considering that possibility.'

She had gone rather pale, I noted almost gladly.

148

'There aren't many people living around here. Where did she live?'

'At *Las Pampas*, the middle house up the road, the one – '

'I know it,' she said decisively, 'though I've never even set eyes on Miss Rainier. I think I inherited my window-cleaner from her but that's about it. Her housekeeper was quite nice to us when the kids and I first moved in, until she found out I wasn't a tragically young widow. When do you say she died? – Miss Rainier, I mean.'

'On the night of the sixth, a Tuesday.'

'I don't remember days precisely, but it's always quiet here.' She shrugged, threw down the cigarette, twitched the huge striped collar of her coat and moved towards the house. 'I can't help you. I noticed nothing unusual, but then why should I?' She gave a fleeting smile, more at than for me. 'I go to bed early.'

The yellow door closed behind her; I found myself scrutinising it, as though it held some clues – which perhaps it did for understanding Samantha Buckle. I could see her and her two children choosing its colour and carrying out its painting competently. That they had decided to paint it at all might have its significance, though scarcely of relevance to the Rainier case.

Standing there, staring rather blankly, I must have looked as foolish as I felt; and I moved hurriedly out of range of those windows from which one of Samantha Buckle's children might well be beadily watching me. Cosgrove had given me a task – just as I'd wanted – but somehow I had funked doing it. Turning out the trivia of my morning for his inspection could be as humiliating as turning out one's pockets. No assurance to myself that I meant to return in the afternoon and talk to Mrs Praed could disguise that.

Yet, when I entered Cosgrove's office to find him alone, writing busily, it was all much easier than I had expected. He glanced up at me as if surprised and momentarily unsure who I was. He surprised me too, because he was almost disguised by a pair of plain steel spectacles which made him look naive to the point of silliness. Perhaps he sensed as much. He began unhooking them awkwardly from behind his freckled ears, faintly grimacing as he put them away in his breast-pocket under his handkerchief.

He interrupted my rehearsed, carefully unstammering explanations so gently that I hardly felt halted.

'That's all right, laddie. I don't know that Mrs Praed's of much consequence to us. Now I've sent poor Bill Burgess to lie down and shake off that dreadful cold of his. If you've nothing more important to do, we might have a wee bite of lunch and you can tell me who you did see.'

I wondered if he would ask me to recommend somewhere, but he led me down towards the sea-front, saying nothing as we walked along the crowded high street. Walking beside him, I realised he was not only quite short but rather frail under his dapper blue plumage. Once he stumbled on the narrow pavement in avoiding a bustling, burdened shopper, but hastily recovered.

Just where the open-topped buses turned round in the summer was the almost circular, timbered and thatched building of *The Creamery*. Through its dark, bottle-glass windows I had often noticed well-dressed, middle-aged women having morning coffee in an interior of old oak and tartan upholstery.

'Nice and quiet,' Cosgrove muttered as we entered.

It was very dim inside and half empty, and we were – I quickly noticed – the only men lunching there. Nobody appeared interested in us, least of all the waitress in vaguely dairy-maid uniform who served us in a dreamy, detached way which was almost soothing. The morning receded, even while I went on expecting Cosgrove to start questioning me soon about it. But he seemed unhurried, and when he did begin talking it was about the seaside and about his childhood in Arbroath between the wars. His parents had kept a small stationer's shop, and he still recalled the elaborate covers of the exercise books, the pen-holders and boxes of nibs, and even sticks of sealing-wax tufted like candles so that they could be lit and melted.

Then he asked me about my childhood. Slowly I stirred my too-milky coffee, thinking. The winter afternoon light was making the room dimmer than ever. It was deserted now except for Cosgrove and myself and an old lady growing shadowy in a corner by the window as she clicked her handbag clasp impatiently, waiting for her bill.

'Not much to tell,' I said at last. 'We moved around a good deal, up in the North. My father had been in the army. He picked up some bug in Burma during the Second War and never got over it. My mother had to look after him a lot.'

'Regular soldier, was he?'

'Yes.' As I said it I could hear suppressed impatience in my tone, perhaps at telling the small lie.

I had been reluctant to start talking and now I suddenly saw my childhood in a series of stark images which I wanted to swap with Cosgrove: my childhood and even my life in Steyndean, with the Jelfs' kitchen and my mother in hers and those other kitchens in shabby lodgings where I had helped her as a boy, always told to move quietly so as not to disturb my father.

'Did you never think of the army for your own career?'

I shook my head. 'No. And my mother wouldn't have liked it. She hoped I'd either go into the police or be a dentist.'

Cosgrove's laugh made me laugh – half unwillingly, as he was quick to see. 'Well,' he said with rapid soberness, 'very useful they both are too, though I don't know that I've heard of them as alternatives before. I think you made the right choice, laddie.'

'I knew I couldn't be a dentist.'

'And so you're a policeman.' He smiled shyly at me across the table. 'We both are. But you're a bright lad. Your career's just starting. Mine's coming to an end. They say extremes meet.'

At that moment I felt happy just being with Cosgrove. I felt I could have told him anything.

'This morning,' I said. 'I'm afraid I wasted time. I'm sorry.'

'Aye. My morning was wasted too. It was no great press conference. More of us than them – and still more of Bill's germs, I'd say. But I'd like to hear what you did and who you did manage to see.'

I found it easy to do as he asked, reporting the banal conversations I had had, while he gazed away towards the window where the sky over the sea showed greenish through the glass and chill.

'That child was pretty unnerving,' I ended by saying. Cosgrove was turning to gesture to the waitress who had at last flitted back among the tables.

'What did you make of the mother?' he asked idly. 'Nice cup of coffee they give you here.'

'She might have been some sort of singer or starlet, I suppose – getting away from it all. I got an impression she wasn't poor. Maybe she's been involved with drugs? . . .'

'Do you think she was speaking the truth?'

'Yes, I do.'

'She didn't tell you the name of that window-cleaner of hers?'

'I didn't ask, I'm afraid, sir.'

We were both standing up now. A mood was broken, but I still felt at ease. Cosgrove paid the bill and went to retrieve his blue hat from the row of pegs where it hung prominently alone.

'I'd like to know his name and if he's a local man,' he said when he returned. 'With Bill Burgess down, you could help me over that. We might pay him a visit. There's little enough to go on as it is.'

Once or twice as we walked briskly back up the high street, I wondered if I should ask him about the case. Had he got a theory? I might learn more if Burgess remained ill for a further day or two, as I hoped he would. Perhaps I would go on to work with Cosgrove, not so much at Steyndean – where the Rainier business would surely soon peter out unresolved and then be forgotten – but in London. I envisaged the team of the two of us. Certainly I was more up-to-date and less uncouth than Burgess, who seemed a strange companion for Cosgrove. With Cosgrove I could show myself as clever as I basically was; he would hear me out and then shrewdly add some human observation. Ours ought to be a formidable combination. It would probably never become famous, but it would have repute in circles where such things mattered. And I heard myself describing Cosgrove to my mother – I would describe him to her at Christmas – as the ideal boss, one with whom I could work as a partner and one who really cared about the people who worked with him.

'Right, laddie,' Cosgrove said as soon as we entered the station. 'Let's see if you can put your finger on the where-abouts of yon window-cleaner.'

'Do you think he's important in the case, sir?' I asked.

'Your guess is as good as mine.'

First I telephoned Samantha Buckle. She was even more openly curt than she had been in the morning. To her the window-cleaner was known only as 'Mr Paul'; she had no idea where he lived.

There was no record of anyone of that name living in Steyndean. I half-hesitated and then decided to ask Jenkins if he knew anything about such a window-cleaner. 'Want him to assist your enquiries?' he asked cheerfully. 'Sounds more like a hairdresser to me.'

But with his wife's help (he pointed out) he was able to discover that Robert Porle was the name of a window-cleaner living in one of the stone coastguard cottages that lay imme-diately behind *The Creamery*. I passed on the information to Cosgrove, who stopped at the desk to thank Jenkins before we set off for Porle's cottage.

'He'll be having his tea,' Cosgrove observed as we approached the row of lighted, uncurtained windows. Each cottage had its protective stone porch, with cockleshells set in the curve of the arch.

'He's having his tea,' said the large, dark woman in a multi-flowered scarlet overall who had opened the door. 'I'm his mother,' she added meaningly, not moving.

'We shan't keep him long, madam,' Cosgrove replied. 'It's a routine police matter, but we think he might possibly be able to help us. May we come in?'

'Is it about his motor-bike?'

'Certainly not,' said Cosgrove drily. 'Mr Porle himself is not the subject of our enquiry.'

She drew back, rather reluctantly, and we stepped into the small, bright, hot room – all the hotter as most of the furnish-ings seemed red – where Porle sat in shirtsleeves eating his tea.

Cosgrove again introduced himself and Porle stared at us, looking flushed but puzzled more than disconcerted. He was much fairer than his mother, about my own age, or a little younger, and rather good-looking in a bold way.

'What's all this then?' he asked curiously.

'Mr Porle, I believe you were employed by a Miss Marietta Rainer. Is that correct?'

'I used to clean her windows – yes.'

'You know she was recently found dead?'

'So someone told me – yes.'

'I am investigating the circumstances of her death.'

Cosgrove's soft voice seemed to hold Porle and his mother fixed in their places, and I felt something of the same tension as I stood beside him. He had perched on a fat red armchair that filled the space between the tea-table and the hearth, where a real fire burnt.

'May I ask you,' he went on, placidly, 'where you were on the night of Tuesday the sixth of December?'

'Here, of course,' Porle said. 'At home.'

'Wait a minute.' Mrs Porle abruptly moved and spoke, advancing on Cosgrove. 'You said it was nothing to do with him, didn't you? What you're here about. So why question him like this?'

'I'm only asking if your son was at home on the night of the sixth.'

' 'Course he was. He always sleeps here. Maybe he went round to the pub for a drink. That isn't a crime, is it?'

'Mr Porle.' Cosgrove was still placid. 'Have you been cleaning the windows at Miss Rainier's up till recently?'

Porle had gone almost the colour of the surrounding furnishings.

'No,' he said at last.

'There you are,' Mrs Porle intervened angrily. 'He hasn't even been near her place for months ...'

'How long, in fact, is it since you stopped cleaning the windows there?'

'About eighteen months or so, I suppose.'

Cosgrove turned slightly towards me. 'The sergeant will tell you that about that time Miss Rainier reported a theft of some money. She named no names, but she mentioned her window-cleaner, though she later asked for the whole matter to be dropped. She couldn't be sure any money had been stolen.'

Mrs Porle was clearly eager to intervene again, but Porle stopped her. 'Belt up, Mum,' he said without vehemence. 'Make us some more tea; I want to talk to the inspector alone.'

She glared at Cosgrove, who appeared unruffled under her gaze despite his demotion. I too could not help looking hard at him, uneasily wondering whether he had foreseen the current of the conversation and what exactly we were going to hear. Porle got up and closed the kitchen door, which his mother had left ajar. He looked oddly rueful and younger with his face still flushed.

'How did you know I used to work up there?'

'At Miss Rainier's?'

'Yes.'

'The sergeant here learnt of it by chance from the lady living at *Belmont* – a Miss or Mrs Buckle – whom you know. of course?'

'I'll say I do. Smashing girl, isn't she?' He glanced up at me for the first time, with an almost conspiratorial smile and a sudden access of physical assurance, confirmed by the flash of his very white, even teeth. 'Classy but really nice.'

'May I ask,' Cosgrove said politely, 'how you found Miss Rainier as an employer?'

'Not too bad,' Porle began awkwardly. 'Quite decent really . . . In her way.'

'Was it she or her housekeeper you saw more of?'

'Her usually – with her using the conservatory and so on.'

'And how did you come to leave? Were you sacked?'

'I sacked myself.'

'Had Miss Rainier accused you of theft?'

'Never,' he said grimly. There was a pause. The heat of the small room was beginning to oppress me; I loosened my coat, but even while shifting I sensed Cosgrove's silent rebuke over any distraction at this moment. Then Porle started to speak again. As he began I felt suddenly, appallingly, sure of what he was going to say.

'I hadn't meant to tell anyone, but now she's dead. Anyway, you needn't believe me – '

'Go on, laddie.' Cosgrove breathed it almost as an endearment.

'I used to go up to her place quite often – to do odd jobs as well as the windows. Sometimes she'd sweep in to watch and we'd get talking. Then she asked me not to use the front door but go to the conservatory. She liked sitting there, whatever the weather. One morning when I was doing the panes in there I came down the ladder smartish, not looking, I suppose, and almost cannoned into her – she was standing so close. I really thought I'd given her a heart attack, or something. Then she said it was her fault.' He paused and gave an embarrassed laugh. 'She said – well, that she'd come close deliberately. Of course she didn't use the word but what it meant was she fancied me.'

We all seemed to be listening intently, including, I suspected, Mrs Porle in the adjoining kitchen.

'Were you surprised?'

'Well, I knew she liked me; I liked her, come to that, though she could be weird. I think I was a bit frightened, really. Her being old and so on. I tried to make a joke of it, you know.'

'What happened next?'

'How do you mean "next"?' For the first time Porle sounded aggressive.

'Afterwards.'

'She saw how I felt – I reckon. Anyway, she grabbed my arm and begged me not to stop coming. She was lonely . . . I can't remember it all. I went on going up there, but I couldn't be natural any more. Then one morning in the summer – summer before last, it was – she took me through the house. Her housekeeper had gone off on holiday . . . we were alone in a bloody big bedroom . . . she threw her arms round me, you know. Christ, it was awful. I just struggled. She really cursed me. I got out; and I never went back.'

'You told no one – not even your mother?'

'Least of all her.'

'Did Miss Rainier give you money?'

'Odd sums now and again, for my work – nothing to speak of.'

'Was there usually cash lying around, in the conservatory for instance?'

'Not that I ever saw.'

'Was money something you ever discussed with her?'

'No, it wasn't.'

'But you knew she was rich?'

'Well, I knew she'd got more money than I had.'

'And on the night of sixth December you are prepared to swear you didn't go back to see Miss Rainier?'

'No, I didn't.'

'Thank you, Mr Porle,' Cosgrove said, hopping up from the armchair. 'I'd be glad if you would come to the police station tomorrow and sign a statement confirming what you have just told us.'

Porle looked horrified. 'Has it got to be written down – all about her and me, I mean?'

'A brief statement only: entirely confidential. It will be most useful.'

'I don't like it much . . . Poor old bag – it wasn't really her fault.'

'You've been most helpful,' Cosgrove said with prim finality. 'We'll wish you good evening.'

Rather awkwardly I followed him out of the cottage. We halted outside and then walked slowly towards the stone parapet which separated the row of cottages from the sea. It was windy now – positively refreshing after the stuffy room – and we could sense more than see the tide on the turn in the darkness below. Cosgrove stood there, gazing out, while I shuffled my feet and waited impatiently for some comment from him.

'Laddie,' he said eventually, so quietly that I had to bend to catch his voice, 'yon handsome window-cleaner could be our man. Do you realise that?'

I clutched the coping with my gloved hands as the wind rose, buffeting us briefly and giving the illusion we were on board ship.

'He'd some sort of motive,' Cosgrove went on. 'He knew her habits and could have nipped along unobserved to the conservatory. Perhaps he tried blackmailing her, or pretended he'd been in love with her all the time. Maybe they quarrelled again, this time seriously, and he struck her.'

'But it could've been an accident. I don't somehow see him killing anyone. Besides, he'd stopped going there months before.'

'We've only his word for that.'

'I think he's innocent, sir,' I said into the wind.

'Do you now,' said Cosgrove drily. 'And do you think he was telling the truth about what happened between the two of them? You met Miss Rainier, after all. Would you have thought her a lady who'd make advances to a window-cleaner?'

I hesitated. 'It's hard to say. I suppose not.'

'Respectable, quite rich, and by no means in her first youth – mightn't she rather be someone Porle hoped to exploit? He could pretend to be a bit gone on her, flatter her and so on.'

'But why should he?'

'For the sake of her money, perhaps.'

'I just don't see it,' I said obstinately.

There was a distinct pause. Cosgrove turned up his coat collar and then stepped back from the wall. 'Believe me, laddie, you don't see these things at first. Bill Burgess could tell you of cases where we've both had to eat our words and throw out all our first ideas. You sleep on it, and if Bill's not better tomorrow you can help me out again.'

There was nothing I could say. Oddly, I felt almost disappointed with Cosgrove. Yet he had uncovered something in the relationship of Robert Porle and Miss Rainier : something I would never have guessed at and which left me disturbed. I longed to be alone, to examine the implications of what Porle had told us, and yet I dreaded doing so.

That night I slept badly, as I knew I would. While I boiled myself a bag of frozen 'mushroom-'n'-chicken casserole' in one of Mrs Jelf's polished saucepans I felt already wilting like those titbits in their plastic envelope. My sleep was punctuated by obscurely frightening dreams. A high wind seemed fiercely rocking the monstrously tall spears of the pampas grasses growing on Miss Rainier's lawn, and I feared one would break under the stress as they swayed and bent wildly, almost to the level of the ground. Somewhere hidden in their centre, as tall and thin as them, was Miss Rainier, I knew; and every time the dry stems creaked and parted I expected to catch a glimpse of her lilac kimono.

Cosgrove had warned me to be early the next morning, but I was late – though I hardly bothered with breakfast and left my unrinsed coffee cup and half a piece of cold toast on the draining board, no longer caring that Mrs Jelf would later find them.

'We're off to Brighton, laddie,' he told me sharply. 'It sounds as if Bill's got a touch of 'flu, but he might be better tomorrow.'

In the car he said little, except that we were going to see Miss Rainier's solicitor. He seemed abstracted, much less perky than usual and perhaps – like me – he felt tired. It was wearisome in the small car, not speaking and just watching the rise and fall of the empty coast road on a dull, damp morning. For some reason, the prospect of the solicitor increased my depression; I thought – for the first time – of the evidence he might have, and then I wondered if Cosgrove had seen him before. It would be reasonable to ask, but in my mood of inertia I said nothing.

Cosgrove must have telephoned to make an appointment. Mr Segar was expecting us – Mr George Segar himself, a clerk solemnly told us as he led us into a dusty room which looked like a film set for a lawyer's office. Segar was florid and big, grey-haired, with a confidently loud voice and a set of seals and chains across his double-breasted waistcoat which added to the actorish illusion. He seated Cosgrove with elaborate courtesy, but left me to find a chair while he resumed his own place behind an ostentatiously bare leather-topped desk.

'When I spoke to Mr William Segar,' Cosgrove began.

'My son,' Segar boomed. As I went on scrutinising him, I guessed how likely he was to be a friend of the Chief Constable's.

'He told me,' Cosgrove went on, 'that Miss Rainier had left no will.'

'That is quite correct, Superintendent.'

'What I failed to ask him was whether Miss Rainier had

previously made a will – or wills – which she afterwards cancelled.'

Segar played thoughtfully with one of his dangling gold-mounted seals. Then he put both hands flat down on the desk and cleared his throat.

'That is properly a confidential matter affecting a client,' he said. 'I am anxious to be of assistance, of course, but I am dubious about answering such a question. My son William,' he added grandly, after a pause, 'would certainly not be in a position to respond. He is still a junior in the firm.'

'Miss Rainier's dead – '

'I'm well aware – '

'And we have the task of establishing how she came to die, Mr Segar. It's not idle curiosity that prompts me to ask if you know of her making and destroying a will, though she might have done so, I realise, without consulting you.'

Segar had grown more florid, and perhaps felt rather flustered. He put up a hand to touch gingerly the set waves of his hard-looking hair.

'Our firm has acted for the family for many years. Marietta Rainier was unusual, even eccentric, I should say, but I cannot believe she would behave in such a matter without my knowledge and advice.'

'Your advice being surely that she should make a will. Was she reluctant to do so?'

'Not at all – that is, she tended to do things impusively . . .' Segar frowned at his own recollections. 'Frankly, hers was a head-strong personality. There was some foreign blood there – Spanish, I've been told. I suppose on reflection it can do no harm now to say that more than once she did make a will, somewhat imprudently drawn in my view, as I made clear to her.'

'Leaving her money away from her family?'

'Yes, that is so, Superintendent.'

'Your son told me that her next-of-kin is a niece, a spinster living in Cornwall.'

'In Truro,' Segar said, enjoying the superior precision of his own remark.

'In Truro,' Cosgrove echoed gratefully.

Abruptly Segar got up from the desk. 'Is it too early for a glass of sherry? Or will you join me in a cup of coffee? I feel remiss in not having offered you something before.'

'Nothing, thank you,' Cosgrove replied. 'I am assuming,' he went on, as Segar slowly subsided, 'that there was some pattern to Miss Rainier's making of wills.'

'A pattern?' It was Segar's turn to echo, and rather blankly.

'That she met someone, perhaps, and – in your own words – impulsively decided to make a will in his favour. I'm assuming, you notice, that the beneficiary was male. Later, it may be, she found occasion to change her mind. Something on those lines, Mr Segar. Perhaps I ought to add that I've interviewed a Robert Porle who was her window-cleaner.'

'I fail to see the connection,' Segar said sternly, 'and I certainly do not recall the name.'

'But with regard to what I ventured to call a pattern . . . ?'

Segar sighed with dignified petulance. 'The subject is somewhat embarrassing. My client was a single lady of some means though no longer rich you understand, and lonely no doubt as she grew older. It is unfortunately true she supposed once or twice that a younger man might, er, might – well, that a relationship might be formed.'

'But nothing came of these affairs?'

'I should hardly use that word, and of course I was never privy to the situation except as her legal adviser. We met rarely. Indeed, I owe it to her memory to declare – as I have gone so far – that for several years she had not sought to make a will. I was somewhat relieved, I confess.'

'Rather ironic for you, as a solicitor.'

'The best interests of our clients are always our concern, Superintendent.' Segar paused after serving up the sentence as if savouring it in lieu of the glass of sherry. 'Do you,' he went on, dropping into a less sonorous tone, 'think the case is nearer solution? It seemed a sad business altogether – quite a shock when I learnt of it.'

'I've greatly appreciated your confidence, Mr Segar,' Cosgrove said, rising from his chair. 'It's been a real help. We're not quite at the end of the tunnel, but I think at long last I see my way.'

'Are you sure I can't tempt you to at least some coffee?'

'I'm afraid we've already taken more of your time than we should.' Cosgrove put out his hand. Segar clasped it in a stately way, ushering us towards the door and murmuring benevolently.

When we stood in the street again, Cosgrove sighed and pushed back his hat. 'Nearly stopped him having his coffee and biscuits at the usual time,' he observed. 'That would have been a serious matter.'

'Are you really clear about what happened, sir?'

He gave me an almost furtive but penetrating glance. 'I'm beginning to guess, laddie, but it's only a guess. Proof's another thing.'

'You think Porle went up there, intending to force her to make a will?'

Cosgrove smiled rather wryly. 'Is that your theory this morning?'

'I was wondering about yours, sir.'

'Aye, I see you were. Hop in the car and let's get back to Steyndean.'

We drove back as mutely as we had come. But now I no longer felt weary, for all my apprehension. In a way, I even felt relief. It had been too testing, too dangerous – I suppose – and yet I doubted if Cosgrove could ever find real proof, despite Porle's testimony.

Anyway, I had gone back often enough to see her without any of his awkwardness. I enjoyed those secret evenings in the conservatory when she listened to me talking of my life. To me she was glamorous, elegant, exotic, neither old nor young. And the conservatory, like the secluded surrounding grounds, had the same glamour and the same security. Ours was a conspiracy quite harmless and happy until she broke it, less crudely than in her approach to Porle, but fatally.

I couldn't stand her hands exploring my body. I grasped them cruelly that night, I know, yet only to stop the mockery of desire I didn't feel and could never have responded to. It was like an unwinding bundle of clothes slowly suffocating me, with musty, faintly scented draperies floating thickly across my mouth and eyes until I fought to tear them away, and she

162

reeled backwards in one sudden, terrible movement which I watched, unable to prevent.

How often had she said I was clever. As I knelt beside her, sick with fear, I wanted to go on being clever for her sake : she would have wished it. I had to be calm too, and I had managed that. I could have faced a bullying investigation, even grave suspicion. I hadn't anticipated the utter emptiness of the days that followed and which seemed to extend before me as flat and endless as the sea at Steyndean on a hot summer afternoon when the crowds turned everything hatefully insipid by their noise and vulgarity.

Cosgrove had proved dangerously disarming. I didn't think it would be difficult to deceive him, but I was surprised that increasingly I didn't want to. Even she had never understood me, I realised more and more – perhaps most bitterly when I heard Robert Porle tell of his experiences which seemed to caricature all I had thought was unique. But Cosgrove ought to understand. In his attitude there would always be something firm, friendly, paternal.

And as the car approached Steyndean, signalled by the outline of the battered black hulk of the windmill abruptly visible on the last rise of the road, I knew that Cosgrove must discover the truth. I would solve the case, I decided; I would tell him everything.

Ellis Peters

THE PRICE OF LIGHT

Hamo FitzHamon of Lidyate held two fat manors in the north-eastern corner of the county, towards the border of Cheshire. Though a gross feeder, a heavy drinker, a self-indulgent lecher, a harsh landlord and a brutal master, he had reached the age of sixty in the best of health, and it came as a salutary shock to him when he was at last taken with a mild seizure, and for the first time in his life saw the next world yawning before him, and woke to the uneasy consciousness that it might see fit to treat him somewhat more austerely than this world had done. Though he repented none of them, he was aware of a whole register of acts in his past which heaven might construe as heavy sins. It began to seem to him a prudent precaution to acquire merit for his soul as quickly as possible. Also as cheaply, for he was a grasping and possessive man. A judicious gift to some holy house should secure the welfare of his soul. There was no need to go so far as endowing an abbey, or a new church of his own. The Benedictine abbey of Shrewsbury could put up a powerful assault of prayers on his behalf in return for a much more modest gift.

The thought of alms to the poor, however ostentatiously bestowed in the first place, did not recommend itself. Whatever was given would be soon consumed and forgotten, and a rag-tag of beggarly blessings from the indigent could carry very little weight, besides failing to confer a lasting lustre upon himself. No, he wanted something that would continue in daily use and daily respectful notice, a permanent reminder of his munificence and piety. He took his time about making his decision, and when he was satisfied of the best value he could get for the least expenditure, he sent his law-man to Shrewsbury to confer with abbot and prior, and conclude with due ceremony and many witnesses the charter that conveyed to the custodian of the altar of St Mary, within the abbey church, one of his free tenant farmers, the rent to provide light for Our Lady's altar throughout the year. He promised also, for the proper displaying of his charity, the gift of a pair of fine silver candlesticks, which he himself would bring and see installed on the altar at the coming Christmas feast.

Abbot Heribert, who after a long life of repeated disillusionments still contrived to think the best of everybody, was moved to tears by this penitential generosity. Prior Robert, himself an aristocrat, refrained, out of Norman solidarity, from casting doubt upon Hamo's motive, but he elevated his eyebrows, all the same. Brother Cadfael, who knew only the public reputation of the donor, and was sceptical enough to suspend judgement until he encountered the source, said nothing, and waited to observe and decide for himself. Not that he expected much; he had been in the world fifty-five years, and learned to temper all his expectations, bad or good.

It was with mild and detached interest that he observed the arrival of the party from Lidyate, on the morning of Christmas Eve. A hard, cold Christmas it was proving to be, that year of 1135, all bitter black frost and grudging snow, thin and sharp as whips before a withering east wind. The weather had been vicious all the year, and the harvest a disaster. In the villages people shivered and starved, and Brother Oswald the almoner fretted and grieved the more that the alms he had to distribute were not enough to keep all those bodies and souls together. The sight of a cavalcade of three good riding horses, ridden by travellers richly wrapped up from the cold, and followed by two pack-ponies, brought all the wretched petitioners crowding and crying, holding out hands blue with frost. All they got out of it was a single perfunctory handful of small coin, and when they hampered his movements FitzHamon used his whip as a matter of course to clear the way. Rumour, thought Brother Cadfael, pausing on his way to the infirmary with his daily medicines for the sick, had probably not done Hamo FitzHamon any injustice.

Dismounting in the great court, the knight of Lidyate was seen to be a big, over-fleshed, top-heavy man with bushy hair and beard and eyebrows, all grey-streaked from their former black, and stiff and bristling as wire. He might well have been a very handsome man before indulgence purpled his face and pocked his skin and sank his sharp black eyes deep into flabby sacks of flesh. He looked more than his age, but still a man to be reckoned with.

The second horse carried his lady, pillion behind a groom. A small figure she made, even swathed almost to invisibility in her woollens and furs, and she rode snuggled comfortably against the groom's broad back, her arms hugging him round the waist. And a very well-looking young fellow he was, this groom, a strapping lad barely twenty years old, with round, ruddy cheeks and merry, guileless eyes, long in the legs, wide in the shoulders, everything a country youth should be, and attentive to his duties into the bargain, for he was down from the saddle in one lithe leap, and reaching up to take the lady by the waist, every bit as heartily as she had been clasping him a moment before, and lift her lightly down. Small, gloved hands rested on his shoulders a brief moment longer than was necessary. His respectful support of her continued until she was safe on the ground and sure of her footing; perhaps a few seconds more. Hamo FitzHamon was occupied with Prior Robert's ceremonious welcome, and the attentions of the hospitaller, who had made the best rooms of the guest-hall ready for him.

The third horse also carried two people, but the woman on the pillion did not wait for anyone to help her down, but slid quickly to the ground and hurried to help her mistress off with the great outer cloak in which she had travelled. A quiet, submissive young woman, perhaps in her middle twenties, perhaps older, in drab homespun, her hair hidden away under a coarse linen wimple. Her face was thin and pale, her skin dazzlingly fair, and her eyes, reserved and weary, were of a pale, clear blue, a fierce colour that ill suited their humility and resignation.

Lifting the heavy folds from her lady's shoulders, the maid showed a head the taller of the two, but drab indeed beside the bright little bird that emerged from the cloak. Lady Fitz-Hamon came forth graciously smiling on the world in scarlet and brown, like a robin, and just as confidently. She had dark hair braided about a small, shapely head, soft, full cheeks flushed rosy by the chill air, and large dark eyes assured of their charm and power. She could not possibly have been more than thirty, probably not so much. FitzHamon had a grown son somewhere, with children of his own, and waiting, some said with little patience, for his inheritance. This girl must be a second or a third wife, a good deal younger than her stepson, and a beauty, at that. Hamo was secure enough and important enough to keep himself supplied with wives as he wore them out. This one must have cost him dear, for she had not the air of a poor but pretty relative sold for a profitable alliance, rather she looked as if she knew her own status very well indeed, and meant to have it acknowledged. She would look well presiding over the high table at Lidyate, certainly, which was probably the main consideration.

The groom behind whom the maid had ridden was an older man, lean and wiry, with a face like the bole of a knotty oak. By the sardonic patience of his eyes he had been in close and relatively favoured attendance on FitzHamon for many years, knew the best and the worst his moods could do, and was sure of his own ability to ride the storms. Without a word he set about unloading the pack-horses, and followed his lord to the guest-hall, while the young man took FitzHamon's bridle, and led the horses away to the stables.

Cadfael watched the two women cross to the doorway, the lady springy as a young hind, with bright eyes taking in everything around her, the tall maid keeping always a pace behind, with long steps curbed to keep her distance. Even thus, frustrated like a mewed hawk, she had a graceful gait. Almost certainly of villein stock, like the two grooms. Cadfael had long practice in distinguishing the free from the unfree. Not that the free had any easy life, often they were worse off than the villeins of their neighbourhood; there were plenty of free men, this Christmas, gaunt and hungry, forced to hold out begging hands among the throng round the gatehouse. Freedom, the first ambition of every man, still could not fill the bellies of wives and children in a bad season.

FitzHamon and his party appeared at Vespers in full glory, to see the candlesticks reverently installed upon the altar in the Lady Chapel. Abbot, prior and brothers had no difficulty in sufficiently admiring the gift, for they were indeed things of beauty, two fluted stems ending in the twin cups of flowering lilies. Even the veins of the leaves showed delicate and perfect as in the living plant. Brother Oswald the almoner, himself a skilled silversmith when he had time to exercise his craft, stood gazing at the new embellishments of the altar with a face and mind curiously torn between rapture and regret, and ventured to delay the donor for a moment, as he was being ushered away to sup with Abbot Heribert in his lodging.

'My lord, these are of truly noble workmanship. I have some knowledge of precious metals, and of the most notable craftsmen in these parts, but I never saw any work so true to the plant as this. A countryman's eye is here, but the hand of a court craftsman. May we know who made them?'

FitzHamon's marred face curdled into deeper purple, as if an unpardonable shadow had been cast upon his hour of self-congratulation. He said brusquely : 'I commissioned them from a fellow in my own service. You would not know his name – a villein born, but he had some skill.' And with that he swept on, avoiding further question, and wife and men-servants and maid trailed after him. Only the older groom, who seemed less in awe of his lord than anyone, perhaps by reason of having so often presided over the ceremony of carrying him dead-drunk to his bed, turned back for a moment to pluck at Brother Oswald's sleeve, and advise him in a confidential whisper : 'You'll find him short to question on that head. The silversmith – Alard, his name was – cut and ran from his service last Christmas, and for all they hunted him as far as London, where the signs pointed, he's never been found. I'd let that matter lie, if I were you.'

And with that he trotted away after his master, and left several thoughtful faces staring after him.

'Not a man to part willingly with any property of his,' mused Brother Cadfael, 'metal or man, but for a price, and a steep price at that.'

'Brother, be ashamed !' reproved Brother Jerome at his elbow. 'Has he not parted with these very treasures for pure charity?'

Cadfael refrained from elaborating on the profit Fitz-Hamon expected for his benevolence. It was never worth arguing with Jerome, who in any case knew as well as anyone that the silver lilies and the rent of one farm were no free gift. But Brother Oswald said grievingly: 'I wish he had directed his charity better. Surely these are beautiful things, a delight to the eyes, but well sold, they could have provided money enough to buy the means of keeping my poorest petitioners alive through the winter, some of whom will surely die for the want of them.'

Brother Jerome was scandalised. 'Has he not given them to Our Lady herself?' he lamented indignantly. 'Beware of the sin of those apostles who cried out with the same complaint against the woman who brought the pot of spikenard, and poured it over the Saviour's feet. Remember Our Lord's reproof to them, that they should let her alone, for she had done well!'

'Our Lord was acknowledging a well-meant impulse of devotion,' said Brother Oswald with spirit. 'He did not say it was well advised! "She hath done what she could" is what he said. He never said that with a little thought she might not have done better. What use would it have been to wound the giver, after the thing was done? Spilled oil of spikenard could hardly be recovered.'

His eyes dwelt with love and compunction upon the silver lilies, with their tall stems of wax and flame. For these remained, and to divert them to other use was still possible, or would have been possible if the donor had been a more approachable man. He had, after all, a right to dispose as he wished of his own property.

'It is sin,' admonished Jerome sanctimoniously, 'even to covet for other use, however worthy, that which has been given to Our Lady. The very thought is sin.'

'If Our Lady could make her own will known,' said Brother Cadfael drily, 'we might learn which is the graver sin, and which the more acceptable sacrifice.'

'Could any price be too high for the lighting of this holy altar?' demanded Jerome.

It was a good question, Cadfael thought, as they went to

supper in the refectory. Ask Brother Jordan, for instance, the value of light. Jordan was old and frail, and gradually going blind. As yet he could distinguish shapes, but like shadows in a dream, though he knew his way about cloisters and precincts so well that his gathering darkness was no hindrance to his freedom of movement. But as every day the twilight closed in on him by a shade, so did his profound love of light grow daily more devoted, until he had forsaken other duties, and taken upon himself to tend all the lamps and candles on both altars, for the sake of being always irradiated by light, and sacred light, at that. As soon as Compline was over, this evening, he would be busy devoutly trimming the wicks of candle and lamp, to have the steady flames smokeless and immaculate for the Matins of Christmas Day. Doubtful if he would go to his bed at all until Matins and Lauds were over. The very old need little sleep, and sleep is itself a kind of darkness. But what Jordan treasured was the flame of light, and not the vessel holding it; and would not those splendid two-pound candles shine upon him just as well from plain wooden sconces?

Cadfael was in the warming-house with the rest of the brothers, about a quarter of an hour before Compline, when a lay brother from the guest-hall came enquiring for him.

'The lady asks if you'll speak with her. She's complaining of a bad head, and that she'll never be able to sleep. Brother Hospitaller recommended her to you for a remedy.'

Cadfael went with him without comment, but with some curiosity, for at Vespers the Lady FitzHamon had looked in blooming health and sparkling spirits. Nor did she seem greatly changed when he met her in the hall, though she was still swathed in the cloak she had worn to cross the great court to and from the abbot's house, and had the hood so drawn that it shadowed her face. The silent maid hovered at her shoulder.

'You are Brother Cadfael? They tell me you are expert in herbs and medicines, and can certainly help me. I came early back from the lord abbot's supper, with such a headache, and have told my lord that I shall go early to bed. But I have such disturbed sleep, and with this pain how shall I be able to rest? Can you give me some draught that will ease me? They say you have a perfect apothecarium in your herb-garden, and all your own work, growing, gathering, drying, brewing and all. There must be something there that can soothe pain and bring deep sleep.'

Well, thought Cadfael, small blame to her if she sometimes sought a means to ward off her old husband's rough attentions for a night, especially for a festival night when he was likely to have drunk heavily. Nor was it Cadfael's business to question whether the petitioner really needed his remedies. A guest might ask for whatever the house afforded.

'I have a syrup of my own making,' he said, 'which may do you good service. I'll bring you a vial of it from my workshop store.'

'May I come with you? I should like to see your workshop.' She had forgotten to sound frail and tired, the voice could have been a curious child's. 'As I already am cloaked and shod,' she said winningly. 'We just returned from the lord abbot's table.'

'But should you not go in from the cold, madam? Though the snow's swept here in the court, it lies on some of the garden paths.'

'A few minutes in the fresh air will help me,' she said, 'before trying to sleep. And it cannot be far.'

It was not far. Once away from the subdued lights of the buildings they were aware of the stars, snapping like sparks from a cold fire, in a clear black sky just engendering a few tattered snow-clouds in the east. In the garden, between the pleached hedges, it seemed almost warm, as though the sleeping trees breathed tempered air as well as cutting off the bleak wind. The silence was profound. The herb-garden was walled, and the wooden hut where Cadfael brewed and stored his medicines was sheltered from the worst of the cold. Once inside, and a small lamp kindled, Lady FitzHamon forgot her invalid role in wonder and delight, looking round her with bright, inquisitive eyes. The maid, submissive and still, scarcely turned her head, but her eyes ranged from left to right, and a faint colour touched life into her cheeks. The many faint, sweet scents made her nostrils quiver, and her lips curve just perceptibly with pleasure.

Curious as a cat, the lady probed into every sack and jar and box, peered at mortars and bottles, and asked a hundred questions in a breath.

'And this is rosemary, these little dried needles? And in this great sack – is it grain?' She plunged her hands wrist-deep inside the neck of it, and the hut was filled with sweetness. 'Lavender? Such a great harvest of it? Do you, then, prepare perfumes for us women?'

'Lavender has other good properties,' said Cadfael. He was filling a small vial with a clear syrup he made from eastern poppies, a legacy of his crusading years. 'It is helpful for all disorders that trouble the head and spirit, and its scent is calming. I'll give you a little pillow filled with that and other herbs, that shall help to bring you sleep. But this draught will ensure it. You may take all that I give you here, and get no harm, only a good night's rest.'

She had been playing inquisitively with a pile of small clay dishes he kept by his work-bench, rough dishes in which the fine seeds sifted from fruiting plants could be spread to dry out; but she came at once to gaze eagerly at the modest vial he presented to her. 'Is it enough? It takes much to give me sleep.'

'This,' he assured her patiently, 'would bring sleep to a strong man. But it will not harm even a delicate lady like you.'

She took it in her hand with a small, sleek smile of satisfaction. 'Then I thank you indeed! I will make a gift – shall I? – to your almoner in requital. Elfgiva, you bring the little pillow. I shall breathe it all night long. It should sweeten dreams.'

So her name was Elfgiva. A Norse name. She had Norse eyes, as he had already noted, blue as ice, and pale, fine skin worn finer and whiter by weariness. All this time she had noted everything that passed, motionless, and never said word. Was she older, or younger, than her lady? There was no guessing. The one was so clamant, and the other so still.

He put out his lamp and closed the door, and led them back to the great court just in time to take leave of them and still be prompt for Compline. Clearly the lady had no intention of attending. As for the lord, he was just being helped away from the abbot's lodging, his grooms supporting him one on either side, though as yet he was not gravely drunk. They headed for the guest-hall at an easy roll. No doubt only the hour of Compline had concluded the drawn-out supper, probably to the abbot's considerable relief. He was no drinker, and could have very little in common with Hamo FitzHamon. Apart, of course, from a deep devotion to the altar of St Mary.

The lady and her maid had already vanished within the guest-hall. The younger groom carried in his free hand a large jug, full, to judge by the way he held it. The young wife could drain her draught and clutch her herbal pillow with confidence; the drinking was not yet at an end, and her sleep would be solitary and untroubled. Brother Cadfael went to Compline mildly sad, and obscurely comforted.

Only when service was ended, and the brothers on the way to their beds, did he remember that he had left his flask of poppy syrup unstoppered. Not that it would come to any harm in the frosty night, but his sense of fitness drove him to go and remedy the omission before he slept.

His sandalled feet, muffled in strips of woollen cloth for warmth and safety on the frozen paths, made his coming quite silent, and he was already reaching out a hand to the latch of the door, but not yet touching, when he was brought up short and still by the murmur of voices within. Soft, whispering, dreamy voices that made sounds less and more than speech, caresses rather than words, though once at least words surfaced for a moment. A man's voice, young, wary, saying : 'But how if he *does* . . . ?' And a woman's soft, suppressed laughter : 'He'll sleep till morning, never fear!' And her words were suddenly hushed with kissing, and her laughter became huge, ecstatic sighs; the young man's breath heaving triumphantly, but still, a moment later, the note of fear again, half-enjoyed : 'Still, you know him, he *may* . . .' And she, soothing : 'Not for an hour, at least . . . then we'll go . . . it will grow cold here . . .'

That, at any rate, was true; small fear of them wishing to sleep out the night here, even two close-wrapped in one cloak on the bench-bed against the wooden wall. Brother Cadfael withdrew very circumspectly from the herb-garden, and made

173

his way back in chastened thought towards the dortoir. Now he knew who had swallowed that draught of his, and it was not the lady. In the pitcher of wine the young groom had been carrying? Enough for a strong man, even if he had not been drunk already. Meantime, no doubt, the body-servant was left to put his lord to bed, somewhere apart from the chamber where the lady lay supposedly nursing her indisposition and sleeping the sleep of the innocent. Ah, well, it was no business of Cadfael's, nor had he any intention of getting involved. He did not feel particularly censorious. Doubtful if she ever had any choice about marrying Hamo; and with this handsome boy for ever about them, to point the contrast . . . A brief experience of genuine passion, echoing old loves, pricked sharply through the years of his vocation. At least he knew what he was condoning. And who could help feeling some admiration for her opportunist daring, the quick wit that had procured the means, the alert eye that had seized on the most remote and adequate shelter available?

Cadfael went to bed, and slept without dreams, and rose at the Matin bell, some minutes before midnight. The procession of the brothers wound its way down the night stairs into the church, and into the soft, full glow of the lights before St Mary's altar.

Withdrawn reverently some yards from the step of the altar, old Brother Jordan, who should long ago have been in his cell with the rest, kneeled upright with clasped hands and ecstatic face, in which the great, veiled eyes stared full into the light he loved. When Prior Robert exclaimed in concern at finding him there on the stones, and laid a hand on his shoulder, he started as if out of a trance, and lifted to them a countenance itself all light.

'Oh, brothers, I have been so blessed! I have lived through a wonder . . . Praise God that ever it was granted to me! But bear with me, for I am forbidden to speak of it to any, for three days. On the third day from today I may speak . . . !'

'Look, brothers!' wailed Jerome suddenly, pointing. 'Look at the altar!'

Every man present, except Jordan, who still serenely prayed and smiled, turned to gape where Jerome pointed. The tall candles stood secured by drops of their own wax in two small clay dishes, such as Cadfael used for sorting seeds. The two silver lilies were gone from the place of honour.

Through loss, disorder, consternation and suspicion, Prior Robert would still hold fast to the order of the day. Let Hamo FitzHamon sleep in happy ignorance till morning, still Matins and Lauds must be properly celebrated. Christmas was larger than all the giving and losing of silverware. Grimly he saw the services of the church observed, and despatched the brethren back to their beds until Prime, to sleep or lie wakeful and fearful, as they might. Nor would he allow any pestering of Brother Jerome by others, though possibly he did try in private to extort something more satisfactory from the old man. Clearly the theft, whether he knew anything about it or not, troubled Jordan not at all. To everything he said only : 'I am enjoined to silence until midnight of the third day.' And when they asked by whom? he smiled seraphically, and was silent.

It was Robert himself who broke the news to Hamo Fitz-Hamon, in the morning, before Mass. The uproar, though vicious, was somewhat tempered by the after-effects of Cadfael's poppy draught, which dulled the edges of energy, if not of malice. His body-servant, the older groom Sweyn, was keeping well back out of reach, even with Robert still present, and the lady sat somewhat apart, too, as though still frail and possibly a little out of temper. She exclaimed dutifully, and apparently sincerely, at the outrage done to her husband, and echoed his demand that the thief should be hunted down, and the candlesticks recovered. Prior Robert was just as zealous in the matter. No effort should be spared to regain the princely gift, of that they could be sure. He had already made certain of various circumstances which should limit the hunt. There had been a brief fall of snow after Compline, just enough to lay down a clean film of white on the ground. No single footprint had as yet marked this pure layer. He had only to look for himself at the paths leading from both parish doors of the church to see that no one had left by that way. The porter would swear that no one had passed the gatehouse; and on the one side of the abbey grounds not walled, the Meole brook was full and frozen, but the snow on both sides of it was virgin. Within the enclave, of course, tracks and cross-tracks were trodden out everywhere; but no one had left the enclave since Compline, when the candlesticks were still in their place.

'So the miscreant is still within the walls?' said Hamo, glinting vengefully. 'So much the better! Then his booty is still here within, too, and if we have to turn all your abode doors out of dortoirs, we'll find it! It, and him!'

'We will search everywhere,' agreed Robert, 'and question every man. We are as deeply offended as your lordship at this blasphemous crime. You may yourself oversee the search, if you will.'

So all that Christmas Day, alongside the solemn rejoicings in the church, an angry hunt raged about the precincts in full cry. It was not difficult for all the monks to account for their time to the last minute, their routine being so ordered that brother inevitably extricated brother from suspicion; and such as had special duties that took them out of the general view, like Cadfael in his visit to the herb-garden, had all witnesses to vouch for them. The lay brothers ranged more freely, but tended to work in pairs, at least. The servants and the few guests protested their innocence, and if they had not, all of them, others willing to prove it, neither could Hamo prove the contrary. When it came to his own two grooms, there were several witnesses to testify that Sweyn had returned to his bed in the lofts of the stables as soon as he had put his lord to bed, and certainly empty-handed; and Sweyn, as Cadfael noted with interest, swore unblinkingly that young Madoc, who had come in an hour after him, had none the less returned with him, and spent that hour, at Sweyn's order, tending one of the pack-ponies, which showed signs of a cough, and that otherwise they had been together throughout.

A villein instinctively closing ranks with his kind against his lord? wondered Cadfael. Or does Sweyn know very well where that young man was last night, or at least what he was about, and is he intent on protecting him from a worse vengeance? No wonder Madoc looked a shade less merry and ruddy than usual this morning, though on the whole he kept his countenance very well, and refrained from even looking

176

at the lady, while her tone to him was cool, sharp and distant.

Cadfael left them hard at it again after the miserable meal they made of dinner, and went into the church alone. While they were feverishly searching every corner for the candlesticks he had forborne from taking part, but now they were elsewhere he might find something of interest there. He would not be looking for anything so obvious as two large silver candlesticks. He made obeisance at the altar, and mounted the step to look closely at the burning candles. No one had paid any attention to the modest containers that had been substituted for Hamo's gift, and just as well, in the circumstances, that Cadfael's workshop was very little visited, or these little clay pots might have been recognised as coming from there. He moulded and baked them himself as he wanted them. He had no intention of condoning theft, but neither did he relish the idea of any creature, however sinful, falling into Hamo FitzHamon's mercies.

Something long and fine, a thread of silver-gold, was caught and coiled in the wax at the base of one candle. Carefully he detached candle from holder, and unlaced from it a long, pale hair; to make sure of retaining it, he broke off the imprisoning disc of wax with it, and then hoisted and turned the candle to see if anything else was to be found under it. One tiny oval dot showed; with a fingernail he extracted a single seed of lavender. Left in the dish from beforetime? He thought not. The stacked pots were all empty. No, this had been brought here in the fold of a sleeve, most probably, and shaken out while the candle was being transferred.

The lady had plunged both hands with pleasure into the sack of lavender, and moved freely about his workshop investigating everything. It would have been easy to take two of these dishes unseen, and wrap them in a fold of her cloak. Even more plausible, she might have delegated the task to young Madoc, when they crept away from their assignation. Supposing, say, they had reached the desperate point of planning flight together, and needed funds to set them on their way to some safe refuge . . . yes, there were possibilities. In the meantime, the grain of lavender had given Cadfael another idea.

And there was, of course, that long, fine hair, pale as flax, but brighter. The boy was fair. But so fair?

He went out through the frozen garden to his herbarium, shut himself securely into his workshop, and opened the sack of lavender, plunging both arms to the elbow and groping through the chill, smooth sweetness that parted and slid like grain. They were there, well down, his fingers traced the shape first of one, then a second. He sat down to consider what must be done.

Finding the lost valuables did not identify the thief. He could produce and restore them at once, but FitzHamon would certainly pursue the hunt vindictively until he found the culprit; and Cadfael had seen enough of him to know that it might cost life and all before this complainant was satisfied. He needed to know more before he would hand over any man to be done to death. Better not leave the things here, however. He doubted if they would ransack his hut, but they might. He rolled the candlesticks in a piece of sacking, and thrust them into the centre of the pleached hedge where it was thickest. The meagre, frozen snow had dropped with the brief sun. His arm went in to the shoulder, and when he withdrew it, the twigs sprang back and covered all, holding the package securely. Whoever had first hidden it would surely come by night to reclaim it, and show a human face at last.

It was well that he had moved it, for the searchers, driven by an increasingly angry Hamo, reached his hut before Vespers, examined everything within it, while he stood by to prevent actual damage to his medicines, and went away satisfied that what they were seeking was not there. They had not, in fact, been very thorough about the sack of lavender, the candlesticks might well have escaped notice even if he had left them there. It did not occur to anyone to tear the hedges apart, luckily. When they were gone, to probe all the fodder and grain in the barns, Cadfael restored the silver to its original place. Let the bait lie safe in the trap until the quarry came to claim it, as he surely would, once relieved of the fear that the hunters might find it first.

Cadfael kept watch that night. He had no difficulty in absenting himself from the dortoir, once everyone was in bed and asleep. His cell was by the night stairs, and the prior slept at the far end of the long room, and slept deeply. And bitter though the night air was, the sheltered hut was barely colder than his cell, and he kept blankets there for swathing some of his jars and bottles against frost. He took his little box with tinder and flint, and hid himself in the corner behind the door. It might be a wasted vigil; the thief, having survived one day, might think it politic to venture yet another before removing his spoils.

But it was not wasted. He reckoned it might be as late as ten o'clock when he heard a light hand at the door. Two hours before the bell would sound for Matins, almost two hours since the household had retired. Even the guest-hall should be silent and asleep by now, the hour was carefully chosen. Cadfael held his breath, and waited. The door swung open, a shadow stole past him, light steps felt their way unerringly to where the sack of lavender was propped against the wall. Equally silently Cadfael swung the door to again, and set his back against it. Only then did he strike a spark, and hold the blown flame to the wick of his little lamp.

She did not start or cry out, or try to rush past him and escape into the night. The attempt would not have succeeded, and she had had long practice in enduring what could not be cured. She stood facing him as the small flame steadied and burned taller, her face shadowed by the hood of her cloak, the candlesticks clasped possessively to her breast.

'Elfgiva!' said Brother Cadfael gently. And then : 'Are you here for yourself, or for your mistress?' But he thought he knew the answer already. That frivolous young wife would never really leave her rich husband and easy life, however tedious and unpleasant Hamo's attentions might be, to risk everything with her penniless villein lover. She would only keep him to enjoy in secret whenever she felt it safe. Even when the old man died she would submit to marriage at an overlord's will to another equally distasteful. She was not the stuff of which heroines and adventurers are made. This was another kind of woman.

Cadfael went close, and lifted a hand gently to put back the hood from her head. She was tall, a hand's-breadth taller than he, and erect as one of the lilies she clasped. The net that had covered her hair was drawn off with the hood, and a great flood of silver-gold streamed about her in the dim light, framing the pale face and startling blue eyes. Norse hair! The Danes had left their seed as far south as Cheshire, and planted this tall flower among them. She was no longer plain, tired and resigned. In this dim but loving light she shone in austere beauty. Just so must Brother Jordan's veiled eyes have seen her.

'Now I see!' said Cadfael. 'You came into the Lady Chapel, and shone upon our half-blind brother's darkness as you shine here. You are the visitation that brought him awe and bliss, and enjoined silence upon him for three days.'

The voice he had scarcely heard speak a word until then, a voice level, low and beautiful, said : 'I made no claim to be what I am not. It was he who mistook me. I did not refuse the gift.'

'I understand. You had not thought to find anyone there, he took you by surprise as you took him. He took you for Our Lady herself, disposing as she saw fit of what had been given her. And you made him promise you three days' grace.' The lady had plunged her hands into the sack, yes, but Elfgiva had carried the pillow, and a grain or two had filtered through the muslin to betray her.

'Yes,' she said, watching him with unwavering blue eyes.

'So in the end you had nothing against him making known how the candlesticks were stolen.' It was not an accusation, he was pursuing his way to understanding.

But at once she said clearly : 'I did not steal them. I took them. I will restore them – to their owner.'

'Then you don't claim they are yours?'

'No,' she said, 'they are not mine. But neither are they FitzHamon's.'

'Do you tell me,' said Cadfael mildly, 'that there has been no theft at all?'

'Oh, yes,' said Elfgiva, and her pallor burned into a fierce brightness, and her voice vibrated like a harp-string. 'Yes, there has been a theft, and a vile, cruel theft, too, but not here, not now. The theft was a year ago, when FitzHamon received these candlesticks from Alard who made them, his villein, like me. Do you know what the promised price was for these? Manumission for Alard, and marriage with me, what we had begged of him three years and more. Even in villeinage we would have married and been thankful. But he promised freedom! Free man makes free wife, and I was promised, too. But when he got the fine works he wanted, then he refused the promised price. He laughed! I saw, I heard him! He kicked Alard away from him like a dog. So what was his due, and denied him, Alard took. He ran! On St Stephen's Day he ran!'

'And left you behind?' said Cadfael gently.

'What chance had he to take me? Or even to bid me farewell? He was thrust out to manual labour on FitzHamon's other manor. When his chance came, he took it and fled. I was not sad! I rejoiced! Whether I live or die, whether he remembers or forgets me, he is free. No, but in two days more he will be free. For a year and a day he will have been working for his living in his own craft, in a charter borough, and after that he cannot be haled back into servitude, even if they find him.'

'I do not think,' said Brother Cadfael, 'that he will have forgotten you! Now I see why our brother may speak after three days. It will be too late then to try to reclaim a runaway serf. And you hold·that these exquisite things you are cradling belong by right to Alard who made them?'

'Surely,' she said, 'seeing he never was paid for them, they are still his.'

'And you are setting out tonight to take them to him. Yes! As I heard it, they had some cause to pursue him towards London . . . indeed, into London, though they never found him. Have you had better word of him? *From* him?'

The pale face smiled. 'Neither he nor I can read or write. And whom should he trust to carry word until his time is complete, and he is free? No, never any word.'

'But Shrewsbury is also a charter borough, where the unfree may work their way to freedom in a year and a day. And sensible boroughs encourage the coming of good craftsmen, and will go far to hide and protect them. I know! So you think he may be here. And the trail towards London a false trail. True, why should he run so far, when there's help so near? But, daughter, what if you do not find him in Shrewsbury?'

'Then I will look for him elsewhere until I do. I can live as a runaway, too, I have skills, I can make my own way until I do get word of him. Shrewsbury can as well make room for a good seamstress as for a man's gifts, and someone in the silver-smith's craft will know where to find a brother so talented as Alard. I shall find him !'

'And when you do? Oh, child, have you looked beyond that?'

'To the very end,' said Elfgiva firmly. 'If I find him and he no longer wants me, no longer thinks of me, if he is mar-ried and has put me out of his mind, then I will deliver him these things that belong to him, to do with as he pleases, and go my own way and make my own life as best I may without him. And wish well to him as long as I live.'

Oh, no, small fear, she would not be easily forgotten, not in a year, not in many years. 'And if he is utterly glad of you, and loves you still?'

'Then,' she said, gravely smiling, 'if he is of the same mind as I, I have made a vow to Our Lady, who lent me her sem-blance in the old man's eyes, that we will sell these candle-sticks where they may fetch their proper price, and that price shall be delivered to your almoner to feed the hungry. And that will be our gift, Alard's and mine, though no one will ever know it.'

'Our Lady will know it,' said Cadfael, 'and so shall I. Now, how were you planning to get out of this enclave and into Shrewsbury? Both our gates and the town gates are closed until morning.'

She lifted eloquent shoulders. 'The parish doors are not bar-red. And even if I leave tracks, will it matter, provided I find a safe hiding-place inside the town?'

'And wait in the cold of the night? You would freeze before morning. No, let me think. We can do better for you than that.'

Her lips shaped : 'We?' in silence, wondering, but quick to understand. She did not question his decisions, as he had not questioned hers. He thought he would long remember the slow, deepening smile, the glow of warmth mantling her cheeks. 'You believe me!' she said.

'Every word! Here, give me the candlesticks, let me wrap them, and do you put up your hair again in net and hood. We've had no fresh snow since morning, the path to the parish door is well trodden, no one will know your tracks among the many. And, girl, when you come to the town end of the bridge there's a little house off to the left, under the wall, close to the town gate. Knock there and ask for shelter over the night till the gates open, and say that Brother Cadfael sent you. They know me, I doctored their son when he was sick. They'll give you a warm corner and a place to lie, for kindness' sake, and ask no questions, and answer none from others, either. And likely they'll know where to find the silversmiths of the town, to set you on your way.'

She bound up her pale, bright hair and covered her head, wrapping the cloak about her, and was again the maidservant in homespun. She obeyed without question his every word, moved silently at his back round the great court by way of the shadows, halting when he halted, and so he brought her to the church, and let her out by the parish door into the public street, still a good hour before Matins. At the last moment she said, close at his shoulder within the half-open door : 'I shall be grateful always. Some day I shall send you word.'

'No need for words,' said Brother Cadfael, 'if you send me the sign I shall be waiting for. Go now, quickly, there's not a soul stirring.'

She was gone, lightly and silently, flitting past the abbey gatehouse like a tall shadow, towards the bridge and the town. Cadfael closed the door softly, and went back up the night stairs to the dortoir, too late to sleep, but in good time to rise at the sound of the bell, and return in procession to celebrate Matins.

There was, of course, the resultant uproar to face next morning, and he could not afford to avoid it, there was too much at stake. Lady FitzHamon naturally expected her maid to be in attendance as soon as she opened her eyes, and raised a petulant outcry when there was no submissive shadow waiting to dress her and do her hair. Calling failed to summon and search to find Elfgiva, but it was an hour or more before it dawned on the lady that she had lost her accomplished maid for good. Furiously she made her own toilet, unassisted, and raged out to complain to her husband, who had risen before her, and was waiting for her to accompany him to Mass. At her angry declaration that Elfgiva was nowhere to be found, and must have run away during the night, he first scoffed, for why should a sane girl take herself off into a killing frost when she had warmth and shelter and enough to eat where she was? Then he made the inevitable connection, and let out a roar of rage.

'Gone, is she? And my candlesticks gone with her, I dare swear! So it was *she*! The foul little thief! But I'll have her yet, I'll drag her back, she shall not live to enjoy her ill-gotten gains. . . .'

It seemed likely that the lady would heartily endorse all this; her mouth was already open to echo him when Brother Cadfael, brushing her sleeve close as the agitated brothers ringed the pair, contrived to shake a few grains of lavender on to her wrist. Her mouth closed abruptly. She gazed at the tiny things for the briefest instant before she shook them off, she flashed an even briefer glance at Brother Cadfael, caught his eye, and heard in a rapid whisper : 'Madam, softly! – proof of the maid's innocence is also proof of the mistress's.'

She was by no means a stupid woman. A second quick glance confirmed what she had already grasped, that there was one man here who had a weapon to hold over her at least as deadly as any she could use against Elfgiva. She was also a woman of decision, and wasted no time in bitterness once her course was chosen. The tone in which she addressed her lord was almost as sharp as that in which she had complained of Elfgiva's desertion.

'She your thief, indeed! That's folly, as you should very well know. The girl is an ungrateful fool to leave me, but a thief she never has been, and certainly is not this time. She can't possibly have taken the candlesticks, you know well enough when they vanished, and you know I was not well that night, and went early to bed. She was with me until long after Brother Prior discovered the theft. I asked her to stay

184

with me until you came to bed. *As you never did!*' she ended tartly. 'You may remember!'

Hamo probably remembered very little of that night; certainly he was in no position to gainsay what his wife so roundly declared. He took out a little of his ill-temper on her, but she was not so much in awe of him that she dared not reply in kind. Of course she was certain of what she said! *She* had not drunk herself stupid at the lord abbot's table, she had been nursing a bad head of another kind, and even with Brother Cadfael's remedies she had not slept until after midnight, and Elfgiva had then been still beside her. Let him hunt a runaway maidservant, by all means, the thankless hussy, but never call her a thief, for she was none.

Hunt her he did, though with less energy now it seemed clear he would not recapture his property with her. He sent his grooms and half the lay servants off in both directions to enquire if anyone had seen a solitary girl in a hurry; they were kept at it all day, but they returned empty-handed.

The party from Lidyate, less one member, left for home next day. Lady FitzHamon rode demurely behind young Madoc, her cheek against his broad shoulders; she even gave Brother Cadfael the flicker of a conspiratorial smile as the cavalcade rode out of the gates, and detached one arm from round Madoc's waist to wave as they reached the roadway. So Hamo was not present to hear when Brother Jordan, at last released from his vow, told how Our Lady had appeared to him in a vision of light, fair as an angel, and taken away with her the candlesticks that were hers to take and do with as she would, and how she had spoken to him, and enjoined on him his three days of silence. And if there were some among the listeners who wondered whether the fair woman had not been a more corporeal being, no one had the heart to say so to Jordan, whose vision was comfort and consolation for the fading of the light.

That was at Matins, at midnight of the day of St Stephen's. Among the scattering of alms handed in at the gatehouse next morning for the beggars, there was a little basket that weighed surprisingly heavily. The porter could not remember who had brought it, taking it to be some offerings of

185

food or old clothing, like all the rest; but when it was opened it sent Brother Oswald, almost incoherent with joy and wonder, running to Abbot Heribert to report what seemed to be a miracle. For the basket was full of gold coin, to the value of more than a hundred marks. Well used, it would ease all the worst needs of his poorest petitioners, until the weather relented.

'Surely,' said Brother Oswald devoutly, 'Our Lady has made her own will known. Is not this the sign we have hoped for?'

Certainly it was for Cadfael, and earlier than he had dared to hope for it. He had the message that needed no words. She had found him, and been welcomed with joy. Since midnight Alard the silversmith had been a free man, and free man makes free wife. Presented with such a woman as Elfgiva, he could give as gladly as she, for what was gold, what was silver, by comparison?

Anthony Price

THE BOUDICCA KILLING

A foolish boy throws a stone at his brother on the mountain-
side, and starts an avalanche – that is how it begins. Not by
accident, but not by deliberate intent either.

A syndicate of City financiers complains that it has been
cheated over certain military and civilian contracts in Britain.

The complaint is unofficial (which it has to be, for no
actual law has been broken), but the complainants are determined to make trouble for the man who has beaten them at
their own game. So they maintain piously that, just as their
lost investment in the new province was originally undertaken
for patriotic rather than commercial reasons, now their sole
concern is for the welfare of the state, that first and highest
duty of every citizen.

Thus is the stone cast, and the avalanche set in motion.

At first, however, it is no more than a shiver on the loose
scree of the hillside. For if the syndicate has indirectly sustained a great loss over its British investment, many others
have also lost their money – and directly – as a result of the
terrible insurrection in that unhappy province.

Two colonies of veterans have been destroyed; vast quan-
tities of military stores and private goods have gone up in
smoke during the sack of Londinium; many thousands of per-
sons, both citizens and freemen, not to mention valuable slaves,
have been massacred – in effect, both debtors and their
property; and many other debtors among the native aristoc-
racy are now proscribed rebels, whose wealth (such as remains
of it) is the legitimate booty of the armed forces, which not
even Caesar himself may safely appropriate.

Yet once in motion, an avalanche may not be hindered –
and a fiscal investigation is inexorable.

This is not because the fiscal inspectors set any store what-soever by the syndicate's patriotism; nor are they usually very interested, all things being equal, in the particular identity of contract-holders, provided such men pay their taxes.

Yet they are also by nature intensely suspicious men, and Gnaeus Alfrenius Cotta is a new name in their files.

Gn. Alfrenius Cotta, recently in a modest way of business in Ostia, but now a major financial power in the City.

Gn. Alfrenius Cotta, who has made a fortune out of Britain, where everyone else had lost money.

Gn. Alfrenius Cotta, who (so it transpires) knows how the dice will fall before they have been thrown.

I : *In the City*

The Colonel of *Arcani* goes to that office between the Capito-line and the Palatine where such briefings are held, under orders to proceed without delay to that Province.

There are present three senior fiscal clerks, together with the Sub-prefect of the Imperial Courier Service, and a freedman from the Palace (whom the Colonel instantly identifies as one of Caesar's principal secretaries-of-state).

One of the clerks speaks first.

He sketches the course of the late British insurrection; which the Colonel understands better than any fiscal clerk, not only because such things are his business but also because he has served in Britain, which (he surmises) is why he is now under orders for the island, and not Hierosolyma (where there is also trouble, as usual).

The clerk concludes : 'Colonel, it amounts to this : after the despatches of the late Decianus Catus, Procurator of the Pro-vince, we received the first true account of the situation from the noble Governor, Gaius Suetonius Paulinus.'

That is good, thinks the Colonel. Caesar's justice has made Decianus 'the late' and Suetonius 'the noble' – which is as things should be.

'By that time the *colonia* at Camulodunum has been des-troyed – '

'And one whole battlegroup of the Ninth Legion,' says the

second clerk, the one with rabbit's teeth. 'Three regular cohorts of the line – *obliterated!*'

He makes it sound like an entry on the wrong side of one of his ledgers. Which for him no doubt it is, thinks the Colonel bitterly. The best footsloggers in the world are . . . expensive -- to a clerk.

'They were ambushed on the march, in wooded country,' adds Rabbit's-teeth. 'It's a situation the legions have never learned to handle. Varus couldn't – and they still can't.'

So Rabbit's-teeth is an amateur tactician. And the nearest thing Rabbit's-teeth has seen to 'wooded country' is the Garden of Lucullus.

The Sub-prefect, who has served in Germany, has the grace to look uncomfortable; the Colonel, who has served in Britain and knows that hell is a dank, dripping, trackless undergrowth without end, merely smiles politely and asks to see the Governor's despatch.

It is short, and to the point.

And, although it is from the noble Governor himself, who one week later won the greatest victory of the reign, over a British horde outnumbering his army ten-to-one, it smells unmistakably of Roman defeat, disaster and death.

Decianus Catus, Procurator of Britain, has fled the Province. The Twentieth Legion has disobeyed orders, failing to march to the Governor's aid, and the Second is too far away; the Ninth (what is left of it) is closely besieged in its camp. Consequently, the Governor must abandon Londinium and Verulamium, which are now indefensible, and retire to his field army in the north-west – one tired Legion with its auxiliary regiments.

If Queen Boudicca and her savages catch him on the road, or if she ambushes his army (shades of Rabbit's-teeth !) before he can conduct that army to his chosen battle-ground, or if she waits ten days until his supplies are exhausted, then Rome in Britain is finished. That must be faced, and plans laid accordingly by Caesar.

Alternately, within seven days, if the Gods favour Rome, the Governor will have the honour of laying a great victory at the feet of Caesar.

So . . . the Governor writes of victory, but expects defeat, like a gambler throwing against a Venus. It is a dead man's despatch, with expectation overshadowing hope.

'Is that clear, Colonel?' says the first clerk.

The room is cooler now. In his youth the Colonel has seen (as the clerks and the freedman have not seen, though the Sub-prefect may have seen) what the savages do to their prisoners. And, remembering a grove on the high chalk downs, he recalls particularly how ingenious the British women were in impaling a young officer of the Batavians, who was his special friend, who was still alive when –

No! That is not a proper memory for a Colonel of the *Arcani*.

The Colonel nods.

'Very well.' The first clerk accepts the nod. 'When the syndicate heard the contents of that despatch, which they did within an hour of its receipt – '

Now the Colonel understands more : one of Caesar's chief ministers is in the syndicate.

' – they commenced to offer their contracts on the open market in the City. And their provincial debts.'

'At a reduced rate?' asks the Colonel, deliberately insulting.

'Not initially . . . You must remember, Colonel, that Decianus Catus had made light of the rising in *his* despatches. Rather, he emphasised the number of slaves taken during the Governor's campaign in the north-west – and the gold mines of the new territories . . . The syndicate made it sound as though they were putting new shares on the market, with new areas for capital development.'

The Colonel nods again, dutifully. High finance isn't so very different from betting on the races : the biggest wins are always to be made on outsiders.

But this race has to be different – and the Sub-prefect is looking decidedly uncomfortable.

'Someone talked?'

Even the first clerk looks uncomfortable. Imperial couriers who talk only talk once – or twice, the second time being when they admit that they talked. Which is positively the last time that they ever talk.

'And then the market fell – and Cotta started to buy?' The Colonel is beginning to enjoy himself, and to like Gn. Alfrenius Cotta, who has evidently beaten the official odds.

'Not immediately . . . The market was nervous – Decianus Catus has a bad name – '

'Nobody bought.' It is the third clerk who speaks, a goat-faced man who has been silent hitherto. 'British investments have never been attractive. The slaves are unsatisfactory, and the cost of mineral extraction is high unless it's under local control. And the loan repayments from the local aristocracies have been unreliable. We should never have invaded the island.'

Rabbit's-teeth nods to that. 'So the syndicate dropped its prices. And then the details of that despatch leaked out – '

'The bottom dropped out of the market,' says Goat-face. 'On the second day – in the afternoon.'

'And then Cotta bought?'

'No,' says Goat-face. 'Then he started to *borrow*.'

'To – borrow?'

'Yes, Colonel. You see – you must understand – this man Cotta is . . . was . . . nothing special, financially speaking . . . Mostly import-export, Massilia-Ostia. Plus a few contracts the bigger groups had missed – only four in Britain – '

'His agent there is his nephew, his sister's son,' supplements Rabbit's-teeth eagerly. 'The youth has – *had* – a minor post on the staff of the Procurator, Decianus Catus – '

'The *late* Decianus Catus,' murmurs Goat-face. 'But . . . the point is, he had no cash on hand. He had to borrow in order to buy.'

'More than borrow,' amends Rabbit's-teeth. 'He called in all his debts – he mortgaged all his property . . . And then he took out second mortgages. He sold his villa at Praenestina – '

'At a loss,' says the first clerk.

'At a loss. And then he mortgaged his sister's property,' says Rabbit's-teeth. 'And *then* he borrowed on the open market!'

Goat-face gestures abruptly. 'He went beyond all reason and prudence – he borrowed on risk-cargoes in transit, even. And he has a reputation in Ostia for good sense – sharp, but sensible – '

'Which helped his credit in Ostia.' Rabbit's-teeth nods.

'He even borrowed from the syndicate – ' Goat-face smiles. 'Short-term, high interest – they took him for a stupid provincial, and he took *them* – '

'But he didn't buy openly,' says Rabbit's-teeth. 'It was all through nominees – more provincials.'

'He bought everything they had, including that palace we're building for the client-king in the south,' says Goat-face. 'By the eighth day – all signed, sealed and delivered. Plus a dozen other contracts from . . . other groups.'

The Prince's ministers had sold out too, naturally.

'He owns half the Province now,' says Rabbit's-teeth. 'If he had a son he'd have to call the child "Britannicus".'

'But he has no son. Only that nephew, whom he exiled to Britain because they mistrusted each other,' murmurs the first clerk. 'Tiberius Alfrenius Martinus . . . Britannicus . . .'

It adds up to one conclusion, and one only. They have been at pains to make that clear.

'So – he knew,' says the Colonel.

'He knew.' Goat-face nods. '*And he knew before we did.*'

It is Goat-face who is the senior clerk, the Colonel decides. It irritates him that he did not guess that more quickly.

But now he does not wish to compound that error.

The despatch he has seen was not the latest despatch, there has to be another –

Queen Boudicca dead, her Army destroyed, the Province saved!

The noble Governor, Gaius Suetonius Paulinus, would have sent that despatch no less quickly than its predecessor. It would have taken maybe a day or two longer, travelling from the battlefield, but it would have taken the same route, under the same absolute priority of the imperial Governor's seal – courier, and fast galley, and courier; relay after relay, the best men on the fastest horses, along the imperial highways. Ever since the Varus disaster, fifty years before, when there had been disgraceful scenes of panic in the City, bad news had always been brought to Caesar first, before being released to the Senate; and even good news, travelling on its own fair wind, is supposed to reach the Palatine Hill first.

192

But if that has been compromised then the Sub-prefect should be looking more unhappy . . .

Which he is not. (And Caesar's freedman hasn't spoken a word either, yet; but then his job is to listen and report back, no more, of course.)

So the Colonel says nothing. And for a moment or two no one else wishes to speak, either.

'And that is the sum of our problem,' says Goat-face finally. (Naturally, it must be Goat-face.) 'He knew – but he could not have known.'

Rabbit's-teeth surreptitiously signs himself against evil.

The first clerk speaks : 'It is the time factor, Colonel . . . No one in his right mind would have risked what Alfrenius Cotta did, unless he was certain. Because he pledged himself, and his freedom, and his life . . . and his family – '

'Three times over,' cuts in Rabbit's-teeth, actuarially.

'But he is in his right mind,' says Goat-face. 'Yet he started raising money *before* Boudicca was defeated. And he began buying *before* the victory despatch had crossed the Narrow Sea to Gaul – '

'Which leaves us with only two explanations,' says Rabbit's-teeth. 'First . . . sorcery – of the worst kind !'

'Um . . . present knowledge of a future event, that is,' says the first clerk. 'The supernatural.'

'Of which there have been cases – well-authenticated cases – ' Rabbit's-teeth is cut off by a look from Goat-face.

'Well-authenticated cases . . . *after* the event.' Goat-face looks at the Colonel dispassionately. 'But there has *never* been a case where the immortal Gods have helped a small business-man to make a large fortune while Caesar himself is sacrificing on the Altar of Victory in the hope of a sign from heaven.'

Rabbit's-teeth is crestfallen. Caesar's freedman begins to look interested.

Goat-face continues to observe the Colonel. 'The noble Governor's despatch foreshadowed a great defeat. But some-one else evidently knew better – and what is more, he knew better enough to convince Gnaeus Alfrenius Cotta, who is certainly nobody's fool, that he knew better, Colonel.'

No one rejects this reasoning.

'Now . . . I think I know *who*, Colonel . . . since there is only one person who could have known.'

The Colonel begins to understand what is required of him. 'What I need to know is *how* – '

The imbecile innocence of the Sub-prefect's expression confirms the understanding : his service has not failed twice.

' – and I want to know quickly.' Goat-face's voice is like marble. 'So . . . this day you will leave the City, carrying Caesar's formal congratulations to the noble Governor, Gaius Suetonius Paulinus – '

II : *In the Province*

Britain is different from Germany in the early autumn. In a few weeks it will be bare, and every gutter will be choked with fallen leaves, but now it is a riot of red and yellow and gold, where Germany is an eternal dark green.

These are the colours which the Colonel remembers, when the world was young and he was a junior staff officer of auxiliaries.

But now it is different in a different way, with the fresh scars of hastily dug ditches and the raw wood of new palisades around every halt on the road to Londinium ; and the town itself a burnt-out horror smelling of damp ash and rotting flesh, in which he sleeps under canvas for one night only, thankful to obey the letter of his orders to the last syllable.

Except that what follows, as he moves on towards the noble Governor's field headquarters, is worse, even allowing for the satisfaction of the crowded prison camps in which the women and children are held (there are no male adult prisoners in the forward areas ; the Gallic irregular cavalry are spearheading the mopping-up operations, and they are head-hunters by both inclination and religion, and they are earning their bounty-money ; so . . . satisfaction and yet death and devastation are always depressing, even when justly imposed on the guilty – and these natives are undeniably guilty).

But tonight he is dining with the Governor himself, as befits his Praetorian rank and his status as Caesar's honoured messenger, carrying greetings from the Roman Senate and People. (What the Governor does not know is that his is a political mission : Caesar has no use for governors who win victories which take the imagination of the Roman Senate and People, such men must be cut down to smaller size – Goat-face has made that abundantly clear in private, with the freedman's nod.

(And that makes his task both distasteful and difficult; distasteful, because he admires the noble Governor's brilliant victory over odds; and difficult . . .

(Difficult, because there is not one shred of evidence so far that the noble Governor has conspired with Tiberius Alfrenius Martinus – and Gnaeus Alfrenius Cotta – to execute a gigantic fraud on Caesar and the City . . .

(Difficult, because the dates check out – the noble Governor was still fighting when Gn. Alfrenius Cotta was borrowing . . .

(Difficult, because when the noble Governor abandoned Londinium nobody, but *nobody*, knew which way Boudicca was marching; indeed, if anything, the consensus was that she would destroy the Governor and his army first, and the town afterwards, for which very sensible reason ten thousand Roman settlers and friendly tribesmen remained there, hoping for the best, and died there very unpleasantly when she stormed the decaying ramparts before chasing the Governor . . .

(*So* difficult that Colonel is almost of a mind to agree with Rabbit's-teeth on the matter of sorcery . . .

(Almost, but not quite. For Tiberius Alfrenius Martinus, nephew to Gnaeus Alfrenius Cotta and formerly a tax accountant with the late, unlamented Procurator, Decianus Catus, is now the trusted military secretary of the noble Governor. And that, in the circumstances of the Procurator's behaviour, is a very curious promotion, which makes no sense at all . . .

(And which, therefore, requires investigation.)

So . . . now the Colonel is dining with the noble Governor, and the last of the food has been removed, and the small talk, though it is apparently continuing, is in fact over –

'Wasn't that young Alfrenius Martinus I saw taking notes at your briefing this afternoon, my lord?' inquires the Colonel conversationally.

'My secretary?' The noble Governor is mellowed by the wine and the day's gratifying head-count. 'You know him?'

'I know his uncle slightly – one of the coming men in the City . . . But I thought young Martinus was on Catus's staff?'

The Governor frowns momentarily, and then smiles in quick succession, no doubt thinking first of his former procurator, whose crass stupidity caused the insurrection, and then of the fate of both procurator and insurrectionists.

'Yes, so he was. But . . .'

The Colonel listens as the Governor, wine-mellowed, talks –

It had been just after the news had been confirmed that the Twentieth Legion hadn't marched : what had already become a serious tribal uprising was something far worse now – it had a Varus-disaster premonition about it now.

The Governor was desperately tired, quite drained by bad news; and, what was worse, he knew he was beginning to despair. Also, the last of the galleys was waiting to slip its moorings, and he had a despatch (which he now believed would be the last of his career) to send aboard, but he had no one to take it down in writing for him.

'Who?' he snapped at the Guards sergeant.

'Alfrenius Martinus – Tiberius Alfrenius Martinus, my lord.'

He didn't want to see anyone, and the name meant nothing to him. But he knew that fear was infectious, and he must not let it spread from him.

'Very well – I'll see him.'

He turned away, waiting until the sergeant had made himself scarce.

Tiberius what-was-his-name was youngish and short and rather fat, and he wore an ill-fitting uniform, and the smell of the infection was already on him.

'Yes?'

Martinus saluted self-consciously and badly, and began to explain what he was, rather than who. Which was a mistake, because at the mention of the Procurator's name the Governor cut him off brutally.

'You are too late. Your master has run for it – and I'm damned if I'm giving you a place on the despatches galley.

Get out!' It was a measure of the Governor's weariness that this death sentence gave him no special satisfaction.

But Martinus stood firm. 'I wasn't too late. I chose to stay, sir.'

'Oh?' The words registered only partially. 'Then that was very foolish of you.'

Martinus swayed, as though embarrassed. 'My . . . my father was a soldier. A-and his father – my grandfather – was a soldier.' He blinked. 'It would have been . . . dishonourable.'

The Governor discovered that he could still be surprised. The fellow was sweating with fright, and he was also ridiculous. But he was nevertheless volunteering to die with his betters – a bloody tax-man – and *that* wasn't ridiculous.

'I know I'm no soldier' – Martinus blinked again – 'but they said . . . in the Officers' Mess . . . that your secretary had run away. So I thought – ' He stopped suddenly, and seemed to take his fear, if not his courage, in both hands. 'They said, if the Army is to have a chance, then Boudicca must attack Londinium first. But they don't think she will . . . But I think there's a way, sir . . .'

The Governor nodded, speechlessly. It would be stupid, whatever it was, it would be stupid. But he mustn't laugh, because this man's 'honour' was like a flower on a dunghill – and his fear was something they possessed in common. So he mustn't laugh.

'Sir – if Boudicca believes that the Procurator is still here in the town . . . They say he had her flogged under her own roof – if she thought he was still here – '

The Governor felt a pang of disappointment. In spite of himself, in spite of instinct and appearances, he had hoped for a miracle.

'Martinus . . .' He edited out the sharpness. 'Martinus, this city – this town – is full of spies. He's gone, the bastard – and they saw him go, Martinus.'

'Yes, sir.' Martinus nodded. 'But not all of them – and the ones who didn't will want to report that he's still here. If we give them something to report – if we give them rumours even . . . We could say the galley grounded in the estuary, and you'd had him brought back – and we could put guards on his house

. . . Just a rumour, sir – that might be enough to decide her . . . Just the outside chance of taking him *alive* – '

Plainly ridiculous. Boudicca knew well enough that Catus had run away, and even if she didn't then the obvious military logic of attacking the army first was the only thing that made sense.

And yet –

'Just the chance, sir.' Martinus bared his teeth. 'If she could lay her hands on him . . .'

Yet there was something about this little fellow which lent force to his words.

Suddenly the Governor caught the undertone of anger beneath the fear.

So that was it, then : if Tiberius Something Martinus had Decianus Catus in his hands now, the bastard would die as slowly as if he'd fallen to Boudicca, Queen of the Iceni!

It had never occurred to him to take such elemental passions into the reckoning, to be weighed against the better strategy. Yet if the image of Decianus Catus impaled living on a sharpened stake could fire a snivelling tax-man, how much more might a well-placed rumour distort Boudicca's judgement?

He was clutching at straws. But they were all he had.

He was also staring poor little Martinus out of countenance.

But he felt better –

'I have a despatch to send. Can you take dictation?'

'Sir?' Martinus stiffened. 'Yes, sir !'

'After that . . . we'll see what we can do with your rumours.' Absurdly, the Governor felt much better. The thought of Martinus drawing his rusty sword against a great hairy Briton might be laughable, but he had seven thousand heavy infantry up the road from this doomed town – Roman infantry, the true Rome – who knew how to use their swords. And Martinus could meanwhile draw his pen to good effect to settle Decianus Catus, whatever the outcome.

The little man was trying to speak again.

'Yes?'

'I was wondering, sir . . . Might I send a private letter – two private letters – with your despatch?' He fumbled beneath the armour. 'I have them here, sir. For you to read.'

'What?' The Governor found he had accepted the letters.

'To my mother, sir. I – I am her only son . . . And – and to my uncle, sir. She is a widow.'

The Governor read the two letters, and as he read them the last of his tiredness and fear fell away from him.

This – *this* – was also the true Rome, here in this unprepossessing little pen-pusher, as surely as in his unbeatable footsloggers.

And these were words he would never forget.

'Very well – send them.' He returned the letters. 'But now – '

Now they were going to beat that damned woman Boudicca.

And that, says the noble Governor, was what they did.

III : *In the Forward Headquarters*

The Colonel is still following the noble Governor into the newly pacified – totally devastated – territory of the Iceni two days later (with that damned woman only a dark memory now), and it is raining. (And that is another thing the Colonel recalls from '96 – the rain.) Off the log corduroys of the camp the lines are already halfway to quagmires.

But the tent of Tiberius Alfrenius Martinus, with its charcoal brazier and its plank floor, is snug and warm – as befits that of the Governor's chief secretary, whom the Governor has been pleased to honour with the rank of acting-colonel for the duration of the emergency.

The chief secretary/acting-colonel is busy drafting tomorrow's operational orders when the Colonel enters the tent.

(The chief secretary/acting-colonel is also still in uniform too, which seems to support the camp joke – that he is so proud of his armour that he sleeps in it. But then it is better-fitting now, the Colonel notes.)

He looks up at his visitor, clearly a little irritated at this interruption of his work. He is a world away – a great victory away, and the Governor's favour away, and a private fortune away – from the frightened tax-man of former days.

So shock tactics are called for : the Colonel tosses his Imperial warrant on to the table, with its seal of life and death uppermost.

To the slave at Martinus's shoulder he says : 'Get out.'

The slave has never seen that seal, and perhaps Martinus hasn't either. But he has heard of it.

'Leave us,' he orders his slave. Then : 'Can I help you, Colonel?'

'You can. And you will.' The Colonel looks round for a seat. There is a stool piled with papers – quartermaster's reports, muster rolls, casualty lists and head-count tallies. He tips them on to the floor and sits down opposite Martinus.

'I don't know how you did it, Tiberius Alfrenius Martinus. But I know you did it somehow.'

Martinus says nothing.

'And I know that you are a liar.'

Still nothing.

'A considerable liar. Not an only son, for example. And your father was a tally-clerk. And his father was also a tally-clerk. For a start – a considerable liar, Tiberius Alfrenius Martinus.'

Martinus smiles . . . as if to say that these are minor matters now.

'Very well !' The stool is uncomfortable. 'Then I'll tell you a story, Tiberius Alfrenius Martinus . . .

'There was once a tax official – a *junior* tax official – who was sent to the south coast of Britain, to Noviomagus, to collect the Procurator's share of the palace contractors' bribes. But when he got back to Londinium – not without difficulty – he found that a revolt had broken out – '

Martinus stirs suddenly, as though he wants to speak.

'No! Don't spoil my story !' The Colonel cuts him off. 'This *very junior* tax official also finds that his master, the Procurator, has already run away. And there is only one galley left . . . and when he tries to bribe his way aboard – with the Noviomagus gold – he is turned away with a sharp sword. Because the last galley is reserved for the Governor's last despatch . . . and no one – no one else – and least of all a damned tax official – is going aboard, at any price.

'So *he* – our minor cog in the broken wheel of Decianus Catus – *he* then goes in despair to the Governor's headquarters, to see if his gold will buy safety there.

'But it won't. Because gold has lost its value in Londinium. It won't buy a berth on the last galley. And all the roads are

cut now, anyway. And the Governor himself is about to abandon the town and march to almost certain defeat, if Boudicca
keeps her head and does the right thing. And then the town
will fall.

'So when he offers his gold to the officers they just laugh at
him – and offer him a breast-plate two sizes too big and a
nasty sharp sword – No! Don't deny it, Tiberius Alfrenius
Martinus – I've talked to them, and I know what happened!'

The stool is quite excruciating, really.

'But now it becomes interesting, because we come to what I
don't know . . . Because you went to the Governor, and you
suggested to him how he might lure Boudicca to Londinium
while he chose his battlefield – very good!

'And you sent two letters by his courier – two Roman letters
to warm the heart of a Roman general on the eve of battle –

*'Mother – I write to you on the eve of battle. I hope to serve
with honour, fighting beside my General and Governor, the
noble Gaius Suetonius Paulinus. Know that I shall not dis-
grace Father's memory, and that, should I fall, my last thought
but one will be of you, and my last of Rome, the Great Mother
of us all. Your loving and dutiful son, Tiberius*

*'Uncle – I write to you on the eve of the battle. The odds are
against us. If I should fall, I charge you by the glorious memory
of my father, your brother, who also gave his life for Rome, to
comfort and sustain my dear mother. Your dutiful nephew,
Tiberius*

' – letters engraved on that general's heart,' continues the
Colonel, gazing on Martinus not without admiration.

'But what is engraved on my heart is . . . that you are a most
ingenious and absolute liar, Tiberius Alfrenius Martinus – and
I want to know *what was in the letters you actually sent*, not
in those which you showed to the Governor.'

He leans forward and taps the seal on the warrant to emphasise this request. But now there is a cast of obstinacy in
Martinus's expression : on the strength of his acting-rank, and
the Governor's favour, and his new wealth, he is still inclined
to cover his dice with his cup and bet on them.

'Pardon me, Colonel – I know of no letters – a few small . . .
inaccuracies, perhaps – slips of the tongue made in a moment

of enthusiasm, no more. But the Governor will forgive them, Colonel. And I know that I have committed no crime' – his eyes flick for an instant to the seal – 'no crime whatsoever, Colonel.'

No crime. And he has the Governor nicely calculated : the noble Gaius Suetonius Paulinus will never admit being taken for a fool by this man, it will be against the dignity of his great victory.

Martinus knows that. He strokes his breast-plate as if to emphasise his knowledge. Nothing can be proved, and the past will bury the past. He is guilty, but safe.

'So, Colonel – ?' The pudgy little hand continues to massage the gilded bronze, which no gentleman would wear at such an hour – certainly no officer –

In that moment the Colonel sees his way, towards which that hand has pointed.

Under his bronze, Martinus must be frightened, because everyone is frightened by that seal.

Under that bronze is a man who knows his law and his rights as a citizen. But not his military law, for a guess –

And under that bronze is a snob, a parvenue and a social climber – as might be expected of a junior tax official –

So . . . the stick and the carrot.

'No crime?' The Colonel pretends to be comfortable. 'It is our belief, as the facts indicate, that you entered into direct communication with the woman Boudicca, without your commander's knowledge or consent . . . whereby you obtained details of her plans, on which you acted – '

'No – '

'*And*, under military law in the field, and in uniform – and with your rank – on my authority alone I can have you flogged and crucified, Tiberius Alfrenius Martinus. Which will get you conveniently out of the Governor's way – '

'*No* – '

The stick has landed squarely on those white buttocks. The man doesn't know his military law – but he has seen what the scourge and the cross-tree can do to a man.

'*But* . . . Caesar is merciful.' Now for the carrot : the Colonel balances himself carefully. 'And he is also grateful – '

Martinus's battle line is bending : surprise has joined fear in the frontal assault.

'Grateful. For it was *you* who put backbone into the noble Governor, Tiberius Alfrenius Martinus – it was you who saved Britain with your treason !'

One last reinforcement is needed. The Colonel calls it up.

'Your uncle is a crude person – rich now, but still crude. Your family's influence requires proper representation in the City . . . In the equestrian order at once . . . and, in due time, in the Senate itself.' By a miracle the words do not choke their speaker. 'All we need to know, before your equestrian sponsors are nominated, is . . . exactly how you know what Boudicca was going to do, sir.'

The line is shattered. Dreams of gentility are too much for it.

'But . . . that is to say . . . I didn't actually *know* . . .'

It is a moment to hold one's breath. And smile, as one colonel to another, encouragingly.

'You are right – I came back, and *he* had gone – ' There is the flare of anger which the Governor saw. 'He had gone, and they laughed at me. I could have crucified him – '

So the Governor had been right, too !

'And I could have crucified my uncle with him – for sending me to this filthy place !'

But the Governor had also been quite wrong too, evidently.

'Then . . . one of the officers said . . . he said I needn't worry. Because in a few days' time we'd all be heroes – or we'd all be dead . . . if we were lucky . . . He said the Governor needed a secretary, and if he took me on at least it would be quick – win or lose – when *she* caught up with us. *Aut Caesar, aut nihil* – one way or the other –

'So I wrote the letters – the real ones –

'*Mother – Do exactly what I order, no more and no less. In two days' time take the enclosed letter to my uncle, Alfrenius Cotta, together with all the monies I have remitted to you to hold for me. Tell him you have just received the letter and instruction from a stranger. Do not tell him of the delay. Do not fail me. Destroy this letter at once. Your loving son, Tiberius*

'Uncle – In haste. The Army has won a great victory. Lon-dinium and the two veterans' colonies have been destroyed, but the rest of the Province is substantially undamaged. I am acting as the Governor's secretary and will delay his victory despatch for six days. I send this letter in advance by a secure messenger. My mother brings it to you with my savings to invest in Britain at your discretion. Act quickly to make us rich. Your dutiful nephew, Tiberius'

The Colonel looks at Martinus incredulously. 'You didn't know?'

Martinus spreads his hands. 'Nobody knew, Colonel. But they all said – all the officers said – that these savages only have one big battle in them. We couldn't get away ... so they'd either wipe us out completely, like Varus. Or we'd smash them to pieces – '

'But you didn't know, man – '

'I knew it would be one way or the other. And if I was wrong, then I bloody well wouldn't be there to admit it. But if I was right – I'd be rich, Colonel.'

'So you gave him your money?'

Martinus smiles. 'I had to make him believe me – and if there's one thing my dear uncle believes, it's money. So I bought his belief with my savings, Colonel – it was an invest-ment, you might say.'

'But you could have ruined him – ?'

'Yes. And that was also part of the investment.' Another, colder memory freezes the smile. 'He would have been ruined – and I would have been dead – '

Martinus pauses for a moment to listen to the incessant sound of the rain on the canvas above him.

' – Dead. But also avenged on him for condemning me to death on this frightful island, Colonel.'

Beyond the downpour there is the distant noise of the Gallic irregulars celebrating drunkenly over the day's trophies.

Martinus brightens. 'But I was right. And now we're both rich ... And being right and rich isn't yet a crime in the City – is it, Colonel?'

Julian Symons

THE FLAW

I

'Drink your coffee.'

Celia sat feet up on the sofa reading a fashion magazine, the coffee cup on the table beside her. 'What's that?'

'I said drink your coffee. You know you like it to be piping hot.'

She contemplated the coffee, stirred it with a spoon, then put the spoon back in the saucer. 'I'm not sure it's hot enough now.'

'I poured it only a couple of minutes ago.'

'Yes, but still. I don't know that I feel like coffee tonight. But I do want a brandy.' She swung her legs off the sofa and went across to the drinks tray. 'A celebratory brandy. Can I pour one for you?'

'What are we celebrating?'

'Me, Giles, not you. I'm celebrating. But you want me to drink my coffee, don't you? All right.' She went swiftly back, lifted the coffee cup, drank the contents in two gulps and made a face. 'Not very hot. Now may I have my brandy?'

'Of course. Let me pour it for you.'

'Oh no, I'll do it myself. After all, you poured the coffee.' She smiled sweetly.

'What do you mean?'

'Just that we've both had coffee. And you poured it. But I gave it to you on the tray, remember?'

Sir Giles got up, put a hand to his throat. 'What are you trying to say?'

'Only that if I turned the tray round you'll have got my cup and I shall have got yours. But it wouldn't matter. Or would it?'

He made for the door and turned the handle, but it did not open. 'It's locked. What have you done with the key?'

'I can't imagine.' As he lumbered towards her, swaying a little, she easily evaded him. 'You think I'm a fool, Giles, don't you? I'm not, that's your mistake. So this is a celebration.'

'Celia.' His hand was at his throat again. He choked, collapsed on to the carpet and lay still.

Celia looked at him thoughtfully, finished her brandy, prodded him with her foot and said, 'Now, what to do about the body?'

The curtain came down. The first act of *Villain* was over.

2

'I enjoyed it enormously,' Duncan George said. 'Is it all right if I smoke?'

'Of course.' Oliver Glass was busy at the dressing-table, removing the make-up that had turned him into Sir Giles. In the glass he saw Dunc packing his pipe and lighting it. Good old Dunc, he thought, reliable dull old Dunc, his reactions are always predictable. 'Pour yourself a drink.'

'Not coffee, I hope.' Oliver's laugh was perfunctory. 'I thought the play was really clever. All those twists and turns in the plot. And you enjoy being the chief actor as well as the writer, don't you, it gives you an extra kick?'

'My dear fellow, you're a psychologist as well as a crime writer yourself, you should know. But after all, who can interpret one's own writing better than oneself? The play – well, between these four walls it's a collection of tricks. The supreme trick is to make the audience accept it, to deceive them not once or twice but half a dozen times, to make them leave the theatre gasping at the cleverness of it all. And if that's to be done, Sir Giles has to be played on just the right note, so that we're never quite certain whether he's fooling everybody else or being fooled himself, never quite sure whether he's the villain or the hero. And who knows that better than the author? So if he happens to be an actor too, he must be perfect for the part.'

'Excellent special pleading. I'll tell you one thing, though. When the curtain comes down at the end of the first act, nobody really believes you're dead. Oliver Glass is the star, and if you're dead they've been cheated. So they're just waiting for you to come out of that cupboard.'

'But think of the tension that's building while they wait. Ready, Dunc.'

He clapped the other on the shoulder, and they walked out into the London night. Oliver Glass was a slim, elegant man in his fifties, successful both as actor and dramatist, so successful that he could afford to laugh at the critic who said that he had perfected the art of over-acting, and the other critic who remarked that after seeing an Oliver Glass play he was always reminded of the line that said life is mostly froth and bubble. Whether Oliver did laugh was another matter, for he disliked any adverse view of his abilities. He had a flat in the heart of the West End, a small house in Sussex, and a beautiful wife named Elizabeth who was fifteen years his junior.

Duncan George looked insignificant by his side. He was short and square, a practising psychiatrist who also wrote crime stories, and he had known Oliver for some years. He was typified for Oliver by the abbreviation of his first name, *Dunc*. He was exactly the kind of person Oliver could imagine dunking a doughnut into a cup of coffee, or doing something equally vulgar. With all that, however, Duncan was a good fellow, and Oliver tolerated him as a companion.

They made their way through the West End to a street off Leicester Square where the Criminologists' Club met once a quarter, to eat a late supper followed by a talk on a subject of criminal interest. The members were all writers about real or fictitious crime, and on this evening Oliver Glass was to speak to them on 'The Romance of Crime', with Duncan George as his chairman. When he rose and looked around, with that gracious look in which there was just a touch of contempt, the buzz of conversation ceased.

'Gentlemen,' he began, 'criminologists – fellow crime writers – perhaps fellow criminals. I have come tonight to plead for romance in the world of crime, for the locked room murder, the impossible theft, the crime committed by the invisible man. I have come to plead that you should bring wit and style and complexity to your writings about crime, that you should remember Stevenson's view that life is a bazaar of dangerous and smiling chances, and the remark of Thomas Griffiths Wainewright when he confessed to poisoning his pretty sister-in-law : "It was a terrible thing to do, but she had thick ankles." I beseech you not to forget those thick ankles as a motive, and to abandon the dreary books some of you write concerned with examining the psychology of two equally dull people to decide which destroyed the other, or looking at bits of intestines under a microscope to determine whether a tedious husband killed his boring wife. Your sights should be set instead on the Perfect Crime . . .'

Oliver Glass spoke, as always, without notes, fluently and with style, admiring the fluency and stylishness as the words issued from his mouth. Afterwards he was challenged by some members, Duncan George among them, about that conjectural Perfect Crime. Wasn't it out of date? Not at all, Oliver said, Sir Giles in *Villain* attempted it.

'Yes, but as you remarked yourself, *Villain*'s a mass of clever tricks,' Dunc said. 'Sir Giles wants to kill Celia as a kind of trick, just to prove that he can get away with it. Or at least, we think he does. Then you play all sorts of variations on the idea, is the poison really a sleeping draught, does she know about it, that kind of thing. Splendid to watch, but nobody would actually try it. In every perfect murder, so called, there is actually a flaw.' There was a chorus of agreement, by which Oliver found himself a little irritated.

'How do you know that? The Perfect Crime is one in which the criminal never puts himself within reach of the law. Perhaps, even, no crime is known to have taken place, although that is a little short of perfection. But how do we know, gentlemen, what variations on the Perfect Crime any of us may be planning, may even have carried out? "The desires of the heart are as crooked as corkscrews", as the poet says, and I'm sure Dunc can bear that out from his psychiatric experience.'

208

'Any of us is capable of violence under certain circumstances, if that's what you mean. But to set out to commit a Perfect Crime without a motive is the mark of a psychopath.'

'I didn't say without motive. A good motive for one man may be trivial to another.'

'Tell us when you're going to commit the Perfect Crime, and we'll see if we can solve it,' somebody said. There was a murmur of laughter.

Upon this note he left, and strolled home to Everley Court, passing the drunks on the pavements, the blacks and yellows and all conditions of foreigners, who jostled each other or stood gaping outside the sex cinemas. He made a slight detour to pass by the theatre, and saw with a customary glow of pleasure the poster : *Oliver Glass in* Villain. *The Mystery Play by Oliver Glass.* Was he really planning the Perfect Crime? There can be no doubt, he said to himself, that the idea is in your mind. And the elements are there, Elizabeth and deliciously unpredictable Evelyn, and above all the indispensable Eustace. But is it more than a whim? Do I really dislike Elizabeth enough? The answer to that, of course, was that it was not a question of hatred but of playing a game, the game of Oliver Glass versus Society, even Oliver Glass versus the World.

And so home. And to Elizabeth.

A nod to Tyler, the night porter at the block of flats. Up in the lift to the third floor. Key in the door.

From the entrance hall the apartment stretched left and right. To the left Elizabeth's bedroom and bathroom. Almost directly in front of him the living-room, further to the right dining-room and kitchen, at the extreme right Oliver's bedroom and bathroom. He went into the living-room, switched on the light. On the mantelpiece there was a note in Elizabeth's scrawl : *O. Please come to see me if back before 2 a.m. E.*

For two years now they had communicated largely by means of such notes. It had begun – how had it begun? – because she was so infuriatingly talkative when he wanted to concentrate. 'I am an artist,' he had said. 'The artist needs isolation, if the fruits of genius are to ripen on the bough of inspiration.' The time had been when Elizabeth listened open-eyed to such words, but those days had gone. For a long while now she had made comments suggesting that his qualities as actor and writer fell short of genius, or had pointed out that last night he had happily stayed late at a party. She did not understand the artistic temperament. Her nagging criticism had become, quite simply, a bore.

There was, he admitted as he turned the note in his fingers, something else. There were the girls needed by the artist as part of his inspiration, the human clay turned by him into something better. Elizabeth had never understood about them, and in particular had failed to understand when she had returned to find one of them with him on the living-room carpet. She had spoken of divorce, but he knew the words to be idle. Elizabeth had extravagant tastes, and divorce would hardly allow her to indulge them. So the notes developed. They lived separate lives, with occasional evenings when she acted as hostess, or came in and chatted amiably enough to friends. For the most part the arrangement suited him rather well, although just at present his absorption with Evelyn was such . . .

He went in to see Elizabeth.

She was sitting on a small sofa, reading. Although he valued youth above all things he conceded, as he looked appraisingly at her, that she was still attractive. Her figure was slim (no children, he could not have endured the messy noisy things), legs elegant, dainty feet. She had kept her figure, as – he confirmed, looking at himself in the glass – he had kept his. How curious that he no longer found her desirable.

'Oliver.' He turned. 'Stop looking at yourself.'

'Was I doing that?'

'You know you were. Stop acting.'

'But I am an actor.'

'Acting off stage, I mean. You don't know anybody exists outside yourself.'

'There is a respectable philosophical theory maintaining that very proposition. I have invented you, you have invented me. A charming idea.'

'A very silly idea. Oliver, why don't you divorce me?'

'Have you given me cause?'

'You know how easily it can be arranged.'

He answered with a weary, a world-weary sigh. She exclaimed angrily and he gave her a look of pure dislike, so that she exclaimed again.

'You *do* dislike me, don't you? A touch of genuine feeling. So why not?' She went over to her dressing-table, sat down, took out a pot of cream.

He placed a hand on his heart. 'I was – '

'I know. You were born a Catholic. But when did you last go to church?'

'Very well. Say simply that I don't care to divorce you. It would be too vulgar.'

'You've got a new girl. I can always tell.'

'Is there anything more tedious than feminine intuition?'

'Let me tell you something. This time I shall have you followed. And *I* shall divorce *you*. What do you think of that?'

'Very little.' And indeed, who would pay her charge account at Harrods, provide the jewellery she loved, above all where would she get the money she gambled away at casinos and race meetings? She had made similar threats before, and he knew them to be empty ones.

'You want me as a kind of butterfly you've stuck with a pin, nothing more.'

She was at work with the cream. She used one cream on her face, another on her neck, a third on her legs. Then she covered her face with a black mask, which was supposed to increase the effectiveness of the cream. She often kept this mask on all night.

There had been a time when he found it exciting to make love to a woman whose face was not visible, but in her case that time had gone long ago. What was she saying now?

'Nothing gets through to you, does it? You have a sort of armour of conceit. But you have the right name, do you know that? *Glass* – if one could see through you there would be nothing, absolutely nothing there. Oliver Glass, *you don't exist.*'

Very well, he thought, very well, I am an invisible man. I accept the challenge. Elizabeth, you have signed your death warrant.

3

The idea, then, was settled. Plans had to be made. But they were still uncertain, moving around in what he knew to be his marvellously ingenious mind, when he went to visit Evelyn after lunch on the following day. Evelyn was in her early twenties, young enough – oh yes, he acknowledged it – to be his daughter, young enough also to be pleased by the company of a famous actor. But beyond that, Evelyn fascinated him by her unpredictability. She was a photographer's model much in demand, and he did not doubt that she had other lovers. There were times when she said that she was too busy to see him, or simply that she wanted to be alone, and he accepted these refusals as part of the excitement of the chase. There was a perversity about Evelyn, an abandonment to the whim of the moment, that reached out to something in his own nature. He felt sometimes that there was no suggestion so outrageous that she would refuse to consider it. She had once opened the door of her flat naked, and asked him to strip and accompany her down to the street.

Her flat was off Baker Street, and when he rang the bell there was no reply. At the third ring he felt annoyance. He had telephoned in advance, as always, and she had said she would be there. He pushed the door in a tentative way, and it swung open. In the hall he called her name. There was no reply.

The flat was not large. He went into the living-room, which was untidy as usual, glanced into the small kitchen, then went into the bedroom with its unmade bed. What had happened to her, where was she? He entered the bathroom, and recoiled from what he saw.

Evelyn lay face down, half in and half out of the bath. One arm hung over the side of the bath, the other trailed in the water. Her head rested on the side of the bath as though her neck was broken.

He went across to her, touched the arm outside the bath. It was warm. He bent down to feel the pulse. As he did so the arm moved, the body turned, and Evelyn was laughing at him.

'You frightened me. You bitch.' But he was excited, not angry.

'The author of *Villain* should be used to tricks.' She got out, handed him a towel. 'Dry me.'

Their lovemaking afterwards had the frantic, paroxysmic quality that he had found in few women. It was as though he were bringing her back from the dead. A thought struck him. 'Have you done that with anybody else?'

'Does it matter?'

'Perhaps not. I should still like to know.'

'Nobody else.'

'It was as though you were another person.'

'Good. I'd like to be a different person every time.'

He was following his own train of thought. 'My wife puts on a black mask after creaming her face at night. That should be exciting, but it isn't.'

Evelyn was insatiably curious about the details of sex, and he had told her a good deal about Elizabeth.

'I'm good for you,' she said now. 'You get a kick each time, don't you?'

'Yes. And you?'

She considered this. She had a similar figure to Elizabeth's but her features were very different, the nose snub instead of aquiline, the eyes blue and wide apart. 'In a way. Being who you are gives me a kick.'

'Is that all?'

'What do you mean?'

'Don't you like me?'

'It's wet to ask things like that. I never thought you were wet.' She looked at him directly with her large, slightly vacant blue eyes. 'If you want to know, I get a kick out of you because you're acting all the time. It's the acting you like, not the act. And then I get a kick out of you being an old man.'

He was so angry that he slapped her face. She said calmly, 'Yes, I like that too.'

By the time that night's performance was over his plan was made.

213

4

In the next two weeks Tyler, the night porter at Everley Court, was approached three times by a tall, bulky man wearing horn-rimmed spectacles. The man asked for Mrs Glass, and seemed upset to learn on every occasion that she was out. Once he handed a note to Tyler and then took it back, saying it wouldn't do to leave a letter lying around. Twice he left messages, to say that Charles had called and wanted to talk to Mrs Glass. On his third visit the man smelled of drink, and his manner was belligerent. 'You tell her I must talk to her,' he said in an accent that Tyler could not place, except that the man definitely came from somewhere up north.

'Yes, sir. And the name is – '

'Charles. She'll know.'

Tyler coughed. 'Begging your pardon, sir, but wouldn't it be better to telephone?'

The man glared at him. 'Do you think I haven't tried? You tell her to get in touch. If she doesn't I won't answer for the consequences.'

'Charles?' Elizabeth said when Tyler rather hesitantly told her this. 'I know two or three people named Charles, but this doesn't seem to fit any of them. What sort of age?'

'Perhaps about forty, Mrs Glass. Smartly dressed. A gentleman. Comes from the north, maybe Scotland, if that's any help.'

'No doubt it should be, but it isn't.'

'He seemed – ' Tyler hesitated. 'Very concerned.'

On the following day Oliver left a note for her. *E. Man rang while you were out, wouldn't leave message. O.* She questioned him about the call.

'He wouldn't say what he wanted. Just rang off when I said you weren't here.'

'It must be the same man.' She explained about him. 'Tyler said he had a northern accent, probably Scottish.'

'What Scots do you know named Charles?'

'Charles Rothsey, but I haven't seen him for years. I wish he'd ring when I'm here.'

A couple of evenings later the wish was granted, although

she did not speak to the man. Oliver had asked her to give a little supper party after the show for three members of the cast, and because two of them were women Duncan was invited to even up the numbers. Elizabeth was serving the cold salmon when the telephone rang in the living-room. Oliver went to answer it. He came back almost at once, looking thoughtful. When Elizabeth said it had been a quick call, he looked sharply at her. 'It was your friend Charles. He rang off. Just announced himself, then rang off when he heard my voice.'

'Who's Charles?' one of the women asked. 'He sounds interesting.'

'You'd better ask Elizabeth.'

She told the story of the man who had called, and it caused general amusement. Only Oliver remained serious. When the guests were going he asked Duncan to stay behind.

'I just wanted your opinion, Dunc. This man has called three times and now he's telephoning. What sort of man would do this kind of thing, and what can we do about it?'

'What sort of man? Hard to say.' Duncan took out his pipe, filled and lit it with maddening deliberation. 'Could be a practical joker, harmless enough. Or it could be somebody – well, not so harmless. But I don't see that you can do much about it. Obscene and threatening phone calls are ten a penny, as the police will tell you. Of course if he does show up again Elizabeth could see him, but I'd recommend having somebody else here.'

This was, Oliver considered, adequate preparation of the ground. It had been established that Elizabeth was being pursued by a character named Charles. There was no doubt about Charles's existence. He obviously existed independently of Oliver Glass, since Tyler had seen him and Oliver himself had spoken to him on the telephone. If Elizabeth was killed, the mysterious Charles would be the first suspect.

Charles had been created as somebody separate from Oliver by that simplicity which is the essence of all fine art. Oliver, like Sir Giles in *Villain*, was a master of disguise. He had in particular the ability possessed by the great Vidocq, of varying his height by twelve inches or more. Charles had been devised from a variety of props like cheek pads, body cushions and false eyebrows, plus the indispensable platform heels. He would make one more appearance, and then vanish from the scene. He would never have to meet anybody who knew Oliver well, something which he slightly regretted. And Charles on the telephone had been an actor whom Oliver had asked to ring during the evening. Oliver had merely said he couldn't talk now but would call him tomorrow, and then put down the receiver.

In the next few days he noticed with amusement tinged with annoyance that Elizabeth had fulfilled her threat of putting a private enquiry agent on his track. He spotted the man hailing a taxi just after he had got one himself, and then getting out a few yards behind him when he stopped outside Evelyn's flat. Later he pointed out the man to Evelyn, standing in a doorway opposite. She giggled, and suggested that they should ask him up.

'I believe you would,' he said admiringly. 'Is there anything you wouldn't do?'

'If I felt like it, nothing.' She was high on some drug or other. 'What about you?'

'A lot of things.'

'*Careful* old Oliver.' What would she say if she knew what he was planning? He was tempted to say something but resisted, although so far as he could tell nothing would shock her. She suddenly threw up the window, leaned out and gave a piercing whistle. When the man looked up she beckoned. He turned his head and then began to walk away. Oliver was angry, but what was the use of saying anything? It was her recklessness that fascinated him.

His annoyance was reflected in a note left for Elizabeth. *E. This kind of spying is degrading. O.* He found a reply that night when he came back from the theatre. *O. Your conduct is degrading. Your present fancy is public property. E.*

5

That Oliver Glass had charm was acknowledged even by those not susceptible to it. In the days after the call from Charles he exerted this charm upon Elizabeth. She went out a good deal in the afternoons, where or with whom he really didn't care, and this gave him the chance to leave little notes. One of them ran : *E. You simply MUST be waiting here for me after the theatre. I have a small surprise for you. O.*, and another : *E. Would supper at Wheeler's amuse you this evening? Remembrance of things past . . . O.* On the first occasion he gave her a pretty ruby ring set with pearls, and the reference in the second note was to the fact that they had often eaten at Wheeler's in the early months after marriage. On these evenings he set out to dazzle and amuse her as he had done in the past, and she responded. Perhaps the response was unwilling, but that no doubt was because of Evelyn. He noticed, however, that the man following him was no longer to be seen, and at their Wheeler's supper mentioned this to her.

'I know who she is. I know you've always been like that. Perhaps I have to accept it.' Her eyes flashed. 'Although if I want to get divorce evidence it won't be difficult.'

'An artist needs more than one woman,' Oliver said. 'But you must not think that I can do without you. I need you. You are a fixed point in a shifting world.'

'What nonsense I do talk,' he said to himself indulgently. The truth was that contact with her nowadays was distasteful to him. By the side of Evelyn she was insipid. A great actor, however, can play any part, and this one would not be maintained for long.

Only one faintly disconcerting thing happened in this, as he thought of it, second honeymoon period. He came back to the flat unexpectedly early one afternoon, and heard Elizabeth's voice on the telephone. She replaced the receiver as he entered the room. Her face was flushed. When he asked who she had been speaking to, she said, 'Charles.'

'Charles?' For a moment he could not think who she was talking about. Then he stared at her. Nobody knew better than he that she could not have been speaking to Charles, but of course he could not say that.

'What did he say?'

'Beastly things. I put down the receiver.'

Why was she lying? How absurd, how deliciously absurd, if she had a lover. Or was it possible that somebody at the supper party was playing a practical joke? He brushed aside such conjectures because they did not matter now. Nothing could interfere with the enactment of the supreme drama of his life.

6

Celia's intention in *Villain* was to explain Sir Giles's absence by saying that he had gone away on a trip, something he did from time to time. Hence the remark about disposition of the body at the end of Act One. Just after the beginning of the second act the body was revealed by Celia to her lover shoved into a cupboard, a shape hidden in a sack. A few minutes later the cupboard was opened again, and the shape was seen by the audience, although not by Celia, to move slightly. Then, after twenty-five minutes of the second act, there was a brief blackout on stage. When the lights went up Sir Giles emerged from the cupboard, not dead but drugged.

To be enclosed within a sack for that length of time is no pleasure, and in any ordinary theatrical company the body in the sack would have been that of the understudy, with the leading man changing over only a couple of minutes before he was due to emerge from the cupboard. But Oliver believed in what he called the theatre of the actual. In another play he had insisted that the voice of an actress shut up for some time in a trunk must be real and not a recording, so that the actress herself had to be in the trunk. In *Villain* he maintained that the experience of being actually in the sack was emotionally valuable, so that he always stayed in it for the whole length of time it was in the cupboard.

The body in the sack was to provide Oliver with an unbreakable alibi. The interval after Act One lasted fifteen minutes, so that he had nearly forty minutes free. Everley Court was seven minutes' walk from the theatre, and he did not expect to need much more than twenty minutes all told. The body in the sack would be seen to twitch by hundreds of people, and who could be in it but Oliver?

In fact Useful Eustace would be the sack's occupant. Eustace was a dummy used by stage magicians who wanted to achieve very much the effect at which Oliver aimed, of persuading an audience that there was a human being inside a container. He was made of plastic, and inflated to the size of a small man. You then switched on a mechanism which made Eustace kick out arms and legs in a galvanic manner. A battery-operated timer in his back could be set to operate at intervals ranging from thirty seconds to five minutes. When deflated, Eustace folded up neatly, into a size no larger than a plastic mackintosh.

Eustace was the perfect accomplice, Useful Eustace indeed. Oliver had tried him out half a dozen times inside a sack of similar size, and he looked most convincing.

On the afternoon of The Day he rested. Elizabeth was out, but said that she would be back before seven. His carefully worded note was left on her mantelpiece. *E. I want you at the flat ALL this evening. A truly sensational surprise for you. All the evening, mind, not just after the show. O.* Her curiosity would not, he felt sure, be able to resist such a note.

During Act One he admired, with the detachment of the artist, his own performance. He was cynical, ironic, dramatic – in a word, superb. When it was over he went unobtrusively to his dressing room. He had no fear of visitors, for he was known to detest any interruption during the interval.

And now came what in advance he felt to be the only ticklish part of the operation. The cupboard with the sack in it opened on to the back of the stage. The danger of carrying out an inflated Eustace from dressing room to stage was too great – he must be inflated on site, as it were, and it was possible although unlikely that a wandering stage hand might see him at work. The Perfect Crime does not depend upon chance or upon the taking of risks, and if the worst happened, if he was seen obviously inflating a dummy, the project must be abandoned for the present time. But fortune favours the creative artist, or did so on this occasion. Inflation of Eustace by pump took only a few moments as he knelt by the cupboard, and nobody came near. The timer had been set for movement every thirty seconds. He put Eustace into the sack, waited to see him twitch, closed the cupboard's false back, and strolled away.

He left the theatre by an unobtrusive exit used by those who wanted to avoid the autograph hunters outside the stage door, and walked along head down until he reached the nearest Underground station, one of the few in London equipped with lockers and lavatories. Unhurriedly he took Charles's clothes and shoes from the locker, went into a lavatory, changed, put his acting clothes back in the locker. Spectacles and revolver were in his jacket pocket. He had bought the revolver years ago, when he had been playing a part in which he was supposed to be an expert shot. By practice in a shooting range he had in fact become a quite reasonable one.

As he left the station he looked at his watch. Six minutes. Very good.

Charles put on a pair of grey gloves from another jacket pocket. Three minutes brought him to Everley Court. He walked straight across to the lift, something he could not do without being observed by Tyler. The man came over, and in Charles's husky voice, with its distinctive accent, he said: 'Going up to Mrs Glass. Expecting me.'

'I'll ring, sir. It's Mr Charles, isn't it?'

'No need. I said, she's expecting me.'

Perfectly, admirably calm. But in the lift he felt, quite suddenly, that he would be unable to do it. To allow Elizabeth to divorce him and then to marry or live with Evelyn until they tired of each other, wouldn't that after all be the sensible, obvious thing? But to be *sensible,* to be *obvious,* were such things worthy of Oliver Glass? Wasn't the whole point that by this death, which in a practical sense was needless, he would show the character of a great artist and a great actor, a truly superior man?

The lift stopped. He got out. The door confronted him. Put key in lock, turn. Enter.

The flat was in darkness, no light in the hall. No sound. 'Elizabeth,' he called, in a voice that did not seem his own. He had difficulty in not turning and leaving the flat.

He opened the door of the living-room. This also was in darkness. Was Elizabeth not there after all, had she ignored his note or failed to return? He felt a wave of relief at the thought, but still there was the bedroom. He must look in the bedroom.

The door was open, a glimmer of light showed within. He

did not remember taking the revolver from his pocket, but it was in his gloved hand.

He took two steps into the room. Her dimmed bedside light was switched on. She lay on the bed naked, the black mask over her face. He called out something and she sat up, stretched out arms to him. His reaction was one of disgust and horror. He was not conscious of squeezing the trigger, but the revolver in his hand spoke three times.

She did not call out but gave a kind of gasp. A patch of darkness showed between her breasts. She sank back on the bed.

With the action taken, certainty returned to him. Everything he did now was efficient, exact. He got into the lift, took it down to the basement and walked out through the garage down there, meeting nobody. Tyler would be able to say when Mr Charles had arrived, but not when he left.

Back to the Underground lavatory, clothes changed, Charles's clothing and revolver returned to locker for later disposal, locker key put in handkerchief pocket of jacket. Return to the theatre, head down to avoid recognition. A quick glance at his watch as he opened the back door and moved silently up the stairs. Nearly thirty minutes had passed.

He knelt at the back of the cupboard and listened to a few lines of dialogue. The moment at which the body was due to give its twitch had gone, and Eustace proved his lasting twitching capacity by giving another shudder, of course not seen by the audience because the cupboard door was closed. Eustace had served his purpose. Oliver withdrew him from the sack and switched him off. With slight pressure to get out the air he was quickly reduced and folded into a bundle. Oliver slipped the bundle inside his trousers, and secured it with a safety pin. The slight bulge might have been apparent on close examination, but who would carry out such an examination upon stage?

Beautiful, he thought, as he wriggled into the sack for the few minutes before he had to appear on stage. Oliver Glass, I congratulate you in the name of Thomas de Quincey and Thomas Griffiths Wainewright. You have committed the Perfect Crime.

7

The euphoria lasted through the curtain calls and his customary few casual words with the audience, in which he congratulated them on being able to appreciate an intelligent mystery. It lasted – oh, how he was savouring the only real achievement of his life – while he leisurely removed Sir Giles's make-up, said goodnight, and left the theatre still with Eustace pinned to him. He made one further visit to the Underground, as a result of which Eustace joined Charles's clothes in the locker. The key back in the handkerchief pocket.

As he was walking back to Everley Court, however, he realised with a shock that something had been forgotten. The note ! The note which said positively that he would be at the flat during the interval, a note which if the police saw it would certainly lead to uncomfortable questions, perhaps even to a search, and discovery of the locker key. The note was somewhere in the flat, perhaps in Elizabeth's bag. It must be destroyed before he rang the police.

He nodded to Tyler, took the lift up. Key in door again. The door open. Then he stopped.

Light gleamed under the living-room door.

Impossible, he thought, impossible. I know that I did not switch on the light when I opened that door. But then who could be inside the room? He took two steps forward, turned the handle, and when the door was open sprang back with a cry.

'Why, Oliver. What's the matter?' Elizabeth said. She sat on the sofa. Duncan stood beside her.

He pulled at his collar, feeling as though he was about to choke, then tried to ask a question but could not utter words.

'Come and see,' Duncan said. He approached and took Oliver by the arm. Oliver shook his head, resisted, but in the end let himself be led to the bedroom. The body still lay there, the patch of red between the breasts.

'You even told her about Elizabeth's bedtime habits,' Dunc said. 'She must have thought you'd have some fun.' He lifted the black mask. Evelyn looked up at him.

Back in the living-room he poured himself brandy and said to Elizabeth, 'You knew?'

'Of course. *Would supper at Wheeler's amuse you this evening?* Do you think I didn't know you were acting as you always are, making some crazy plan. Though I could never have believed it – it was Dunc who guessed how crazy it was.'

He looked from one of them to the other. 'You're lovers?' Duncan nodded. 'My dreary wife and my dull old friend Dunc – a perfect pair.'

Duncan took out his pipe, looked at it, put it back in his pocket. 'Liz had kept me in touch with what was going on, naturally. It seemed that you must be going to do something or other tonight. So Liz spent the evening with me.'

'Why was Evelyn here?' His mind moved frantically from one point to another to see where he had gone wrong.

'We knew about her from having you watched, and all that nonsense about Charles made me think that Elizabeth must be in some sort of danger. So it seemed a good idea to send your note to Evelyn, so that she could be here to greet you. We put the flat key in the envelope.'

'The initials were the same.'

'Just so,' Dunc said placidly.

'You planned for me to kill her.'

'I wouldn't say that. Of course if you happened to mistake her for Liz – but we couldn't guess that she'd put on Liz's mask. We just wanted to warn you that playing games is dangerous.'

'You can't prove anything.'

'Oh, I think so,' Dunc said sagely. 'I don't know how you managed to get away from the theatre, some sort of dummy in the sack I suppose? No doubt the police will soon find out. But the important thing is that note. It's in Evelyn's handbag. Shows you arranged to meet her here. Jealous of some younger lover, I suppose.'

'But I *wasn't* jealous, I didn't arrange – ' He stopped.

'Can't very well say it was for Liz, can you? Not when Evelyn turned up.' The door bell rang. 'Oh, I forgot to say we called the police when we found the body. Our duty, you know.' He looked at Oliver and said reflectively, 'You remember I said there was always a flaw in the Perfect Crime? Perhaps I was wrong. I suppose you might say the Perfect Crime is one you benefit from but don't commit yourself, so that nobody can say you're responsible. Do you see what I mean?' Oliver saw what he meant. 'And now it's time to let in the police.'